Iris Wildthyme and the Celestial Omnibus

edited by Paul Magrs
and Stuart Douglas

Published by Obverse Books
www.obversebooks.co.uk

First Published April 2009
This edition published August 2012

Cover Design by Mark Michalowski

With thanks to Piers Britton, Anthony Dry, Jay Eales, June Hudson, Scott Liddell, Mark Michalowski and Lars Pearson

Printed and bound in Great Britain by 4edge Limited

For Julie and Jeremy, with love

ALSO AVAILABLE FROM OBVERSE BOOKS

THE OBVERSE QUARTERLY

1.1 Bite Sized Horror
1.2 Senor 105 and the Elements of Danger
1.3 The Diamond Lens and Other Stories
1.4 Zenith Lives!
2.1 Tales of the City

IRIS WILDTHYME

Iris Wildthyme and the Celestial Omnibus
The Panda Book of Horror
Miss Wildthyme and Friends Investigate
Iris: Abroad
Wildthyme in Purple

FACTION PARADOX

A Romance in Twelve Parts

NOVELS

The Ninnies
Skaldenland

Contents

Introduction

Katy Manning

Out the extraordinary mind of Mr Paul Magrs exploded Miss Iris Wildthyme – transdimensional adventuress and ratbag. A woman of indeterminate age and with enough energy to illuminate Blackpool's Golden Mile (Vegas too on a good day) her incandescence dimming only in rare moments of heart-wrenching depression fuelled by a few too many – or six – G&T's, no slice!

Iris' most treasured possession is her No. 22 double-decker Putney bus. A sputtering heap that hurtles through time and space causing chaos and mayhem in many an unsuspecting galaxy, with the aid of the lugubrious, petulant Panda. Like a comedic Martha and George, hand in straw paw, they bicker and battle as only true friends can, righting wrongs and wronging rights...

There are no hidden agendas with our Iris. What you see is comfortingly what you get. But slowly, as the stories unravel, we are able to peek into a past that helps us to understand the hidden depths of this formidable, funny, quirky, caring, rock 'n' roll roustabout.

Of course, I play Iris, a character that rules the other personalities that dwell within me with a piece of 2' X 4'. Paul Magrs has a total understanding of women, and an ability to write from the woman's planet of Venus, alongside Willie Russell and Alan Bennett. Add just a big dash of Gothic sci-fi and a splash of Lewis Carroll and you've got it – God help you!

A Gamble with Wildthyme

Steve Lyons

The sound of a door crashing open broke a silence that might have lasted forever.

The intruders, a moment ago running for their lives, faltered to an apologetic halt as a billow of dust preceded them along the nave of the ancient church.

'This is it,' whispered Brandon, a tall, rake-thin fellow nursing a few remaining tufts of grey hair. 'This must be the place. You can sense it, can't you? It reeks of history!'

'It reeks of summat. Mould, I'd say,' said Iris Wildthyme. You know what she looks like. She was carrying a stuffed panda bear tucked under her left arm. Under Brandon's arm, there was a painting in an ornate frame.

'There's always been something about an old church,' he breathed, 'a sort of ambience – and they haven't built them like this one in years.' He moved gingerly forward, appreciating the cracked vinyl flooring, the retractable seating, the table altar draped in a faded blue cloth and the rusted sound system.

'May I remind you both,' said the panda bear, tartly, 'that we have a small but generously-equipped mercenary force on our heels. Hence the fact that I have been whisked off my feet and bundled underarm like an unwanted cardigan.'

'They won't start a fire fight in here,' said Brandon confidently. 'This is a listed building, an exemplar of the old brutalist architecture.'

'Good,' said Iris, collapsing into a seat. 'Then I can get me breath back while you tell us what the heck's going on here, and you can start with that painting.'

'You don't know?' said Brandon. 'But... but I thought you were fellow believers. When you saved me from that ambush at the station, I thought...'

Iris waved a hand airily. 'Oh, you don't want to go reading too much into anything I do, chuck. Sometimes, I just get swept along in the romance of a moment.'

'He has stolen that painting, I hope you know,' said Panda. 'You and your mad impulses, woman, you have entangled us with a common miscreant.'

'I did not steal the painting,' Brandon objected. 'I just...' He screwed up his face, trying to conjure the right word. 'All right,' he conceded, 'I stole it. But I was saving it, really. This painting...' He thrust it into Iris' lap. 'This painting is a map to the greatest secret in the world, a secret that some people would see lost forever.'

'Oh dear. Are you certain about that, chuck?' Iris gave him a look of pure pity. Panda, who had squirmed about in her grasp until he could see the canvas, reacted to it with a theatrical groan of distaste and a roll of his eyes.

'Cos it just looks to me,' said Iris, 'like a picture of some dogs playing poker. Mind you, it is quite good, isn't it? You can tell what it's supposed to be, like.'

'That picture,' said Brandon, 'was painted over two centuries ago. It is one of the few great works of art to have survived the purges.'

'Although,' said Iris, her brow furrowing, 'you know, it does ring a bell.'

'But search for its name on the net, and you'll get no hits. Nothing at all.'

'Trouble with my memory these days is, you can't always tell which bells are connected to which ropes, if you see what I mean.'

'Not that an image on a screen would have done,' continued Brandon. 'Nor would a print, even if I could have found one. No, to uncover the entire, true meaning of *A Friend in Need*, we have to look not just at the surface but beneath it.'

He had produced a plastic torch-like device, which shone a blue light onto the canvas. 'You see?' he said. 'On the wall behind that St Bernard there: a painting within a painting. What better way to suggest that something has been covered up?' He twisted a dial, and the light grew more intense, penetrating, until it seemed to peel away the top layer of paint itself.

'And this,' announced Brandon, 'is what Cassius Coolidge originally painted.'

Visible now behind the St Bernard's head was a white-framed window, beyond which stood the incongruous shape of a red double-decker bus.

'Oh, sod it!' exclaimed Iris, rooting in her handbag for a bottle of vodka and unscrewing the cap. 'Sod it, sod it, sod it!'

'*We have the church surrounded, Mr Brandon,*' came an amplified voice from outside. '*You and your floozy can come out now and hand over the painting, or things can get rather unpleasant for you.*'

'It's coming back to me now,' sighed Iris, 'at least some of it is. Everything at stake... and old Cash, of course. He'd been doing cartoons for the local paper, but he said I inspired him to try a broader medium. Ooh, I gave him such a clout when I saw what he'd done, put my old bus in one of his artworks.'

'It always has to be about you, doesn't it?' huffed Panda. 'What about me? I suppose I am to be relegated once again to the role of facilitating your expository dialogue, am I? And you still haven't put me down.'

Iris plonked the stuffed bear down on the seat beside her. 'What I still don't get,' she said to Brandon, 'is why here? Why an old church in Scunthorpe?'

Will Brandon recalled a lecture he had once given to a hall full of rapt students.

Well, in fact, there had been no students, what with Brandon actually being a fishmonger. No hall, either. He had provided those details himself, with his mind's eye. His real audience had been Tilly, his best friend and flatmate.

'*A Friend in Need* is brimming with symbolism,' he had said, 'if you can just open your mind to it. Consider the grey bulldog in the foreground of the painting, passing a card to his partner beneath the table. What else could that dog represent but Great Britain? And the brown bulldog receiving the card... er, that must be Great Britain too. The card, of course, is the ace of clubs, which in cartomancy represents great power, wealth, war, it depends who you ask really. Note also that the lampshade above them, its stark red colour drawing our eyes towards it, has six sides. It is surely no coincidence that the hexagram symbol occurs in so many of the major world—'

'Oi,' snapped Iris. She was on her feet, jabbing a finger under Brandon's nose. 'Less of the daydreaming. I asked you a question, buster!'

'The numbers,' said Brandon. '*A Friend in Need* is full of numbers: one-eleven on the clock, the four aces on display, the value of chips in the pot. But there was still something missing, and today I uncovered it. Two-two, the number on the bus. The key that allowed me to crack Coolidge's code and come up with a grid reference.'

'But for heaven's sake, man, why?' cried Panda. 'What is all this for?'

'Evidence,' said Brandon. 'Evidence that we have been visited by aliens.'

'If that's all you're after, luv,' said Iris, 'you should have just said.'

'Aliens from an alternative Earth,' Brandon went on, 'from another version of Great Britain. I believe that, two centuries ago, they conspired with our government. We combined our science with theirs to create the ultimate weapon of war.'

'And, of course,' hooted Panda, 'the ideal hiding place for such a weapon would be right here, where no one would think to look for it.'

'An ace in the hole, you might say,' agreed Brandon, immune to the bear's mocking tone. 'Now we only have to find the final clue. A symbol on the wall or the floor or something. A club, perhaps.' He dropped to his knees and began to search.

'Er, look, Mr Brandon,' said Iris, wringing her hands awkwardly, 'I don't quite know how to break this to you, but—'

'You're barmy,' said Panda helpfully. 'Touched in the head.'

'No offence, luv, but this theory of yours, the aliens and the numbers and all, well, you have to admit it is a little bit... it is sort of... it's... well, it's bollocks, really, isn't it? Oh, no, don't look at me with those cow eyes. Maybe you're right, maybe there is a message about aliens in that painting. I just think it might be a bit less... oblique than you've been assuming. Let me try to explain.'

'In the meantime,' said Panda, 'the highly-trained killers encamped on our doorstep might be somewhat less inclined to shoot us all down dead if we were to restore that, ah, charming piece of art to its owners, don't you think?'

Brandon had been listening to all this with a stunned look, but now his eyes hardened. 'No! No, you're wrong. Because those men, those soldiers out there, they weren't sent by the gallery. They represent an altogether more insidious force, a clandestine cabal that will go to any lengths, including murder, to protect their secrets. So great is their hatred of this painting, of Coolidge's dogs, that they even call themselves... MIAOW!'

'MIAOW?' gasped Iris. 'The Ministry for Incursions And Ontological Wonders? What would they be doing mixed up in this palaver? Unless... oh, no...'

For the second time in as many minutes, a door crashed open – this one a smaller door that, Brandon assumed, accessed a smaller room – and through this door burst a motley assortment of dogs, each walking upright, each brandishing a weapon.

There were seven, all told, led by an overly-coiffured grey poodle. She held her head at a haughty angle, her lips in a sneer of contempt and her dainty white hairdryer-like gun in a delicate grip. She was flanked by a pair of squat bullmastiffs, their short arms wrapped about heavy laser assault rifles. Snapping and drooling behind these came a dachshund, a couple of beagles and a red tricolour border collie.

'Thank you, Brandon,' the poodle yipped. 'I will take that painting from you now, if you please.'

Brandon let out a yelp of alarm. 'Tilly! What are you doing here? How did you get out of the house? No, no, wait a second... How come you can talk?'

'Why is it always the voice they fixate upon?' sighed Tilly. 'Don't they ever notice the opposable thumbs?'

It was at that moment that a further four intruders, human this time, dressed in black combat suits, came smashing in through the windows on ropes.

A short, heavy-set man with small, dark eyes and a thick moustache landed by Brandon's side and thrust a pistol to his temple. 'You were warned, Mr Brandon,' he growled. 'My name is Lincoln, and I have been hired by the Ministry for...'

His voice tailed off as he caught sight of Tilly and her entourage. His eyes flicked toward them, then back to Brandon, to Iris, to each of his three comrades, and back to the dogs again in mounting disbelief.

The dogs, all seven of them, had their weapons trained on Lincoln's head.

The pistol dropped from his suddenly numbed fingers.

Nobody could be sure, afterwards, who had fired the first shot. There was no doubt, however, as to who had brought the brief but violent altercation to an end.

Brandon did try. He screamed something about the architecture and threw himself on top of the Coolidge painting, shielding it with his body. Lincoln was shouting too, ordering his men to stand down in the face of such obviously superior firepower, but they were panicking too hard to hear him.

'We have to get out of here,' cried Panda, scurrying about at knee height. 'Iris, my dear, where are you? I can't see you. My legs, too short. You have to pick me up, for pity's sake, somebody pick me up!'

It was Iris who stopped it, who was suddenly in between them all, an implacable force, her eyes blazing with resolve. 'Now look,' she roared, 'there will be no argy-bargy here!' As the dust settled in silence around her, she looked at first a little surprised and then quite pleased with herself.

'That's more like it,' she said. 'Now, I'm not one for blowing my own trumpet, mind, but... you, soldier boy!' She pointed to Lincoln. 'First chance you get, you whistle up your contacts at MIAOW. Tell them you've had a brush with Iris Wildthyme, and see how that puts the wind up 'em. As for you lot...' She rounded on Tilly and her canine cohorts. 'They have another name, a special name, for me on Dogworld. They call me *Ka Faraq Kweethri*!'

The dogs, to her evident satisfaction, each took a step back from her.

'*The Oncoming Hangover*?' gasped the dachshund.

Iris' chest deflated. 'Oh, is that what that means? I had hoped for something more portentous.'

Lincoln's mercenaries were emerging from cover, dusting themselves down, applying medikits to their energy burns, doing what they could about scorched jackets and melted plates of body armour. The dogs, in contrast, were untouched, except that one of the beadles had been grazed by a bullet and was looking a tad dazed.

'This is none of your business, old woman,' Tilly hissed. 'This is between Dogworld and Earth. It is a matter of pride!'

'Ah,' said Iris, 'now we're getting to the meat of it. Secret Service, right? And there's something in that picture, something you want kept hidden.'

'I knew it!' cried Brandon. All eyes turned on him, and he shifted from foot to foot nervously, the disputed painting wrapped tightly in his arms.

'I wouldn't expect a humanoid to recognise the ancestor of one of our greatest statesmen,' sniffed Tilly, 'but to us, the pedigree is unmistakable – and the act in which he is depicted in that painting a vile slur upon his dynasty.'

'Oh, you can't mean Griff,' laughed Iris, 'the cheating bulldog?'

The bullmastiffs bristled, and one of them snarled, 'You insult the betrothed of the Princess herself!'

'Two years I have spent on this cesspit of a world,' said Tilly. 'Two years, erasing every image, every mention of that painting from your databases, tracking down tea towels and napkins and biscuit tins on eBay so that they can be destroyed.'

'But the original was well guarded,' surmised Iris, 'and you can't afford to be seen, can you? Art theft by space dogs, there wouldn't half be a fuss on the news services. Word would get back home, and suddenly that painting would be getting more attention than it's had in a hundred years. There'd be a scandal!'

'Brandon was the perfect dupe,' said Tilly. 'He'll believe anything you suggest to him. I left a few books lying about the house, whispered a few words in his ear while he slept, slipped a tea towel into the kitchen.'

'So, it *was* you,' said Brandon. 'Grabbing me by the pyjamas, shaking me, screaming, 'For pity's sake, just take the hint and steal the damn painting, you moron!' I thought I'd dreamt that. I… I have been dreaming about talking dogs a lot.'

'Then all you actually want to do is take the painting and leave?' said Panda. 'Well, I for one have no problem with that. Godspeed.'

'If only it were so simple,' said Tilly. 'But you've seen us now, everyone in this building – and that means you must die.'

'What?' cried Lincoln. 'You can't do that!'

'I'm afraid we can,' said Tilly. 'Your people have insulted Dogworld. According to our laws, compensation is due. I set the price at seven lives, and cheap at that. Guards, you may fire at will. Destroy the painting first!'

'No, no, wait!' cried Iris, 'I'll play you for them! I'm serious, please, just hear me out a second. You say you have a claim on our seven lives. Well, I have something your Princess wants, that her family has coveted for generations.'

'Oh, Iris dear,' cried Panda, 'you mustn't!'

'There is nothing you can offer me,' sniffed Tilly, 'nothing I could want from you. My mission here is almost done, at last. *A Friend in Need* will be gone, every copy of it vanished without trace, and no one will even know. Soon, it will be forgotten.'

'And I'm sure the Princess will be dead chuffed about that,' said Iris, 'until she finds out what you could have won.'

She was rummaging in her handbag again, and she gave a squawk of triumph as her hand emerged clutching a pack of dog-eared playing cards. 'I knew they were in there somewhere. The very deck with which I challenged your forefathers in 1903. Only this time, lady, I've a stake of my own to put up. My most treasured possession, you might say. My bus, for our seven lives! Think about that, Tilly, just think about what it could mean to you: the whole of time and space at your four paws.'

And for a moment, the poodle looked tempted. Until Brandon chimed in:

'And for the painting!'

Iris shot him a frustrated look, but Brandon was unrepentant. He didn't know where the courage had come from to step forward, to speak out for the first time in front of an actual audience, but there it was, and the words were flowing freely from him:

'OK, so it may not look like much to you, but that painting is a part of my history. And it's accessible, and it's fun, and it excites my imagination, and it wouldn't have been copied so many times over if an awful lot of people hadn't loved it. *I* love it. If that doesn't make *A Friend in Need* worthwhile, important even, if that doesn't make it art, then I don't want to know what does.'

Panda buried his face in his hands. Lincoln's jaw gaped open. The dogs looked angry. But Iris just grinned, and gave Brandon an approving nod before she turned back to Tilly. 'You heard the man,' she said. 'I'll stake my bus against our lives and the painting. I'd say that's still a pretty good deal, wouldn't you?'

They found a trestle table in the church's back room, and cleared an area in front of the altar where it could be set up. Without being told to, the mercenaries had holstered their guns, accepting that they were the prisoners here.

Tilly detailed the bullmastiffs to stand guard over the front and back doors while she, the remaining four dogs and Iris took their seats.

'And we're satisfied that this is a prudent and viable plan, are we?' said Panda.

'It worked last time,' shrugged Iris. 'Some Dogworld General, it was, got taken by a snake-oil salesman in New Jersey – well, you've seen what this lot are like for their pride, not to mention their small print. We wound up playing five-card draw for three bridges, a small lake and the mining rights to Hoboken and Newark.'

'But you won that time,' said Lincoln. 'I mean, you did win, didn't you?'

'Well, not won, exactly. It was more that my opponents forfeited the game. When Cash saw that Griff one passing the ace...' The dachshund, to Iris' left, growled at her, and she took the hint and left the sentence unfinished. 'But don't you fret, chuck, I'm a bit of a demon at cards if I say so meself.'

She leaned back in her chair, swigged the last of her vodka and smacked her lips.

'It might help,' said Panda, 'if you could keep yourself upright, you old lush.'

Iris was not so much shuffling the cards as mushing them together, catapulting half of them across the table. Brandon gaped in horror. This was all his fault. He had placed their lives – the lives, if he understood correctly, of everyone who lived or had ever lived or would ever live – in those unsteady, liver-spotted hands.

Then, he noticed something odd.

The backs of the cards were patterned with red and green spots of varying shades – and in the centre of each one, their shapes picked out by clusters of the darker spots, Brandon could see letters. And numbers. *6S, QD, 9H, 4H...*

Iris' deck was marked – and marked so clearly, so blatantly, that no one could have missed it. Brandon held his breath, waiting for one of the dogs to see, to react to this insult. Noticing his expression, Iris threw him a cheerful wink.

Tilly looked at the painting, still in Brandon's hands, and she tutted. 'Humans!' she said. 'Only you could have produced such a piece of work, let alone fought so hard to preserve it. I swear, I will never understand the attachments you can form to such trite, crass ephemera.'

'Aye, well,' said Iris, 'you Dogworld lot never did know much about art, did you? I expect that comes from your all being colour blind.'

She began to deal.

Sovereign

Mags L Halliday

Iris was scrunched up against the headboard, the bleached candlewick covers clutched to her chest. Shadows, cast by the icy white moonlight, swirled across the wallpaper of the room as, at the frost-patterned window, something *scritched*.

'Oh lummie,' she whispered, 'this was meant to be a break from it all!'

Iris parked the bus at the bottom of the orchard, where it wouldn't be overhung by branches. Outside was a cold January in 1960, with yellowing snow clouds glowering above the horizon. She wrapped herself up and took the path through the bare fruit trees. Beyond the low wall that marked the boundaries of the house was a bleak landscape of dark fields and moorland. In the shadows, a heavy frost still lay despite the sunshine. The old Georgian house sat on the rise, sheltering from the wind. Silhouetted against the horizon beside it was a thick copse, the bare trees sharp black against the white sky. The main lane down to the road led into the woods, where the branches closed in on themselves and created a tunnel.

Iris knocked at the house's front door. 'Coo-ee!' she called, trying the latch. Before she could lift it, the door was pulled violently open and a girl barged out. She was hauling her coat on as she turned and shouted back behind her.

'...and I don't care about your stupid ideology! I'm going out with Luke!'

An older woman followed, her paint-splattered indigo work clothes in contrast to the sharp red of the girl's duffel coat.

'Belle! Don't you take that – oh, hello Iris – don't you take that tone with me! Come back here!'

Belle tossed her bobbed black hair and stormed out of the yard, hugging herself tight against the cold.

Iris cocked her head. 'Teenagers, eh, Aggie? We were just as bad ourselves.'

Agnes Inglewood huffed, letting a thick cloud of her breath form in the freezing air. 'Sorry, this is no way to welcome you back. Come in, love, and I'll get the kettle on.'

Iris stepped over the threshold and sighed with relief to be out of the cold. 'You look like you need something stronger, chuck, and I won't say no meself.'

Belle stomped up the lane, letting the barren trees close over her head. The mud from the autumnal rainstorms had frozen into ruts and ridges that refused to let her walk as fast as her fury deserved. Where water still lay were smooth puddles of ice, waiting for the unwary. Under her thick wool duffle coat her hand-me-down cotton dress was too thin and the wind found its way inside and made her shiver. She stopped in the midst of the copse and scowled.

She'd have to turn back, of course.

It was another hour until Luke was due to arrive in his dad's Land Rover to collect her. If she waited out here till then, she'd catch her death. Besides, there was no way she was going to a dance in Saint Brigid in these clothes. Jane, who ran the village scene with an eyebrow of iron, would raise it a little and then whisper a lot about poor dear Belle who lived up there with the crazy ladies.

The cold January sun was already vanishing below the horizon, leaving only a narrow band of amber uplighting the storm clouds. She'd not put her torch in her pocket before rushing out of the house, so she reluctantly turned back before darkness could made the lane treacherous. Above her, the naked trees were joined together and the empty nests of the crows who normally roosted there hung like malignant growths. There were no birds, not even the frantic calls of the evening chorus from the orchard beyond the house, and no rustlings in the undergrowth. She'd not noticed any squirrels bouncing through the skeletal leaves looking for unfrozen stashes either. Normally, her stomp up the lane would send birds dashing upwards chittering with alarm and annoyance. Belle felt the fine hairs at the nape of her neck prickle, as if the storm were coming or someone was watching her.

She huffed, her annoyance pouring out her like steam, and started back up the lane.

They took their drinks into the studio attached to the house, where a paraffin heater dried the air and took the nip off it. Iris greeted Dana, who was sat on an old slumping sofa. She was a rakishly thin woman with an asymmetrical fringe, a jumper falling off one shoulder and a Gitane permanently in the corner of her mouth. Iris settled beside her with a 'budge up!'.

Dana raised an eyebrow and exhaled a long plume of smoke. 'Belle still sticking it to the man?'

'To the woman, yes. I know, I know,' Agnes waved her drink around as if deflecting unspoken comments. 'It's all very well to believe in non-conformity, and I did raise her to challenge rules – and there's a record of schools she's been expelled from for that – but it's different when it's your own child rebelling against you.'

'By dating a farm boy.'

'She says she loves him. I just don't want her thinking he's all there is, or that any man is.'

The grumble of an engine, revving as it bounced down the track, cut through the workshop and another slam of the door suggested Belle had both come back and gone again.

‘Well, I need to brew coffee and start work,’ Dana said and slinked out. The library of the house was her den, where she would chain smoke and swear over manuscripts all night.

‘So,’ Iris said once they were alone, ‘you sent me a psychic postcard asking for my help. What’s the problem? Belle?’

‘If only. Belle worries me but she’s her own person in the end. No, the problem my old comrade, is that my muse has gone.’

‘Well, ‘ere I am now, chuck, and...’ Iris tailed off as Agnes shook her head and gestured around the studio. The walls held up stacks of abandoned canvases and the tables were deep with discarded sketches. Abstracted figures who should have danced fluidly across the compositions, as they had used to, looked stiffly uncomfortable. Iris was a knew what she liked kind of art appreciator and she knew that Agnes’s paintings were no longer connecting, no longer expressing meaning. Something, some hard to define energy, was missing. Her dark hair, once as glossy as Belle’s, held white at the temples, and her hands seemed stiff. Agnes started flipping through the unfinished paintings: they were half-formed and somehow half-hearted.

‘I’ve always painted, Iris, always worked. I can’t verbalise like Dana or you. For thirty years I’ve expressed myself through my work, through my hands. I put up with the wandering mind of that tutor at Slade, I worked the artistic scene right through the ‘30s and into the war. Remember those blacked out nights in the attic studio on Denmark Street?’

Iris nodded, and poured Agnes another drink. ‘Do I ever? There was that night in ’41, before you were shipped down here to be a land girl, when the bombs were falling all around but you wouldn’t go down to the shelter until the painting was finished.’

‘Anton was so mad at me for that. He was always worrying, writing every day from barracks. He was so pleased when I got dragged out of London, even though he’d spend half his leave getting down here.’

Iris was silent. Anton had been on train, heading westwards, that was hit by a bomb outside Plymouth. Everyone in his carriage had died.

‘And now?’ Iris asked.

‘ ‘A change has come upon me,’ as the lady cried. The Change. And the spark has gone. I’ve not painted anything worth a brass ha’penny for the best part of two years. My agent is becoming impatient. If Dana wasn’t so damn in demand, I’d not be able to keep up the payments on this place. I need my spirit back, Iris, and I know you can help me.’

Belle should have known the dance would be disappointing after all that hassle. Saint Brigid’s tiny assembly rooms, above the Duchy Inn, had been built for Regency quadrilles and no amount of crepe paper could disguise the faded gilt.

Someone had managed to fit a small mirror ball, and it refracted light into the damp-speckled mirrors and the handfuls of couples on the dance floor.

Everyone from St Brigid's, and the surrounding hamlets and farms, was there. Every girl between fifteen and twenty-two, and every boy under twenty-five who wasn't off on National Service, anyway. Adam Trevartha was just back from Malaysia, showing off his tan and muscles. Jane and her coterie were admiring him, to the annoyance of their own boyfriends.

And Luke was ignoring her. He was over in the corner, where Jack Penhallow had stashed crates of brown beer under a trestle table and was doing a roaring illegal trade. Luke was head and shoulders above the others. Since they'd all left school at fifteen, he'd worked on the Tremen farm and grown tall and blond, like wheat in sunshine. He was more confident than he had been at school, and she had found it surprisingly easy to accept his kisses and embraces, and to let his hands roam freely. But he could easily shut himself up: she'd mention a book he'd not read, or something foreign, and all the sun would go from his face. Like now.

Local bands had been playing skiffle covers of songs she didn't know. Belle had heard better jam sessions when Agnes's London friends decamped to camp in the grounds all summer and she'd said as much. Luke taken offence as one of his friends was playing at the time and was refusing to dance with her now the disc jockeys had started up. Jane, who had been the unofficial head girl at school thanks to her ability to rule the social scene, sneered loudly about how black the music being spinned was, souring Belle's mood further.

Why had she thought this was somewhere she wanted to be? With girls who looked down at her outmoded clothes and wayward mother, and boys who wondered if she would be more willing because of it. With Luke off drinking with his friends, she leaned against the wall, arms and brows crossed. But her annoyance hadn't spread to her toes, and they tapped out the beat without her knowing it.

'You look like you want to dance,' someone said and she looked up to see a young man standing in front of her.

Unlike the other boys, he was dressed in a sharp dark suit, with tight trousers and a skinny tie. His thick black hair was cut sharply short, with two tiny elfin curls resting in front of his ears.

'Belle?' he asked and she recognised the blue eyes beneath the short fringe.

'Alex?'

Alex had lived up on the moor beyond their house with his father, a drunkard. He'd caught the bus to school each morning, waiting with her and Luke at the crossroads. Then one day a few years ago he'd not shown up. His mum had reappeared, they said in the village, and taken him off with her to that London. His father, not exactly noted for being social anyway, had retreated further into his bottles and had turned up his toes a few weeks back. Alex must have come back to clear out his cottage. Belle put her hand into his and let him lead her onto the dancefloor.

And he could dance. Where he'd learnt she didn't know, as this wasn't the gawky boy she'd known back then, and his polished shoes gleamed as he grabbed her, spun her and mirrored her moves. Her scowl lifted and she started to laugh.

When the records gave way to another skiffle band, Alex pulled a face and they left the floor. Luke was waiting where she had been stood, his face as angry as hers had been.

'What d'you think you're doing? Showing me up, dancing with some stranger?'

'He's not, though. It's *Alex*!'

Luke looked Alex up and down, his sneer more apparent than ever.

'Come back with your new-found London ways, have you? Well, Belle's my bird, and she dances with me.'

He took Belle's arm. 'Come on, we've got to go.'

'Hang on, I don't want to go yet. And I'm not mad at anyone anymore. We can stay for the next dance set, can't we? I want to dance, baby...'

'I said already we had to head off around now: Dad needs the rover back before dawn.'

'But...'

Belle turned to appeal to Alex, only to find Jane had come over and had grabbed his attention. She was leaning on his arm like he wasn't the same boy she'd taunted as 'Acne Marrack' at school. Maybe she didn't even recognise him yet?

She had no other ride home, so she'd just have to go with Luke. It was too cold to walk the five miles, and the lack of phone at the house meant she couldn't call and convince anyone to come and fetch her. Which they probably wouldn't, or would do but she'd pay for it with a lecture.

In the carpark, Luke's headlights caught a steel grey Vespa scooter with a bedroll tied to it.

'I bet we could go over that and barely feel a bump,' he said. Belle shivered in the unheated cab and pulled her coat closed.

'Let's just go home, eh?'

He crunched into gear. 'The long way around, yeah?'

'No, just home. *Please*.'

'You little cock tease, Belle,' he said and they drove in silence. Occasional snowflakes glimmered in the light beams but failed to settle.

'Here you are then: home,' he said.

They were at the turning into the lane through the copse. Belle stared at Luke. He shrugged and looked ahead into the night. 'You said home, Belle, and your house's boundaries start here, so I reckon you're home.'

Belle continued to stare at him for a minute, then shoved the door open and hopped down onto the iron-hard verge. 'You're bloody pathetic, Luke.'

'Pathetic, am I? You'll see, my girl.'

Belle slammed the land rover's door and watched as he drove off. After the rear lights had vanished around the curve of the road, she hunched up inside her coat. Her numb fingers checked the toggles were done up and pulled the hood up. She had at least thought to shove her torch into her pocket this time, and she switched it on. The beam threw sharp shadows across the lane and into the monochrome trees. She was chattering with the cold, but the ground was so uneven that she daren't run.

There was a heavy rustling in the trees above her. Probably the snow starting to fall more heavily, or the wind getting up. She just wanted to get home and go to bed without getting an earful from Agnes about earlier. Home and buried deep under the blankets, with a hot brick by her toes and her old toy cat to hug.

She felt a whoosh over her head. Belle stopped and lowered her hood so she could hear. She always hated how muffled her senses were with it up. The bare branches of the trees were clacking together, and the faint light of the full moon could be glimpsed through scudding clouds.

'Hoo!'

She nearly dropped the torch as the screech came from all around her.

'Stop it!' she called, 'stop pissing about, Luke! It's not funny.'

Except it was far too unearthly to be made by a human. And it was far louder than any owl she'd ever heard before. She veered towards the edges of the path as she tried to find its source, catching her clothes on the frozen long grasses that cut like blades.

'Hoo! Hoo!'

It was behind her.

Belle looked back, her hair and hood almost obscuring her view. There was a man on the path behind her. A tall shadowy silhouette picked out by the intermittent moon.

She screamed, and swung to face him, bringing her torch around.

'Hoowa!' the shape screeched and leapt into the air faster than her shaking torch could follow. She glimpsed tawny feathers and wide, wide wings, and cruel talons stretched towards her.

He had...it had...

'Belle? Belle!'

Torches were coming from the house, wielded by strong women who were rushing to protect her.

Iris tucked the heavy blankets in around Belle, and pulled the candlewick bedspread high.

'Do you want the light on?' she asked, proud of her maternal abilities.

'Just the landing light, Iris, thanks. I'm not a little girl any more.'

'No you're not. You've two boys – young men! – fighting for your attention. Lucky you!'

Belle didn't look convinced but smiled anyway. Iris checked the hot milk – laced with more brandy –and went back downstairs.

Finding her child in the woods, her stockings ripped and her whole body shaking with fear, Agnes had taken firm charge. They'd got Belle inside, wrapped her in a blanket and settled her by the ever burning range in the kitchen. She'd poured her daughter a brandy, 'for medicinal purposes' and they'd listened with relief to her description of the creature that had so frightened her.

'Thank god,' Agnes said when Iris rejoined her. 'I imagined something so much worse.'

Iris poured her a drink and sat on the rug before the range, next to her friend's chair.

'You don't think it's a what d'you call it? A false memory. Avoiding the truth, do you?' She had to ask. Didn't like to, but had to. DNA was still unravelling in an Oxford lab in 1960, but Iris had equipment aboard the bus that could unpick it in the blink of an eye.

'No! No. Come on, Iris, I remember all that business with the vampires on Hampstead Heath in the thirties. And Belle isn't prone to lies, or fantasies.'

The wind was starting to clatter around the chimney tops now, and the predicted rough night was descending on them. Thin howls of draughts moved the curtains and rattled the windows. Before they had heard Belle's screams, they had been battening down the studio. Switching off the paraffin heater, as it was better to freeze than to burn to death, and stuffing rags around the windows. Dana had hauled in a basket of logs from the woodshed, and Agnes had brought in the shovel to prop up by the door. Iris had been tasked with putting a candle and matches in all the bedrooms, in case snow brought down the power lines. The kitchen was warm and snug, though, so that the storm seemed remote

'And now we've a man in the form of a bird,' Iris said.

'Or a bird in the form of a man.'

'Well, I've never come across any vampire owls, anyway.'

'There's local stories. A well over at Saint Pryddin's gets dressed as an owl each spring. And there's something about a curse, and Merlin—'

'Oh, that man. If he were responsible for everything they say he was, he'd need to have lived hundreds of years. Mind you...'

'Listen!'

Above the rising wind, they heard something rattling in the eaves.

'A loose slate,' Iris said but Agnes had stood and was staring upwards.

The rattle came again, more like a scrabble now. With a stutter, the lights went out. Upstairs, Belle screamed.

They ran up and Iris flicked the light switch frantically. 'The bloody wind's brought the lines, pet,' she said into the darkness as she found the matches and lit the candle she'd left on the chest of drawers. She pretended not to see her own hand trembling as wildly as the flame.

Up here the scrambling was louder, and there was something above it. Some kind of wild call. Agnes had grabbed her daughter and hugged her close.

'It's the storm breaking, is all,' Iris tried, but the animal sounds from above them called her a liar.

By morning there was perhaps six inches of snow blanketing the countryside and the storm had blown itself out. They'd decamped to the kitchen and lounge in the night, where they would be close to the fires and happier in numbers.

Agnes set to as soon as the morning broke, shovelling a path from the kitchen door to the woodshed. Then she started work on restoring the generator. Iris found all the fixings for a large breakfast in the larder but was grateful when Belle took control of the pans.

'I never was much of a domestic goddess,' she admitted, 'except that one time on Kikirooka. I'll get more wood in.'

The snow crumped under Iris' boots as she hauled the full basket towards the house.

'Ooh, me creakin' back,' she exclaimed enthusiastically, faintly disappointed no-one had rushed to help her. She leaned back theatrically, stretching her spine. The sun sparkled on the frosted windows just above her head, and on the window sills topped with snow. Her eyes widened. In the wood of the sill were large gouges. Even from her angle, she could see the pale cream of freshly exposed wood. Last night, something big and clawed had rested outside Belle's window.

Around noon, when snow was starting to loosen and slide down the roof, they all went outside to spot where slates had fallen or were loose. Belle tried to act normally, but she felt buzzed: as if she was drunk on champagne. Like a bubble was centred around her, watching and waiting. The snow damped down noise and made the air like crystal. They spoke quietly, unlike themselves.

Until Dana, wired on caffeine from another all night redrafting session, suddenly curled snow into a ball and flung it at Belle. It missed, but Belle shrieked and dashed after the writer. The battle skidded across the front garden, their boots slipping on the sparkling snow, until the burr of an engine cut through the air.

'If that's Luke,' Dana suggested, 'tell him to get screwed.'

But Belle didn't recognise the engine's voice. They turned towards the copse and watched as a steel grey moped emerged. Alex was wrapped inside a thick parka coat, ex-military, with gloves and a scarf.

'They said down at the post office that you still lived up here, so I thought I'd stop by,' he said, drawing down the scarf.

Dana raised an eyebrow at him. 'Well, and haven't you grown up just dandy?' she asked.

'Hello, Dana. I read your last collection. Wild stuff.'

Belle felt herself starting to blush as Agnes and Iris prowled around the corner of the house. She wasn't sure why: it wasn't as if Agnes hadn't often had Alex over for tea when he was a skinny lost boy with no promise of a meal at home. It just felt that this was a different boy: this collected and hip young man was too cool to be exposed to two eccentrics like her mum and Iris.

'Alex?' Agnes asked. 'Well, I can see why Belle barely recognised you. Want some lunch? It's lucky dip stew, I'm afraid, but there may be some dumplings.'

'Thanks, Mrs Inglewood, but I was just coming over to see if Belle wanted a quick spin?'

'I think you can call me 'Aggie' now, young man. I was never a Mrs anyway. And is that thing safe?'

Belle was already tightening her scarf and brushing the snow off her coat.

It was, she admitted after five minutes, not the warmest way to get around. And they couldn't talk like you could in a car. And, well, there were other things that were easier in a four wheeled vehicle. But her arms could circle his waist, and feel every movement of his muscles against her as he controlled their speed. They stuck to the main roads, heading up onto the moors near his father's cottage. Cresting Menheer Tor, he pulled over and cut the engine.

The hills tumbled away from them. The air was so crisp and clear that she could see the Atlantic on three horizons. The cold wind brought the faint tang of salt inland, along with seagulls who soared overhead looking for food. The fleets must not have sailed in the storm last night. Breathing out, she felt the last of the night's fears escape, and a new tingle replace them.

Watching Alex, she knew why he breathed on his hands a few times to warm them. And she felt her head tilt as he took her face in his hands and traced her lips with his thumb. 'You've become the most gorgeous creature, Belle,' he said. His lips touched hers, briefly, uncertainly.

'I didn't want to come back, but someone had to clear the cottage. I never wanted to see the place again. All that misery and silence. And then when I saw you in the hall...I remembered all the good things as well. And they all involved you.'

'Alex...Luke...'

He dropped her face, and she felt the loss of warmth immediately.

'Don't tell me you buy into that shit. All that belonging to one man rubbish. You're not his 'bird', you're your own self.'

'And you'll be gone in a week, like you were never even back here. I'm not a quick lay for anyone who shows me any attention either.'

They scowled at each other, but the cold was too bitter to stand.

'Come on, I'll take you home.'

Back at the house, he let Agnes cajole him into the kitchen for a warm drink and submitted himself to what she doubtless thought was a subtle grilling on his intentions and prospects. Belle cringed and glowered in the corner but was more afraid of leaving.

When they heard a deeper engine growling down the lane, Belle's urge to flee got stronger but Iris patted her arm. 'Let's just see, eh? An' if it all gets too much you can always run away with me on the bus. I've a panda you'd love but he's refused to leave London...'

She let Iris prattle on, a river of noise that held her rising alarm in check as Luke walked into the kitchen. He nodded, impassively.

'Alex.'

'Luke.'

'That your hairdryer in the yard, then?'

'Yeah. Still driving your dad's rover?'

Belle saw the muscles in Luke's jaw twitch at just the same moment that Alex carefully put down the cup he'd been drinking from.

'Belle?' Luke asked. 'Could I have a word, private like?'

She wasn't sure that she'd forgiven him for leaving her at the top of the lane. Not after that thing had spooked her. But she nodded and led him into the lounge.

'Well?'

'Well, I'm sorry. You were right. I was being pathetic. I just, well, didn't like it. Seeing you dance with another man like you ought to have been dancing with me. Seeing you smile at him like I thought you could only smile at me.'

Luke closed the distance between them and chucked her under the chin so that she looked up into his brown eyes. All she could see in them was concern and hungry emotion.

'No,' she said, quietly. 'I'm sorry I was being such a mare. I was in a mood before we even got there.'

Luke reached down and took one of her hands. His callused thumb traced patterns on its palm, like it had done elsewhere on her before, and she leaned in as her body responded.

'So,' he asked into her hair, 'Am I forgiven?'

'If I am.'

He hugged her close, his long arms reaching around her. She heard the front door of the house slam and looked up.

'Leave it, Belle. He'll be gone in a week, and I'll still be here and you'll still be mine.'

She stilled in his arms.

'Belle?'

'I'm just not sure I want to be anybody's right now.'

'What's that mean? Are you breaking off with me?'

Belle shook her head. How could she explain? Finally, all those stories Agnes had told, all those arguments about not just doing what was expected, made sense. She didn't know what she wanted and she wasn't going to make a decision just because it was the easiest one. And she knew she'd struggle to explain it to Luke.

After he'd gone, scowling, she collapsed onto the sofa and tried not to cry. Iris came in first, with a cup of tea and a hug.

'I just don't know what to do, Iris!'

'Do what you feel is right, chuck, and never pay no mind to what anyone says. Your mum doesn't want you settling for someone just cause they're there, and others would say you'd be crazy to leave him for a boy you've barely seen for five years.'

'And what would you say?'

'I'd say it's up to you, pet. Throw 'em both over if you don't want 'em. But they both want you.'

Iris scrunched up against the headboard, the bleached candlewick covers clutched to her chest. Shadows, cast by the icy white moonlight, swirled across the wallpaper of the room as, at the frost-patterned window, something *scritched*.

'Oh lummie,' she whispered, 'this was meant to be a break from it all!'

'Gerron out of it!' she yelled, reaching for the candle beside her.

There was a hard thump, as if something had recoiled from the window in alarm. Iris nodded with satisfaction. Her theory was right: the creature was after Belle specifically. This was Belle's room, and it had sheared away when it had realised Belle was not within. Iris had produced some lame excuse about draughts to take it, preying on Belle's good mannered upbringing and her own apparent age to engineer a swap.

'Iris? Are you alright?' Agnes was in the doorway, shielding her candle from the draughts.

'I'm fine. Where's Belle?'

'Downstairs. She fell asleep on the sofa and I didn't like to wake her.'

'It's her it wants. Let's get down there!'

Running down the stairs, they saw the front door was open. Belle stood in the yard, flurries of snow swirling around her head. She was shining her torch upwards, dancing it about in search of something. Dana stood close by, a trench coat over her shoulders. They could see something in the darkness, some shape which shied away each time the torch beam got near. Its call echoed through the air.

‘It’s on the roof again, Dana,’ Belle yelled as more slates smashed to the ground.

Dana was slotting cartridges into the shotgun she had crooked in her arm. ‘I’m not putting up with this,’ she said as she locked it. ‘I’m on a bloody *deadline*.’

She squinted past her Gitane and let one barrel off. With a hoarse caw of alarm, the creature rose. Right into the path of Dana’s second barrel. She squeezed the trigger as it went through her sights.

‘Winged it,’ she said with satisfaction and broke the gun open. ‘Knew that Roedean education was good for something.’

‘Yes, but where’s it gone?’

Dana shrugged. ‘Probably into the wood. We can’t look for it at night, but at least now I can get some quiet.’

Belle slept on the sofa, Iris having explained the real reason she’d taken her room. She’d thought she’d never sleep, knowing that the owlman had been fixated on her, but the fuzzy warmth from the fire and Dana’s familiar curses from the library let her drift away. She woke when Iris bustled in, a bacon sandwich in hand and another on a plate.

‘Aggie wants us to go over to Luke’s farm. His dad’s had a ham ready for her for the last week and we’re all but out of meat.’

The lane was still relatively clear of snow but the sun was melting the last on the treetops so that it fell in sudden wet outbursts on them. Iris had dug a wheelbarrow up from somewhere in the yard and was dragging it along behind them. Out on the main road, the snowmelt was running and they splashed along. Iris was telling one of her long tall stories, like Belle was still a little girl to be amused by fantasies.

The purr of the scooter’s engine carried easily in the stillness of the morning, so she was ready when it came round the bend towards them. Alex looked unsure for a moment, before Iris heartily greeted him. ‘Well, and how are you today?’

‘Fine, Miss Wildthyme. Just taking some of my father’s books over to yours, in fact. I thought Dana might like to have a look through before I sell them.’

‘Ooh, let’s have a gander! I’m a bit of a bibliophile meself.’

Belle hopped from foot to foot, impatient and embarrassed. Alex got off the scooter and unstrapped the box from the back, flipping it open so Iris could take a look. She started thumbing through enthusiastically with a mutter for every title. Alex moved nearer to Belle, cautiously.

‘Are you alright, Belle?’ he asked. He was hunched into his coat, with his hands deep in the pockets. His blue eyes darted up to catch hers briefly and then fell back to his shoes. This was more like the gawky boy she had grown up with, all angles and frowns. She found herself swinging her torso from side to side: she might have been keeping herself warm in the freezing air, but she was mainly keeping herself from her sudden urge to embrace him.

'I'm OK,' she said.

'Good. Me too.'

Iris butted over. 'No you're not. You're favouring your right arm like anything. I could hear it in the way you handled the brakes.'

'It's nothing, Miss Wildthyme—'

'Iris.'

'Iris. Just came off on a corner yesterday. It was all the snow.'

'Let's see.'

'Really, it's just some bruising. Look.'

He pulled the glove off his right hand and showed her the grazed raw and rapidly bruising skin.

'Humph. I'll give you ten bob for the Tennyson. Dana's already got it and the dealer down in Darstow is a crook.'

Belle rolled her eyes and caught Alex grinning at her.

'Come on *auntie*,' she said, taking Iris' arm and winking at the boy, 'we need to get that pork before dark.'

At the farm, Mr Tremen greeted Belle with familiarity and Iris with a nod of the head. He was a big man, like his son, with a sun-crumpled face, salt and pepper hair and a pipe.

'Tha' boy's in the sheds, if you're wanting 'im,' he said.

'We're just after the pork, actually,' Iris said quickly.

'Ah. Well, tha's in the cool house. You knows the way. I'll get Luke to come help you.'

Belle led them round. She wasn't sure why her heart skittered at the thought of running into Luke so soon after Alex had given her that melting look. She did love Luke: he was broad and made her feel safe, and he could make her laugh like a drain. And he liked her. She noticed when he found them that his lower lip was split; the raw edges white in the cold.

'Afternoon, Belle. Do you want to come inside for a tea? I was just taking a break anyway.'

It was tempting but Iris interrupted. 'We need to be back before dark, Luke, so we'd best get the pork first.'

'Ok.'

Inside the cool house was no warmer than outdoors. In the high rafters, hams hung from hooks like giant mothballs. Iris had manoeuvred the wheelbarrow in and Belle spread a muslin cloth across it. Luke got a hook on a long pole from behind the door and reached up to catch the string around one. He grunted as he lowered it into the cloth, wincing as he untwisted the hook.

'Are you alright, chuck?' Iris asked.

'Just pulled a muscle last night. Had to get the fodder out to the animals in that snow and twisted the wrong way.'

'Humph.'

They wrapped the ham in the cloth and Luke helped Iris get the wheelbarrow back out on the path. 'Ooh, I'm not so young as I was,' she said perkily. 'I just need to powder me nose and we'll be heading back.'

Before Belle could stop her, Iris had scooted off around the corner to the outdoor privy. Luke came close and nudged Belle with his boot. She looked up and saw his brown eyes watching her.

'I'm losing you, aren't I?' he asked.

'What? No. I...'

'Oh, maybe not to Alex. You're not so daft as all that. But you live in a world of books and wild thinking. I'm just the boy from the farm, and everyone reckons one day I'll have the farm and a good farmer's wife to go with it.'

'And they don't think I'm farmer's wife material? Who are they to judge?'

'No-one. Everyone. Anyway, I'm just saying there's more to me than just this farm and you know that somewhere inside you. Don't...don't give me up.'

She leaned over and kissed him on the lips, feeling the cut on them with her tongue.

Iris and Belle were nearly back at the house, trudging up the lane, when Belle felt Iris glancing at her speculatively. 'What?'

'Well....you don't believe that tripe they told you, did you?' Both your beau's with grazed knuckles and bruised ribs. And one with a cut lip.'

'Why not?'

'Why not? If Alex came off so bad as to skin his knuckles raw, how comes his gloves were undamaged? If Luke really had twisted wrong throwing bales to the livestock, he'd be in traction. Nah, it's obvious.'

Belle waited patiently. Iris dropped the wheelbarrow to the ground and raised her eyebrow.

'They were fighting over you. Actual fighting. Fisticuffs!'

'Don't be daft, Iris, and help me get this ham inside.'

Iris sat before the fire and stroked the long wing feather she had found on the path just before dark. Belle had curled herself up under a blanket with a book in her lap and Agnes was sat on the hearth rug ripping old newspaper into strips to make firelighters. It was the first time Iris had seen her friend's fingers making anything since she'd arrived. Iris studied the tawny stripe in the feather, and the blood on its shaft.

'Dana?' she called.

The writer stopped in the hall and glanced in.

'On a deadline,' she said brusquely.

'I know that. But come in for a few minutes and rest. I want to pick your brains.'

Dana grumbled but settled next to Belle.

'I've been wondering something,' Iris said. 'Aren't you the least bit curious about the creature haunting this house?'

Dana blinked.

'Of course. It's an interesting anthropomorphic resonance. And it's interesting that it is happening now, as Belle steps into womanhood and...'

'...and I'm losing mine?' Agnes finished, sitting back on her heels.

Dana shrugged. 'I'd say you were both finding new ways of seeing things.'

'...and so we *are* seeing things? You think it's a shared delusion?'

Dana smiled at Belle. She stabbed her Gitane out.

'When you were little, when Aggie first offered me room and board here if I'd just mind you whilst she painted, I would tell you stories. Do you remember?

'We'd make a tent from the clothes horse and a sheet before the fire, and sit indian style inside. And you wanted so many stories that I told every one I knew. Of the goblin market, of Robin Hood, of Camelot, of the dancing red shoes and the dog with eyes the size of saucers. Of tin soldiers and of running off with the raggle taggle gypsies – oh!

'And of the owlman.'

Agnes stopped ripping at the papers. Iris didn't dare ask anything, for fear of reminding Dana of her deadline.

'I'd been researching,' Dana said. 'Looking into the myths of Cornwall. I thought I was going to be the next Tennyson. Luckily, I got over it. But I retold those myths I found to you as you clamoured for more stories.

'The owlman of Zennan, he was called, and what was said of him was this:

'That once a man so loved his sweetheart that he wanted to stand vigil over her all day and all night. He loved her so that he was jealous of the dark that hid her and the night breeze that caressed her skin. But each night, as he stood watch, sleep stole over him and he began to think she had a lover. So he went to the north, to Tintagel, and begged the old man in the cave for a potion. Merlin – for what other wizard would live in that crazy tower of rock? – agreed but there would be a condition. The man from Zennan, not caring, took the potion and drank it in a single draught. It was then that Merlin told him the condition: henceforth, the man could see his sweetheart by day as a man or by night as an owl. But he could never spend the night with her as a man unless he was her true love and she saw through the creature to the man within.'

'It's...'

'Yes, a version of the Gawain and the loathly lady.'

'And did she?'

'Did she what?'

'See her true love?'

Dana lit a new cigarette and broke the spell.

'Oh yes. But the point is that what's been haunting this house is a manifestation of that story: a psychical phantom.'

'Why did you shoot at it then?' Iris asked.

'All this screaming and upset in the night: it seemed like a good way to disperse the hold it had. I *am* on a deadline.'

Dana drained her coffee and headed back to her room. Iris sat by the fire still, twirling the feather in her hands.

'Humph.'

Belle pulled her sweater on over her pyjamas and stamped into her boots. There was no escaping from chores. It was going to be near freezing outside, but she could run to the woodshed and hauling the basket back was always sweat inducing. Agnes was making porridge and coffee and Belle knew she'd enjoy breakfast more if she knew she didn't have to go back outside again.

The uncleared snow in the yard wouldn't melt for days yet, not until the sun could reach into every shadow, so she slowed down when she saw the dark slashes drifting against the woodshed door. Closer, she realised they were feathers, like the one Iris had found yesterday. Closer still, and she realised the door to the woodshed was ajar.

She could sense something – someone – was within. Very quietly, she let the basket fall to the snow. Inside the shed, just to the right of the door, the small hatchet would be resting. The large axe stood there too, but she wouldn't be able to wield that.

She pushed the door wide enough to let her slide in, her hand gliding across until it felt the handle of the hatchet. There was rustling, and the sharp tang of blood stinging her nose.

'Hello?'

Her eyes adjusted to the dim light. Huddled in the shadows, where the stock of wood was already low, was the owlman. He reared back, a low hiss protesting at her intrusion. His tried to stretch his wings wide, tried to launch himself into the air. There was no clearance though, and his bloodied right wing didn't respond properly. The impact of Dana's shot. He wasn't going to attack, he was scared. She let the hatchet drop back against the wall.

'I'm sorry,' she said, 'you've been hurt.'

As she approached, he tried to rise again with his talons extended. Wickedly curved and sharp, they made her hesitate, before his wing collapsed under his weight again. His beak snapped at her. There was no way of getting close, not without being injured herself.

If it were a normal bird, she would throw a towel over it so she could approach without panicking the creature.

'Stay there,' she said, backing away.

There was a big tarpaulin in the garage, but she was going to need help.

They laid the creature on the sofa in the lounge, still wrapped in the tarpaulin. One talon was free but the material was so tightly bound that it could not move. He shifted within the cocoon, and Belle put her hand on his chest. She could feel a panicked heart beating fast within. She brushed her hand along his form and murmured hushes and cooing towards him.

'So,' Iris asked quietly, 'Who do we think he is?'

'Does it matter?' Agnes asked. She was twitching, her hands fluttering up to her chin or tracing patterns on the furniture.

'It does to her,' Iris said. Belle had crouched down by the sofa now, still whispering reassurances and promises. She had discarded her red coat when it had been ripped by a talon as they captured the creature, and in the firelight she suddenly looked older and wiser than her years. She glanced up at the older women.

'I know who it is,' she said, 'it's my true love.'

Iris and Agnes exchanged glances. They both knew that right now that simple certainty was the least complicated thing in the world. Iris held her breath as the shape beneath the tarpaulin quivered and moved. The exposed talon retracted, shuddered and twisted until what had looked like a talon looked like a battered and bare foot. That didn't tell them anything.

Did Belle even know who it was, Iris wondered as the girl leaned forward and loosened the tarpaulin. As the light hit his eyes, the boy within it gasped and shrank back.

'It's OK, you're OK,' Belle said, and folded the tarpaulin aside.

Alex's skin was golden in the firelight, the angry bruises and shot peppering his right side dappling him. For a moment, his eyes were the yellow gleam of a bird's, before he blinked and they came back human.

The last of the snow was melting, and the first faint warmth was returning to the air as Iris entered the hibernating orchard. The bus was at the end, where the road ran close, and Panda would be waiting anxiously – or not so anxiously – at a bar in Soho for her to return.

Back in the yard, Belle had just squeezed a holdall into one of Alex's panniers. Iris had offered them a lift back to London. She'd taken to the young couple and thought they'd handle a life of adventure and derring-do very well. But Alex had demurred: they would be having enough adventures of their own and, besides, he liked the way Belle held him on the scooter.

So Iris had pootled around to the studio, to see if Agnes felt like a change of scenery. She had stopped in the doorway though. Ever since the morning they had taken the owlman in, Agnes's hands had been restless. Now sketches littered the tables and the painter stood in front of a canvas, charcoal in hand. A new figure was taking form, against a purple-blue winter landscape. His wingspan was dark and wide, reaching across the whole canvas, and a red-caped figure curled itself close. And, though the style and subject was new, Iris knew Agnes had found her muse again. She closed the door of the studio and headed home.

Iris Wildthyme and the Unhappy Medium

Cavan Scott & Mark Wright

The babble of expectant voices washed over Hilary. This was the moment he loved, standing in the wings, listening to the gentle hubbub of the general public finding their seats. He couldn't see them, but he knew they were there. The electricity in the atmosphere before a show was addictive and he was like a junkie aching for the sweetness of a new hit.

Catching himself in the cracked, scuffed mirror that stood in the wings of the theatre, Hilary smoothed his already immaculate hair back, his hand laden heavy with rings. He could almost hear his dear old Ma's voice, echoing around the pullies and wooden walkways of the flies. 'You look a million dollars, me babber. A real star.'

If only she had lived to see this. She had been right for all those years. Hilary Mercer had been meant for great things. She had supported him through the lonely darkness of the wilderness years. Working by day as the security guard of the local SaveMart and living the dream at night. The stale smoke and faded velvet seats of the working men's clubs. The desperation of the talent contests. When his Dad had grumbled that Hilary was wasting his life chasing a singing career, Ma had encouraged him to get back up in front of the band. And after they'd split over creative difficulties she'd still believed in him, even though the crowds at the open mike comedy clubs had jeered him out of the spotlight.

It had been worth it though, all those years working his way up the business. It had even been Ma's idea. Well, sort of. One day, over a supper of SaveMart Value scotch pies and watery mash, Ma had launched into one of those one-way conversations only mothers could have.

'You'll never guess who's died,' she suddenly announced, chewing on a fork-full of marrowfat peas. 'Margaret?'

'Who's Margaret,' Hilary had replied, half-listening to Ma and half-watching an item about the fight to stop a telegraph pole being erected in Chipping Sodbury on the HTV news.

'Margaret! You know, Margaret! Goes to bingo, gammy leg, daughter ran away with Mr Shulpa from the corner shop.'

Hilary had shrugged and reached for the Daddies sauce that Dad had been commandeering since the meal began.

'Of course you knew Margaret,' Ma continued gamely. 'Can't believe she's gone. Heart attack. There they were clearing up the tea things after her spiritualist meeting down the community hall when she toppled over in her seat, clutching her chest. She was gone before she hit the wood laminate. Mrs Gibson always does a good job on that floor...'

Hilary had looked up, his attention peaked suddenly.

'Spiritualist meeting? Here? In Knowle?'

'Oh yes. Margaret had the gift. Went a couple of times myself. Must have told you. She channelled your Auntie Gertie a couple of times. Gert spooky it was. She had the gift.'

'What, like a psychic?'

'Not much of one,' Dad had cut in. 'Didn't predict that all those cream cakes she shovelled in her gob were clogging up her arteries did she?' He nodded sagely and rustled his paper.

Ma had shot Dad a look, saying he shouldn't speak ill of the dead. The old man snorted and said that now that Margaret was gone, the dead weren't likely to talk back. Ma had tutted and started to clear up the dinner plates, wrestling Dad's away as he tried to mop up the last of the gravy with a limp slice of rapidly dissolving SaveMart bread.

'They've had to cancel next weeks' meeting as there's no one to lead it. Mrs Moon at number 74 is gutted. She was going to try to contact her late husband to see where he'd put the sandwich toaster before he died. She's been looking for it everywhere.'

Mrs Moon never found her Brevil, but the spiritualist meeting hadn't been cancelled. Hilary had gone straight around to the community centre manager's place and offered his services. Yes, of course he had the gift. Of course he could commune with the spirit world. The manager had been unsure but, in the face of an angry mob of women of a certain age, gave Hilary his big break.

The rest, as they say, is history. Hilary had gone down a storm. Of course, it had been a load of old rubbish, but he'd watched enough daytime TV in the security office of the SaveMart over the years. He'd seen countless psychics hawking their wares, offering vague messages from beyond the veil. What did he have to lose? It was all just an act anyway. All just sparkle and showbiz. And he spoke that language fluently. He'd slipped in a little banter, the odd wink and flirt and before he knew it the community centre was packed.

It all happened so fast; the night the talent scout had dropped by, getting on the club circuit, the appearance on Richard and Judy and then the big one, Dead Scary, the paranormal investigation show on True Life TV. Three seasons on and Hilary Mercer, psychic to the stars, had a book in ASDA's best-seller list and was here, at the Catford Broadway theatre on the second leg of his sell-out UK tour.

Ma would be proud. She should be. She was even part of his act. She'd passed away just before the first episode of Dead Scary aired and so, in a stroke of genius, Hilary had slipped her into the patter. She was his spirit guide, helping him through his experiences with spirit folk in whatever haunted house the team was investigating. The press lapped it up. The mum and son team. Perfect.

'You're on, Mr Mercer.'

The skinny, vacant looking stage manager, who didn't look a day over 22, didn't even glance up as she ushered Hilary onto the stage, but he didn't care. As the Dead Scary theme blared around the auditorium, the sound of the applause washed over him. These were his people. This was his destiny. This was his drug.

Half an hour later and they were eating out of the palm of his well-moisturised hand. The first message had been easy. 'Ma', his ever loyal maternal spirit guide had introduced him to a red-head female ghost who loved shoes and whose name began with, hang on, he could see it, but it was so faint; was it 'E'? No. A 'C'?. Yes, definitely a C. At least five punters had thrust their hands up but he'd picked on the eager looking woman in the first row. It turned out he was channelling her mother Christine who wanted to tell her daughter that the decision she was losing sleep over – and wasn't there always a decision that had to be made – would turn out all right and she would be with her every step of the way. It had run like clockwork. A few non-specific predictions, a couple of historical ghosts for the theatre and they were well on the way to the interval.

Then it happened.

Everything changed.

'Alright my loves, I'm getting someone else coming through. Someone larger than life. Someone with something to say,' Hilary had announced, emphasising the West Country twang in his voice that Woman's Own had called 'winsome and charming'. 'Walk them into the light, Ma. Help them communicate from beyond the grave. I can hear you dear heart. Talk to me. Talk to Hilary.'

'Oh thank heavens for that, Hilary. I thought I'd never get through to you, lovey. Where have you been when you're Auntie Iris needed you?'

Hilary's brow crinkled for a second at the sound of the voice. Somebody having a joke – there was always one. Clearing his throat, he called for quiet in the audience.

'Please, ladies and gentlemen. If you could refrain from shouting out. I must have complete silence if I am to communicate with those from beyond.'

'From beyond what? Hilary luv, what are you chuntering about? Now, you've got to listen carefully as we haven't got a lot of time. Panda is trying to hold them back, but he's up to his little polyester knees in the bloody things.'

Hilary glared out at the audience, searching for whichever joker was trying to derail his show – probably some scally from Lewisham. 'Seriously, whoever that is,' Hilary said sternly, 'this isn't time for mucking about. Communing with the dead is a serious business and demands much concentration.'

There was a small, nervous ripple from the audience. Hilary caught a couple in the front row flashing a confused, sideways glance at each other.

'You're not wrong chuck.' replied the voice, *'Although personally I'd wish they just bugger of out of it. I don't know, a girl takes the wrong turn and all hell breaks through.'*

When the second voice joined the conversation, Hilary was beginning to feel a little sick. He was hot, the collar of his shirt feeling tight and sticky against his skin.

'Iris,' the new voice said, sounding more than a little peeved. *'Have you got through yet. I can't hold this lot off much longer. They're trying to skin me alive. I've given out a few good punches up the hooter, but soon all I'll have left is my not inconsiderable wit.'*

'Don't worry Panda, luv,' the woman replied, *'I've got our Hilary on the line. He'll be able to help.'*

Hilary felt his knees buckle and the sea of heads in the auditorium began to blur and swim before his eyes. The penny dropped. This wasn't some joker in the audience. The voices were inside his head.

Oh God! The voices were inside his bloody head...

From the corner of his vision Hilary could see the Stage Manager waving her scrawny arms, trying to get his attention. And then there was a moment of clarity as the faces of the audience came into focus. The auditorium was deathly silent and Hilary was suddenly painfully aware that every eye in the theatre was on him, but he could only let his mouth flap open and shut like a goldfish. Finally the words came as he murmured uncertainly into the void:

'Do you... Do you know me?'

'Do I what?' The woman asked, *'Of course I know you, you daft bugger! Would I forget me own brother, well, half-brother, well, computer generated hyper-intelligent personality avatar? But we haven't got time for this. You need to help me!'*

'I do?' Hilary said, weakly.

'Yes, you do,' The second voice cut in. It was deep, cultured and aloof. And if he didn't know better, it sounded a little slurred. Drunk, even. *'Has running that disco in Malaga sent you potty? You'll never guess what the drunken old gasket has done now, Hilary old son. I warned her. I told her nothing good would come of it, but oh no. Would she listen? I know a short cut, Panda. Will get us there in no time Panda. It'll get us killed more like!'*

'Oh put a sock in it, Panda! I've done it hundreds of times before. Cut a corner across the spirit plane, as simple as undoing an eunuch's thong! Nothing to it. It's just that this time, well, I think I had the map upside down and there was a ciggy burn where the exit from the ring road was. We've got a little lost. Ended up in some kind of, well, service station on the loop road around limbo.'

Hilary wasn't even aware that the curtain had started to come down and there were angry shouts from the audience. He was just standing there, listening in shock to a disembodied conversation that seemed to involve him somehow, even though he had no idea how he was hearing it.

'Service centre...' he mumbled absently.

'...on the loop road around limbo,' the woman – Iris was it? – repeated. *'The teeny-tiny problem is that the bus isn't supposed to hang around in the shadow dimensions; plays havoc with the suspension... Oh, and we're under attack.'*

'Under attack...'

It must be stress, Hilary thought. Nervous exhaustion. The Chuckle Brothers had warned him about that last month when they shared a bill at the Weston-super-Mare Playhouse, but he'd ignored them, saying he could handle doing the tour, the book signing and the mid-week lottery draw. Ma would be proud.

'Yes, under attack. Why do you keep repeating every bloody word I say? We've got a little dispute with some Ectovores, denizens of this little bit of the void. They said we'd parked in their space and now the buggers are laying siege to me bus. Panda's trying to stop them getting on board but they've jammed the doors open. We only pulled in to use the lavvy, and we've not even been able to make it over to the little shop. Panda's furious because he was looking forward to getting a Ginsters and a copy of Razzle.'

'From a service centre in limbo...'

Hilary didn't even try to stop the little thread of dribble that was hanging from the corner of his mouth. Maybe he was having a stroke. Perhaps that's why he couldn't really feel himself being shaken by the security guard who was telling him to snap out of it.

'Iris,' the male voice, who Hilary assumed was this Panda fellow, shouted, *'something is happening. The Ectovores are fading away. They're vanishing. Retreating. We're saved! Hurrah!'*

That's good then, thought Hilary as his legs finally gave way and he buckled to the stage floor. He could just about hear the security guard shouting for someone to call for an ambulance and the stage manager trying to placate angry punters who were trying to storm the stage to demand their money back.

Perhaps it wasn't a stroke. Perhaps it was a full-on brain haemorrhage.

'Oo 'eck, blimey, Panda. They're not retreating. I've used the bus's pan-dimensional phone to form a connection to Hilary, and those 'orrible spectre things must've sniffed out the chance to break into reality. They're transferring themselves down the line, piggy-backing on the signal.'

'You mean, those sinister spectral savages are going to attack Earth, all because you tried to reverse the charges?'

'I'm afraid so Panda. Hilary luv, you better prepare yourself. You've got trouble on the way. They're no laughing matter, I can tell you.'

But Hilary wasn't laughing. He was giggling. Giggling at the sight of the security guard above him who was now sporting a rather fetching range of bony tentacles that were bursting out of his overstretched black t-shirt. Giggling at the maw that was stretching out of his skull. Giggling at the glowing red eyes that burnt behind the guard's retinas. Giggling as the thing that used to be the stage manager ripped an angry punter's head clean from her shoulders. Stroke. Brain Haemorrhage. Whatever it was, he'd obviously gone stark, raving mad.

'That's the last of them, Iris,' he heard Panda shout, *'How's Hilary doing down there?'*

'Goodness knows Panda,' the woman called Iris replied. *'He's not saying 'owt. He's just laughing!'*

'Laughing?'

'Aye. The poor lad's gone doolally-tap!'

'I always knew he wasn't up to the job...'

I wonder who they're talking about, thought Hilary as the creature-formally-known-as-a-human reached down a bone-encrusted arm and grabbed the front of his suit jacket. He was hoisted up as if he was a rag doll, right into the gaping wound of a mouth that dribbled with pungent, yellow saliva.

What big teeth you have, Grandma.

'Who are you calling Grandma, you cheeky sod,' the female voice shouted, *'I don't know what's wrong with you, but I'm not going to stand by here while you're ripped apart by a bunch of Ectovores. The psychic bridge is well and truly established and if those monsters can get through to you...'*

The world shifted. Well, let's face it, the world had been positively jigging about since Hilary had stepped onto the stage, but this was different. One minute he was staring into the business end of something particularly nightmare-inducing, its vile slobber splashing down his face and the next everything went a bit wibbly. The creature blurred and was replaced by a psychedelic haze. Hilary was suddenly aware he was shooting through a tunnel of vivid colour towards a blazing, white light. This was it then. He'd gone. That had been weird, but thankfully brief. As his body was pulled upward he wondered if Ma would be waiting for him. With waves of calm washing over him, Hilary shut his eyes and...

... cried out in shock as he suddenly dropped face down onto a bright mauve and decidedly threadbare carpet.

'Who, in the name of John Le Mesurier, is *that*?'

Hilary groaned. So the crazy voices were here in heaven too. Just his bloody luck.

'Buggered if know, Panda luv,' replied the female. 'Hilary, is that you?'

Hilary considered raising his head to look around, but thought lying face down was probably the lesser of two evils.

'Perhaps he's, you know, rejuvenated or whatever your lot call it?' suggested Panda. 'The Change.'

'Not likely. If it was one of my own people I'd be able to recognise him by his BO. No-matter how many faces and bodies we get through, no-matter how our personalities change, we always smell the same. In many ways, we have the same smell. No, whoever this is, this isn't Hilary Wildthyme.'

'So who the blazes is he then?'

'There's only one way to find out, my little chuckie egg.'

Hilary felt himself being turned over by a pair of thin, yet surprisingly strong hands. Oh well, he thought, no escaping it now. Time to meet my maker.

Somehow he'd never expected his maker to be wearing a hat *that* big or a pair of ear-rings that would have made Pat Butcher blush.

'Are you all right, luvvie? Can you hear me?'

'Of course I can hear you,' Hilary snapped back, raising a ring-laden hand to his throbbing head. 'I may be dead, but I'm not deaf!'

'Dead? Who said anything about being dead?' said the woman, who he could only assume was Iris, her lined face creasing into a frown. 'You're as alive as me and Panda.'

Hilary's gaze wandered to the improbable sight of a stuffed toy that appeared to be peeking around Iris' tiger-print stockinged legs with bright, curious beads.

'Alive? Are you telling me that that toy is alive?'

'Toy?' the bear bellowed in indignation, 'TOY?!'

'Oh, don't mind him,' said Iris, shushing her furry companion, 'his bark is worse than his bite. He hasn't got any teeth anyway. Now, I think I know where you're coming from. You thinking you've popped your cogs and this place is heaven...'

'It isn't?' Hilary asked weakly.

'Good God no. Heaven is dull as ditch water. I spent three weeks there once, trying to win back the Ark of the Covenant from the Angel Gabriel in a game of Gin Rummy. No, my name's Iris Wildthyme and this is me time travelling bus.'

'Oh, and I'm invisible as well as a toy am I?' moaned the bear.

'And you've met Panda of course. Who might you be?'

'H... Hilary Mercer,' Hilary stammered, 'Psychic to the stars.'

Iris clapped her gloved hands.

'That explains it then!'

'Explains what?' Hilary asked.

'The mix-up. I was trying to call Hilary Wildthyme, my sort-of half brother. Runs a nightclub in Malaga in 2108 with a Naxian called Roger. Long story. But the bus latched onto you, another Hilary with psychic abilities.'

'So you dialled the wrong number then?' Panda asked, his voice dripping with accusation.

'Nothing of the sort, Panda. Wildthyme's Law, Rule Number One: keep pushing buttons and you'll get through eventually. Do you know how difficult it is to make a cross-dimensional call, especially when you're under attack from phantom nasties? By the look of my scanner-doobrey 'ere,' Iris waved something that looked suspiciously like a lady-shave with Christmas lights stuck on to it, 'our Hilary here is a level 15 psychic. He'd have to be a strong one for Ectovores to pass over to him so easily.'

'What are you talking about?' Hilary asked, finally pushing himself up onto his elbows, 'I'm not a psychic. It's all an act, a...' he hated this word, but it was the best to describe the situation, 'sham.'

'Not according to the bus. Even if it was only a latent ability you're a bona fide medium if these readings are to be believed, duck.'

Hilary could only gape. It seemed the decent thing to do.

'Haven't you forgotten something, Iris?' said Panda, but Hilary wasn't listening. He was sitting there, on the grimy carpet of a time-travelling bus, looking at a mad old bat and her talking stuffed bear, trying to take it all in.

'I'm a real psychic,' he whispered to himself.

'What's that Panda luv?' Iris asked.

'It's all true,' Hilary murmured.

'Those extra-dimensional hooligans?' Panda replied.

'Oh my God!' Hilary shouted, 'Those monsters. Eating my audience. It really happened.'

A word slipped past Iris' fulsome lips that Hilary didn't recognised but could tell from its tone was a swear word that would make Gordon Ramsey wince. In a second she had darted to the front of the bus and jumped into the driver's seat.

'Hold onto your stomachs,' she called over her shoulder, 'We're on our way. The bridge is fading by the second, but if I'm quick we can get back to Earth.'

There was an incongruous ding-ding from a hidden bell somewhere within the workings of the bus and the engines roared. The vehicle lurched and Hilary fell back again, thankfully landing on something soft.

'Charming!' came the muffled complaint from Panda.

Outside the windows, the now familiar multi-coloured mist churned and broiled, and the metal shell of the vehicle protested at the onslaught. *I think I preferred it when I thought I was going mad*, thought Hilary.

'We're coming in,' shouted Iris and as with a thundering trump, the mist outside parted. Hilary wasn't even surprised to see that the bus was standing in the foyer of the Broadway Theatre. 'I once saw the Krankies here,' Iris said.

Panda's beads lit up when he saw the sweet counter. 'Perhaps I can get a Ginsters after all.'

'Oh belt up, Panda! Right,' started Iris, hefting herself out of the seat, 'I've brought us in a few minutes before we snatched you into the vortex. If I've done me sums right, the Ectovores are just starting to arrive.'

Hilary allowed Iris to bundle him out of the concertina doors of the bus and into the spookily deserted foyer. Panda hopped down after them and the three of them crept up the doors that led into the stalls. They carefully creaked the doors open a crack and peered through.

Sure enough, the tableau within showed the security guard beginning his monstrous transformation as Hilary lay prone on the stage floor. The angry punter was screaming her tonsils out as the stage manager followed suit, but at least her head was still firmly connected to her neck.

'Oh god, it's going to happen again,' Hilary moaned, 'They're going to die.'

'Not if I've got anything to do with it, petal. Now, Hilary, I need you to be brave. You're going to have to go out there, peg it over that stage and touch yourself.'

'Don't be filthy!' hissed Panda.

'No, no I mean touch your other self. Grab his hand, sooth his worried brow, anything. But you need to do it sharpish before those things fully manifest in this dimension.'

'Iris, isn't that going to be awfully bad for the space-time thingy,' Panda asked disapprovingly. 'People aren't supposed to meet themselves.'

'Abso-bloody-lutely,' cackled Iris, 'Exactly what we need. Go on, Hils, what are you waiting for?'

Hilary looked pleadingly from Iris to Panda and back again. Aren't you... aren't you coming with me?'

'No, luv. We need to wait in here. You'll see why.'

'But those creatures...'

'Won't even know you're there. Now, shift it!'

And with that Iris half-kicked, half-shoved Hilary through the doors. Before he knew what was happening, he was skidding down the centre aisle towards the stage, himself and the mutating security guard. He looked back for a split second to see Iris, a velvet gloved hand raised in a thumbs up of encouragement. Panda just rolled his beads.

'Go on, Hilary luv. Grab yourself and hope for the best.' And with that, the doors closed and they were gone.

This is insane, Hilary thought as he scrambled over to his earlier self. This is crazy, Hilary thought, as he reached out for his earlier self's shoulder. You're mad, Hilary thought, as his deranged earlier self looked in his direction and giggled shrilly.

His hand brushed his other self's suit and the universe exploded.

The babble of expectant voices washed over Hilary. He ignored them for now. All he was concentrating on was the scrap of paper in his hand. Around him he could make out the bustle of Lewisham Hospital A&E department.

So mundane.

So normal.

Dear Hilary,

Sorry we couldn't hang about but as you can imagine, after such a release of temporal energy, I've been running round like a blue-arsed menian dustfly clearing up... Panda has been banging on about playing fast and loose with the web of time, but hey, a girl's got to have a hobby.

I hope you're feeling champion and survived the effects of the blast. No doubt you're going to have a sore head for a few days but you'll be right as rain come the weekend. You're probably wondering what happened, so I'll try and put this in layman's terms. When you touched your earlier self, the paradoxical nature of the encounter caused a big hole to rip in the fabric of space-time. Usually this would be what we like to call A Very Bad Thing, but I gambled that the energy release would rush into the psychic bridge. As luck would have it, I was bang on the money. The shock of suddenly having to cope with a burst of energy ruptured the bridge and sucked the Ectovores back home. Job's a good 'un!

My good old bus protected me and Panda from harm and my scanner-doobry that I slipped into your pocket when I was manhandling you from the old lass kept you safe and sound. Clockworks technology you see. Well, actually you probably don't. Just as well, as is the fact that the localised time-storm would have fried its circuits. Panda's always bellyaching that I leave more xenotech on primitive worlds than the British secret service leave official secrets on the train. Do me a favour will you? Pop it into a jiffy bag and send it to 'The Forge, Dartmoor.' They'll know what to do with it.

Hilary looked up to see the charred remains of Iris' lady-shave on the bedside cabinet.

Anyway, thanks for your help chuck and sorry for getting you into all of this. Daresay you gave your audience a treat though. They'll be talking about your lightshow for years.

Maybe we'll bump into each other again, one of these days.

Until tell, take care of yourself.

Your Auntie Iris

x

PS You might notice some side-effects from your little adventure. Nowt to worry about. You'll know what to do...

Hilary let the letter fall to his lap. They'll certainly be talking about it for years. Iris' gadget may have kept him safe but the temporal energy had played merry hell with the Catford Broadway theatre. Most of the wood in the building had regressed back to trees and collapsed in on the audience. He dreaded to think what the insurance company would make of it.

Of course, that was the least of his worries. All around him in the cubical eager faces stared at him. Not punters. Not fans. But ghosts. Real spirits and spooks. Whatever Iris had done to his career she'd also opened something in his mind. The one thing he was certain; this was no longer a cheap act. He'd never be alone again. There would always be someone needing him, even if they had been dead for ages.

But for the moment, he didn't care. There, behind all the phantoms jostling to get his attention, one translucent face lit up in a wide, beaming smile. It was positively beaming. Hilary grinned back.

Ma looked so proud.

Future Legend

Stuart Douglas

Now that it's all over the whole mad adventure seems a little bit unreal. I think I come out of it rather well and Iris, I suppose, emerges with some credit. But as for that Jenny! I'll be having words with her the next time I see her, the great useless...traffic warden.

I mean to say, there I was in the jaws of almost certain messy death and yet admirably keeping my cool whilst composing a series of witty email bon mots, and there was Jenny, resting with her feet up in her sunny Darlington headquarters, drinking little cups of espresso, nibbling on illicit chocolate Hobnobs and completely failing to come to my much needed rescue.

She claimed later that she hadn't realised I was being serious, but I ask you, Tom my boy – have a look at these emails and tell me they weren't the heartfelt cries of a bruised soul, defiant and unbeaten, but in dread need of succour from his absent friends...

From: panda@thebigredbus.uni
To: jenny@miaow.gov
Subject: This isn't Darlington, Toto

Well Jenny, this has all gone rather badly, I must say. Obviously, I refuse to blame you for my predicament – after all it's hardly your fault that the bloody postman couldn't find your top secret HQ (though sticking the damn place underneath the indoor market does seem a teensy bit paranoid to me.)

Still, I digress. Nerves, you know. They make me natter on like Iris on ASDA gin, they make you...well we both know what they make you do; I'm hardly unique in watching you do the mad sprint lav-wards, am I?

Anyway....no, I don't blame you in the slightest. I blame Iris, the booze-pickled old lush.

It was she, when all's said and done, who forced me off the bus. She who left me no choice but to abscond. She who made my continued presence an impossibility.

She who called me a cut-price Paddington!

PADDINGTON! A fictional bear of surpassing stupidity and rapacity; a poor man's Pooh, even, begging for food and shelter like some Peruvian gypsy at the door. A scrounger, she called me you know: a mumper and a taker. An ingrate and a sponger.

As good, she said, as Scottish.

And all over a half bottle of tonic water! Not even a half bottle, if truth be told: a third full at best. Which I never touched in any case, I need hardly add.

It was unbearable. Worse even than that time when I called her clone son a tiny bit implausible. She cast that up for months afterwards when he turned out to be a sentient YouTube video. As though the way he kept going all blocky and grainy looking wasn't a pretty big clue!

All of which explains why I put myself up for sale on eBay. I mean to say, I could hardly jump off at the next stop, could I? Not with my legs.

No, get myself sold as a rare item to some avaricious, yet tasteful, collector back on Earth, I thought, and then hitch my way up to you in Darlington.

It all seemed so easy in the planning stage, but then I

From: panda@thebigredbus.uni
To: jenny@miaow.gov
Subject: We'll always have this airing cupboard

Oh damn and blast. Sorry about that, dear heart – I pressed 'Send' by mistake and off the message went, prematurely spent.

And I get a woeful signal in this sodding cupboard at the best of times, even without the problem of my lack of fingers and this phone's perversely tiny buttons.

But never mind: brave heart and all that. Back to the earlier stages of my ongoing tale of woe.

If you remember, I had decided to sell myself into temporary chattel slavery on eBay and my listing had proven gratifyingly successful ('Desirable 20th century collectable Panda Plushie. Rare MOC' – only the MOC was actually false advertising, I think, though it's a measure of my fury that I never baulked at plushie.).

The bidding had been quite ferocious, if truth be told, and my little auction had raised the cockle-warming sum of two hundred pounds and fifty-one pence: money which I intended to use to hire a taxi to take me to MIAOW (North-east Division HQ) from wherever on Earth I was delivered.

So I bought one of those self-sealing boxes, stuck an address label on (do you know where Mountweazel is, incidentally? Anywhere near you?), and lay back for a nice relaxing kip as I sped my sleepy way through hyperspace. Between you and me, I was quite looking forward to the trip. Iris and I had been rubbing each other up the wrong way for a while, and this wasn't the first time harsh words had been spoken.

Personally, I think she misses Tom and resents the fact that I'm not him. Iris is never quite the same without some trim gay man around the place with whom she can compare notes about leather trousers and feather boas and the like.

Neither of which, as a hand-stitched Panda presented in his own immaculately brushed fur, is exactly an area of my own expertise.

For my part, I suppose it's possible that I've been a little fractious lately, but who can blame me, the way I'm treated?

A few weeks ago, for instance, we managed to prevent this old freighter crashing into prehistoric Earth and killing all the dinosaurs (even if it did take Iris seventeen goes before she managed to get Tom off in time), and the old bag got so pissed afterwards that she forgot I was with her and left me on that smelly rust bucket for a fortnight. Two weeks with no greater intellectual stimuli than a half-daft cook who claimed that he knew the location of one of the Atlantises and the real identity of someone called Bianca, and prophesised that Tom was one day destined to rule a land of giant scorpions. Totally hatstand, of course.

(You wouldn't have liked it there in any case – one working toilet for fifty permanently half-cut crew. I've seen less busy facilities at CC Blooms on the London Road on a Friday night).

But I'm wandering off the point again. The point is that our friendship has cooled a bit recently.

The other and more pressing point is that I never arrived in Darlington (you already know that, of course), but ended up here instead.

In what, unless I'm very much mistaken is the bottom of an airing cupboard a very long way from Earth indeed.

Little did I know how far, Tom! I won't keep you hanging though...

From: panda@thebigredbus.uni
To: trafficwardenjenny@yahoo.co.uk
Subject: Mind Your Language!

[I'm sending this to your home address as I doubt very much whether the machine which filters your MIAOW email will allow this through]

Fuck, fuck, fuck, fuck, fuckity fuck. I've seen who's holding me prisoner in this glorified broom closet – and it's those fucking Pussyworld cat bastards.

Fuck.

You never met the PussyWorlders, did you? Awful, awful creatures with the most appalling vices. Also very vicious and prone to throwing people off of high places in an altogether uncivilised manner.

Apologies for the bad language, by the by. As you know I abhor vulgarity for the sake of it (if only Iris were the same!), but I do think in this case that my shock justifies the lapse. Also I don't know if you noticed but I do think that that first expletive heavy sentence could be moulded into a Haiku with little effort – just chuck in 'Winter' between a couple of fucks and you're off and running)..

From: panda@thebigredbus.uni
To: jenny@miaow.gov
Subject: Help!!!!!!!!!!!!

Enough of the cool and suave persona, I think. Time to panic and scream for help like a proper travelling companion.

Get me out of here, Jenny. Or contact Iris and get her to do it. Whatever reason they have for kidnapping me, I'll bet you it's not intended to do little old me any good.

For a start, they all talk in some kind of code. I can't understand a bloody word they say: it's all hisses and soft clucking noises, like foxes in a house full of particularly trusting hens.

And this cupboard – I suppose I should call it a cell since I'm being held in it, but I can definitely see jackets hanging from a railing above me – this cell is very peculiar. There's no bed, for a start, and so I've been forced to sleep on a pile of old green rubber something or others I found lying in one corner. Rather creepily, whatever the something or other was before I converted it into Panda bedding, it had arms and legs and even what appear to be rudimentary fingers! I'd worry that I was napping on the skin of the vanquished enemy of my feline captors were it not for the fact the rubber is about two inches thick and anything which previously inhabited it appears to have had no knees. So unless you've had something come through the Flap recently which walked as though it had permanently soiled itself, I think we can assume it's some kind of dressing up costume.

The only other thing in here is an irregularly shaped lump of scratched and dented Perspex. I can't think what it's possibly for. Definitely not a pillow though. I tried.

Tell Iris that I've only seen two of the pussies so far and that they've taken to wearing some kind of armour since last we met. At least, the two I saw had metal plates across their backs and encasing their front legs, and one also had a sort of silver half face plate covering one eye and the top of its head.

Do reply, Jenny. I'm not sure if I have this phone set up properly for receiving messages but on the off chance...

And tell Iris to hurry...

I rather like that email actually, if I can say so without undue modesty. It reads rather like a little novel, with the apparent fear of the opening section shown up as obvious subterfuge by the manner in which our hero calmly takes note of his surroundings and gathers intelligence about the enemy. I put myself very much in mind of a young Jimmy Cagney at the end of 'Angels with Dirty Faces' there actually.

Anyhow, you may want to get a big box of tissues to hand now Tom (no, not for that, you mucky pup). This next message is heart-breaking stuff, all raw emotion and feelings laid bare...

From: panda@thebigredbus.uni
To: iris@thebigredbus.uni
Subject: The Gin Genie

Hey ho,

Just a quick note, dear Iris, in case you don't get here in time and I end up with my stuffing smeared across the four corners of this closet, and my glassy eyes even glassier than usual.

I want to apologise for pinching the last of your tonic water.

I've got no excuse other than the fact I'd poured myself a generous measure of Bombay Sapphire and the only tonic to be had was the one you'd marked 'BUGGER OFF PANDA' in purple felt tip.

I admit to feeling a mite annoyed at you being such a hog, but that's no excuse for not only taking a splash for my gin but also using the rest to shine up some of the little fortune I keep in my special tartan purse (it didn't work either – next week I'll go back to using spit and my buffing cloth, I think).

That was sheer bloody minded vindictiveness of the pettiest variety, I have to admit.

Anyhow, things are looking a bit grim here, between these blasted cats talking gobbledygook and time passing with no sign of you and the good old bus coming to save the day. Yesterday, one of the cats came and took away the lump of Perspex and the rubber stuff, and another one poked me in the stomach with a needle of some sort. That reminded me of the time that you, Tom and I went to that acupuncturist in Lowestoft and he turned out to be one of your lot who had retired and then inexplicably come over all evil. Lucky you had that lighter and those fireworks in your handbag, eh?

Good times, eh? Good times...

Must go, I can feel myself welling up and you know tears matt my fur something awful.

Love
Panda

I bet you're absolutely crying your eyes out by now Tom. I know I am. I was then as well, you know – it was sheer bravado there at the end, where I say I'm welling up. I'd already overflowed that well, I can tell you.

But let us say no more about that. Dear brave Panda exhibiting supreme courage, even when it seemed all was lost.

But no, let's not even mention it.

Incidentally, do you remember The Acupuncturist at all? Tall chap with mutton chop whiskers. Played the accordion and farted a lot. Iris was raging about having to blow him up, if you remember. She said we should have spotted him earlier, and I suppose she had a point – it was a pretty unlikely anagram after all. Still, there was no need for the horrendous tantrum she threw. Really, you'd think we'd wanted him dead!

Which reminds me...

From: panda@thebigredbus.uni
To: jenny@miaow.gov
Subject:

Iris is dead. Those pussy swine got to her somehow, and killed her.

And before you ask, yes I do know for a fact. Two of those feline fiends came to see me this afternoon and told me the news in person. They had obviously decided to stop talking in code, because I could understand every word they said but how I wished that I couldn't as they pulled me out of the cupboard and thrust me willy-nilly into an equally grubby looking corridor.

'Your friend Ms Wildthyme is dead,' said the biggest one – a tortoiseshell with metal paws and back – as he shoved a long thin object into my paws, wrapped up in an old copy of the People's Friend.

'This will confirm that fact,' he said.

The two of them stepped back as I pulled the paper off, obviously worried that I might make my move and incapacitate them in a single furious assault.

Underneath the paper was the gear-stick of the Bus. It was a bit more chipped than when last I saw it, but as it had obviously been wrenched from its fitting that was hardly a surprise. It was definitely Iris' gear-stick, and we both know she would never let anyone vandalise her Bus while she had any way of stopping them.

Iris is dead.

The cats both had their heads tilted quizzically, neither taking their eyes off me as they waited for my reaction. My first thought, genuinely, was to launch myself at them, striking left and right in berserker abandon until overcome by sheer weight of numbers. Let others find my broken little body surrounded by those of my enemies and let them learn how a Panda dies.

[sorry Tom, that last bit still chokes me up. That was such a moving image, don't you think? Bit out of character for me, mind, which just goes to show how grief can hit us for six. Though I'm wasting my talents just being Iris' companion, I should be her chronicler too, if you ask me. It'd make a pleasant change to have our adventures reported with a bit of flair and panache, frankly.]

Luckily I came to my senses in time and recognised that attacking the brutes armed only with a short metal pole with a decorative knob on the end was probably unwise. Instead, I stood for several minutes turning the stick over and over in my paws, thinking about happier times.

Imagining Iris driving the bus through the pouring rain on our way to the Reading festival, flicking her fag ash out the window and letting the rain come in and soak one side of her face. Remembering when she ferried passengers round London in the Blitz until some pompous twit in a bowler hat called her 'my good woman' and said the Bus was filthy. Even the time she got pissed at one of Tony Hancock's parties and tried to run over Kenny Williams.

In the end I settled for glaring at them, letting them know with my eyes that one day a reckoning would come [goodness, I really have a knack for this kind of stuff, don't I?].

As it happens, they responded to this silent accusation by grabbing the gear stick back and shoving me ahead of them, down the endless grey corridor.

Those murderous animals pushed and prodded me forward for what felt like ages. They made no allowance for my little legs either, and my stitches caught more than once on razor sharp metallic claws, ripping and spilling my precious stuffing in thin trails behind us. I began to despair then, Jenny, and between my own misery and the loss of Iris I found myself weeping again, even as I half-realised that the path was coming to an end and a large metal door lay directly in front of me.

That was about twenty minutes ago and we've been stood here like idiots since then waiting for it to open. I'll send this just now and mail you again if anything happens.

Oh what am I going to do without Iris, Jenny?

Interesting fact, Tom. It's only in the moments of our greatest despair that we can truly appreciate good news.

So when one of the cats walked up to me just a minute after I sent that last email to Jenny and grabbed my phone from its secret hiding place in the bottom of my Adventures Bag, my spirits were as low as I believe they could ever go.

And when the cat the hissed in my ear 'We will take that now. I'm sure your friend Ms Wildthyme must have received your messages by now. She is surely on her way here to save you,' I missed the implication entirely for a moment, then gave out such a whoop of delight that I was actually slightly embarrassed.

'Iris is alive!' I shouted. 'You haven't killed her!'

'No,' said the cat, with that smug self-satisfaction which makes the Pussyworlders so unattractive, 'Not yet.'

It struck me suddenly that even though Iris was still alive, something terrible must have happened to her.

How else to explain the broken gear-stick, which without the shadow of a doubt came from the Bus?

I intended to take the matter further with my captors, but with a hearty shove the larger of the two pushed open the great metal door and the smaller quickly hustled me through.

On the other side lay a vast field filled with pussies arranged in strictly regimented rows beneath a dull red sun, each of them unnaturally still. There was faint smell of used kitty litter in the air and for all that the day was bright, it was really quite cold. The scene had something of the feel of twilight about it, I thought later, dim and cool and tinged pink by the sun. It left me feeling momentarily more melancholy than scared or worried, though I'm not convinced that that constituted much of an improvement.

Off to my right as I looked out from the gate was some kind of platform, raised from the grass on stilts and decorated in quite a lot of slightly tatty and very tacky silver and gold bunting. Seated on what was obviously intended to be a throne but looked to my experienced eye more like the passenger seat from a 1974 Ford Cortina jazzed up with a faux leather interior, was some kind of Boss Cat. A king, perhaps, given his completely metal head, or maybe a High Priest since he was chanting something which I couldn't quite make out.

In the middle of the field were the ranks of the pussy army and to the left was what seemed to me to be a bloody big pile of rubbish. I could see old prams and sets of rusty springs towards the front, sticking out from assorted torn tyres and ripped mattresses, and to the rear mini-mountains of wrecked cars and abandoned fridges. A couple of dozen cats were scuttling about amongst the rubbish, pulling and heaving at things I couldn't make out properly and then carrying them in front of the cat army and past the chanting Boss Cat.

'What's that then?' I asked, gesturing vaguely in the direction of the heap of tat. Even in times of peril it's always worth taking an interest in what's going on around you, Iris told me once. Especially in a time of peril, actually, and it seemed pretty sound advice to me.

'It is the Disinclination of Flossie Ta Numara Op Orange the Fourteenth,' the nearest cat hissed at me, 'Look on it in wonder.'

'Righty-ho,' I said, 'will do. And why's it called that?'

The cat looked a bit shifty and shuffled from one set of paws to the other. 'No-one's really sure. It used to be called the Big Pile of Old but Useful Stuff in my grandmother's day, but then General Matthews pointed out that didn't sound very *modern*, so it's been the Disinclination ever since then. Now shut up and get moving!'

He poked me right where my stuffing lives with the metal rod he was carrying, and I was left with no choice but to scurry forward in the direction of the parade of ancient rubbish and the pavilion. It was difficult to keep moving fast enough, and my paws and side were killing me, but as I got nearer I could at least see what was being carried and hear what the Boss Cat was saying.

'Behold the Hidden Mechanism!' he was bellowing as I got within earshot, though I couldn't see whatever it was he was referring to. I did notice that Boss Cat had Iris' gear stick in one hand, though.

'Behold the Likeness of the Arch Deceiver!' the Boss Cat shouted out as four cat acolytes strode past him, each holding the corner of a suspiciously light looking white marble statue, on which was etched the face of a curly haired man I recognised as a one-time friend and lover of Iris (or so *she* claimed, the libidinous old trollop).

'Behold the Key to the Clockworks' he continued, and this time I gave a little start of genuine surprise, as a single acolyte in robes of sapphire and cracked emeralds walked slowly in front of him. On a gold cloth carefully cushioned by his paws lay the grimy lump of Perspex which I had only recently tried to use as an impromptu pillow.

So that's what one of the fabled segments of the Key to the Clockworks looked like? I'd heard of them of course (who hasn't in our line of work?) but it still came as a shock to actually see one, never mind one which only the day before yesterday I'd cursed for its unyielding and non-fluffy nature. Collect all six segments to the Key, legend had it, and fit them together to form a single perfect cube, and the gateway between Universes would be yours to open at will. Iris claimed to have once been sent on a quest by some super powerful being to collect all six pieces, but apparently she'd got into a bit of trouble while collecting the final piece and had ended up chipping a big chunk off one corner, with the result that the damn thing didn't fit together any longer.

In the time it took me to think all this, the pillow carrying acolyte had presented the segment to the Boss Cat and the ceremony had moved on to its next stage.

Boss Cat stood up with the segment in one hand and Iris' gear-stick in the other, and turning slowly in a full circle pointed with them at the various piles of old bits and pieces. As I followed his hand, I noticed things which I had missed in the parade – the pile of green rubber 'skins' from the cupboard for a start, but also a huge pile of cheap plywood cabinets, a mountain of cuddly toys and what appeared to be a forest of battered and broken vacuum cleaners (the ones that people on Earth use to clean carpets, not the ones the Carpathian Stellar Engineers use to sterilise retail micro-universes.)

To be honest, I'd become a bit distracted looking round at all these odd fragments and remnants and it took me a few seconds to realise that Boss Cat has stopped shouting. Imagine my shock, Tom, when I turned to see why and discovered he was pointing at me!

'Bring forward the bear' he shouted. Before I could say a word in protest, my cat guard gave me a good hard shove and I fell my length on the ground.

'Watch now, little bear' the guard knelt and whispered in my ear.

'Watch wha..'

Well I never got a chance to finish the question because the Boss Cat raised Iris' gear-stick above its head and brought it down with a smash onto the top of the segment of the Key.

For future reference Tom, hitting one of the six most powerful objects in the known Universe with a key component of a time machine navigation system makes one hell of a loud bang. Louder even than that Mouse on Mars gig you dragged me along to last year, if you can imagine such a thing.

The noise was so...well, *noisy* that when I saw a circular hole appear in the air directly above the podium I believed for a moment that I was actually seeing the sound wave. It was only when a familiar red Routemaster bus came battering through the hole, being driven by woman screaming '...had to use a bloody umbrella...', that I recognised it for the wormhole in space-time it really was, and knew that Iris had come to the rescue!

Shame she's not a better driver though. With a screech of brakes that I recognised from long exposure and the usual grinding, groaning sound of tortured gears being put through their paces, Iris and the Bus hit the ground hard, clipping one end of Boss Cat's podium and then careened into the massed and still resolutely unmoving ranks of the cat army

I'm squeamish, as you know Tom, and simply cannot abide the sight of blood, so I shielded my eyes from the carnage which seemed destined to result. Had I been thinking straight I might have wondered at the relative lack of screams, or that the only sound I could hear was that of shrieking brakes and splintering wood, but it's fair to say I was heading for shock by the fastest possible route at that point. Suffice to say, I lay on the ground with my eyes tight shut for a minute or two at least, and only cautiously opened them when I could hear no sound at all.

The sight which greeted me was unexpected to say the least.

Iris was just emerging from the Bus, straightening her leopard skin coat and pulling her hat down firmly onto her head.

The Bus itself was as it always was, imperturbable in the face of whatever trouble Iris managed to get it into, and sat idling quietly.

The cat army though was in a terrible state: smashed and broken, and crushed and snapped and smooshed to pieces. Bits of cat warrior were scattered across the field where the Bus had thrown them; a hand here, a leg there, a head some distance over there. All of which would have been horrific in the extreme had it not been for the fact that each member of the army was merely a crudely painted wooden facsimile of a cat warrior rather than the real thing.

I don't mind admitting, Tom, that I was confused. I turned to say that very thing to my guard, but before I could utter so much as a syllable, he had grabbed me by the scruff of my neck and hoisted me up in the air – a position I considered undignified for a Panda of my breeding.

'Put me down at once!' I commanded him in my best Miss Brodie voice, but it had no effect on him, so I switched my attentions to Iris.

'Iris!' I shouted as loudly as my small lungs would allow, 'Iris!'

She must have heard me because she looked over in my direction and waved. 'In a minute, love,' she shouted back, gesturing with a recently lit Sobranie at the wreck of the pavilion. 'I need to have a word with this one first.'

Typical.

I hung there for several minutes, with nothing to do but watch Iris talk to Boss Cat and listen to the hydraulic joints in my guard's metal arm creak quietly. Attempts to engage my captor in conversation failed miserably, in spite of my trying such innocuous conversational gambits as the parlous state of the Georgian State Ballet and the awfulness of Westlife's late period freeform jazz albums.

I had just decided that maybe he was more of a sports fan and was about to ask him for his views on the outrageous new bridle rules for international polo, when Iris hove back into my limited view.

'Right then you,' she said, 'Put the panda down.'

My guard looked over to his superiors for confirmation, but Iris was clearly in no mood for hanging around.

'NOW!' she positively roared (I was so proud of her at that moment, Tom, she was utterly majestic) and as if by magic I was released and fell with a none too gentle thud onto the ground.

'Give us a minute here, ducks,' she said to the cat and, taking my paw, led me away from everyone else.

'Right then Panda. What the hell is going on here? How on Earth did you manage to get yourself here? Do you even know where here is?'

She took a mighty puff on her fag and gave me such an accusatory stare that it was all I could do not to burst into floods of tears.

'No Iris, not really.' I said humbly. 'I don't know what's going on or where I am – I couldn't even understand what those bloody cats were saying until half an hour ago. I was aiming for Darlington,' I concluded lamely.

'Well you missed, you silly animal.'

I let that go (Iris can be quite unsympathetic at times, as you know Tom) and settled for asking where we were then, if she was so bloody smart. I have my pride, after all.

'We're at the end of everything, lovey. This is the cathouse at the end of the universe and these lads are the dancers at the edge of time. Just take a look around you.'

I slowly turned round again and where before I'd seen a heap of cosmic tat and bric-a-brac now I saw a dying civilisation trying to make sense of the wonders which surrounded them but which they could never hope to replicate. The smell wasn't cat litter as I'd so glibly said before, but fear – fear of the end of all things and the death of all that mattered. The red sun coloured the tops of the massive forest deep crimson and black like blood drying and caking round a wound, and the occasional gusts of wind carried with them a hint of dry leaves and desert sand.

Iris placed a hand on my shoulder and looked at me with such compassion and sadness that I felt as though she and I were utterly alone. She beckoned me closer and leaned down to get near enough to whisper in my ear.

'BOO!' she shouted and I fell over in fright.

'Sorry, I couldn't resist messing with you,' she laughed as I crossly picked myself up, 'We *are* at the end of time though. That's why you couldn't understand what they were saying until now – too far away from the Bus. This planet is orbiting the only remaining working sun in the entire Universe and it's not got much time left. A year, maybe eighteen months. So what's left of the Pussyworlders need to find somewhere to go quick sharp before everything goes belly up. And that's where you come in, you daft Panda.'

I like to think I'm fairly quick on the uptake, but I confess I wasn't sure what I could do to help. I said as much to Iris, but she simply shook her head slightly and beckoned to Boss Cat (who had been standing a little apart from us, waiting patiently for something) to come over.

'The problem's obvious, is it not?' he asked as he walked towards us. 'We cats cannot stay here or we will shortly die – but this is the only place in the entire Universe which can support cat life at all. Everywhere else the suns are dead and the planets are either clouds of dust and ash or freezing, airless rock. So, painful though it is to admit, we had to kidnap you and bring you here – using our segment of the Key as I'm certain you will have already surmised, Ms Wildthyme – knowing your friend would come and get you.'

Iris held up a hand to stop Boss Cat from continuing. 'Before you say anything, chuck, don't even think I'm taking you anywhere back in time. You know everything that's ever happened. That would make you far too powerful and dangerous anywhere in the past.'

She sighed. 'I'm sorry but I really don't know what you expect me to do. There's nowhere for you to go even if I agreed to take you. I appreciate that you acted in the best interests of your people and I'm sure that Panda here won't hold a grudge. But there's nothing either of us can do, so we're going to leave now. Coming, Panda?'

Iris held her hand out to me as though it were the most natural thing in the world for us to be standing on the last planet in the Universe, right at the end of time, talking to a cat with a metal head about time travel.

For a moment, it actually looked as though Iris' quick chatter and grab routine had worked.

I took her hand and she made to hoist me up into her arms. Quick as a flash though, my guard (who I'd forgotten all about) grabbed my other arm and with a sort of twist and shimmy that I admit left me flabbergasted, ended up with me in one arm and a great big pair of scissors in the other.

'Enough of your prattling, you ignorant, vain old woman!'

Boss Cat's voice was surprisingly deep and authoritative and, to my astonishment, was enough to halt Iris momentarily dead in her tracks. Before she could recover her wits, Boss Cat had gestured and half a dozen cats armed with an assortment of swords, knives and metal rods had surrounded her.

'Now you will be quiet and listen to me, or Franz here will cut your little Panda into several pieces.'

I'll be quite frank, Tom – I was on the verge of soiling myself as the guard took one of my lovely paws and placed it surprisingly gently between the scissor blades.

'I'm listening,' said Iris coldly.

'You dismiss us at your peril, Ms Wildthyme. You ignore our hopes and dreams for the future and expect to leave us here to die, while you drive away to safety in your ridiculous bus. For a century or more we have planned this moment, searching dead planet after dead planet, replacing our dying bodies with plastic and metal, all the while looking for a working time machine. And we never found one, not in a hundred years of looking. But we did find the wreckage of a bus.'

He held the gear-stick up above his head and shook it like a spear (which made him look just a teensy bit mad, if you ask me). The cats surrounding us gave a cheer, but it was weak and half-hearted and I could tell their hearts weren't in it.

'*Your* bus, Iris Wildthyme. Sitting in a ruined car park in what remains of Hyspero City. We couldn't move it and it seemed as dead as everything else there, but we did manage to snap off this loose part of the drive system. And, combined with the Segment, even a small part of a time machine is enough to do all manner of interesting things. Like snatch a toy bear (*TOY BEAR!*) or open a wormhole in time through which a loud and thoughtless old gypsy might choose to come.'

The look on Iris' face at that point would have been a picture if I weren't so concerned with the possibility of spending the rest of my life as Pegleg Panda. Anger at being called old was mixed with suspicion that she was about to be forced into doing something ill-advised, and I could sense that it wouldn't take much for her to go off on one, as Jenny used to say. Boss Cat never gave her time to say a word, however.

'Look around you, Iris,' he said, 'This is all that's left of my people. A bare dozen out of the millions who once defended our empire. A dozen males and no females, and an army of painted wood which would fool no-one but an utter fool. We are a threat to no-one, Iris. Take us home.'

'No.'

I could see Iris hated saying it but even I realised that she had to. Who knew what kind of mischief the PussyWorlders could get up to with all their future knowledge?

'Then your friend ends up as scraps, Iris. After which we will kill you and take your bus in any case. I'm certain that we can get it working ourselves. Do you really want that to happen?'

Iris slowly took her cigarette case out of her pocket and lit one of her long black fags (there's no denying she's got class, that girl; it's one of the reasons I put up with her occasionally appalling behaviour).

'I might have an idea' she said.

Iris had already told me all about the Obverse; that strange mini Universe which was hidden inside our own in some mysterious way, and from which she currently claimed to have come.

'Do you know what a ship in a bottle is?' Iris had asked one drunken night not long after that business with the Wonderland secreted beneath the London Underground.

Well I'm a bright boy and I could tell where she was heading. 'Ah,' I'd said brightly, 'and the Obverse is the ship is it?'

'Not quite, lovey' she'd said, 'The Obverse is the bottle. But only if you imagine that the bottle is sitting in a bloody enormous empty warehouse. Then the huge warehouse would be this Universe and the tiny bottle sitting in the middle is the Obverse.'

'So what does the ship represent?' I'd asked.

'That's...something else entirely,' she'd said, avoiding my eye. 'Let's just leave it at that for now.'

And now we were heading there in a Bus full of murderous metal pussies!

It hadn't needed much to convince the cats to agree to Iris' idea. Faced with otherwise certain death, they were all but tripping over themselves to come up with reasons why Iris' plan would work splendidly.

'Everything's totally different in the Obverse,' one had remarked excitedly as he climbed onto the Bus. 'We won't know anything more than anyone else does.'

'We won't have any spaceships so it's not like we can actually go anywhere' said another to general agreement.

'Are there cats there?' another had asked Iris, who began to shush him, then smiled at him instead and quietly said 'Oh lots and lots of them. Girl cats too' before going back to her head count.

Boss Cat (whose name unexpectedly turned out to be General Matthews) couldn't be found for a while, but was eventually tracked down to his ruined pavilion where he was packing some bits and pieces into a bag. Once he was ushered onto the Bus by yours truly, we were ready to get going.

Iris was standing in front of the driver's cabin, obviously about to give one of her rambling if rousing speeches. I was quite looking forward to hearing it, to be honest, since I'd never heard her give a speech sober before.

'Everyone grab hold of something. This is likely to be a bumpy trip.'

Well that *was* disappointing.

She headed for her seat and I followed her through and watched as she took the Segment from her bag and, with infinite care, clicked it into a space on the dashboard next to the original, unmarked gear stick. The whole Bus gave an unusual shudder that I'd never felt before. Without any apparent period of transition the air seemed far warmer, almost muggy in fact, and I could feel my fur starting to matt in the suddenly moist atmosphere. Iris turned the engine on and shoved the Bus into first gear.

Two things happened simultaneously.

First, the Bus shot forward, nearly stalled, and then barrelled with a concussive roar through the swirling hole which had appeared in the air directly in front of it. Swirls of madly twisting Vortex gunk shot through with a glittering red thread shimmered and shimmied outside the bus windows like the contents of a really huge Fruit Corner yoghurt.

Secondly, Boss Cat Matthews pulled *his* gear-stick out of his bag and swinging wildly in order to keep Iris back, grabbed me by the scruff of the neck.

Before anyone could do anything he had thrust me towards an open window and the deadly vortex outside. It was only by throwing out my every limb that I managed to wedge myself this side of total destruction.

'I don't trust you, Ms Wildthyme' he hissed. 'From the very beginning of this enterprise I have said that it was unfortunate that the only time traveller we could find was the infamous Iris Wildthyme, transtemporal drunkard and mistress of the half empty gin bottle.' He shrugged. 'Still, you were all that was available and we knew we could easily lure you in with this pathetic creature.'

I was aware that several of the cats were remonstrating with the General and when I cautiously opened one thin slit of an eye I saw two or three of them approaching him and being driven back by the swinging gear-stick.

'Now,' he continued, 'this panda is insurance against your not doing *exactly* what I say. When we arrive in this new universe of yours, you will not as previously discussed take us to a deserted planet at the very edge of space and leave us there to fend for ourselves. We have no wish to live our lives as grubby farmers, devoid of female company and the finer things in life. No – instead you will take us home to Pussyworld, where we can be reunited with our own kind. We have kept our blood pure for millions of years, Ms Wildthyme! Alone amongst the races of the Universe, we have retained our perfection of form. We have refused to sully that perfection through inter-breeding. We kept the faith, Ms Wildthyme, and now that faith is being rewarded. We shall return home in triumph and raise a *real* army using the force of arms of our Obverse brethren and our own knowledge and experience. We will crush all who stand before us in a tidal wave of pussy power!'

He was ranting by now (why do I spend so much time round people who think that ranting is an acceptable means of everyday communication?) and obviously realised it, because he stopped suddenly and went on in a far more measured tone, 'I take it that there is a Pussyworld in this universe?'

Iris nodded without taking her eyes off him. 'There's a planet there, yes. But I don't think you want to go there like this. And I don't think your friends want to go anywhere with you at all.'

One of the cats – my guard from back on the planet I think – spoke up.

'This isn't our way, General,' he said. 'This isn't what we agreed. We'd just ask for help you said.'

There was a general murmur of assent. The General turned round slowly, his eyes never leaving Iris and his hand never leaving my neck.

'Is that so?' he said, and lashed out with the gear stick. The knob of the stick hit one cat flush on the forehead, throwing him sideways into the driver's cabin, where his flailing metal claws slashed across Iris' seat, cut a deep score along the dashboard and sheared straight through the base of the *other* gear-stick. The cat crumpled in a heap of fur and blood and metal at the base of Iris' seat, unmoving.

'Anyone else. No? Right then. Take us to Pussyworld now, or out your little friend goes.'

As he spoke, the General pressed a little harder on my back, and one of my paws lost its grip on the edge of the window, forcing me to twist myself painfully to avoid falling into the Vortex. Iris moved forward to help but the General waved the gear stick in her face and, with her shoulders slumped, she turned back towards the drivers seat.

Oh, I thought all was lost then, Tom. The General had me caught and Iris cornered and since he'd already killed one of his own people, his ruthlessness was beyond question. There seemed to be nothing any of us could do to stop him.

I should have more faith.

Iris bent down to move the dead cat out of the way and as she straightened up and laid the body on a chaise-longue, she quickly spun round and hammered the other gear stick hard down on the General's metal head.

With a dull *THUNK* the stick skidded off the shiny steel skull and the General swung his stick in an arc which Iris did well to skip back from.

You should have been there, Tom, it was damned exciting stuff. Lunge – parry – sly pull of a rug from underfoot – riposte – attempted kick in the goolies – chucking of assorted pots, pans and decorative pill boxes – jump on sturdy table (that was the General, not Iris) – the fight had it all. The General dropped me to the floor almost immediately so I climbed to both safety and an excellent view on top of that laundry basket that Iris keeps her ceremonial robes in.

The two gear sticks were throbbing with weird time energy by that point, with Blinovich gubbins sparking and flashing as they cracked against one another. Iris was breathing pretty heavily and the General had her on the defensive, forcing her back against the LP rack on the rear wall as he hacked down at her and she struggled to get her feet free of entangling raffia mats and discarded pashmina.

For a moment my heart was in my mouth as the General kicked Iris' legs out from under her and raised his gear-stick high above his head. I tensed my little legs and was just about to leap from the laundry basket onto the murderous swine when the other cats charged en masse at the General, bowling him over and sending him flying through the air.

I swear that in my mind's eye the next minute or so is all in slow motion. I can see that shiny metal head first in view and then gone as the General spun a wide circle through the air. In the background I can see Iris half fallen against some Tammy albums, her hair askew and curling over her face, her mouth gently opening. The group of charging cats are ever so slowly skidding to a halt and collapsing in a heap against the front of the bus.

And I'm reaching out and flicking the catch on one of the windows. The window towards which the General is helplessly spinning.

Briefly it looks as though he might save himself. Moving so slowly that I become impatient with my own memory, the General reaches out with the gear-stick he's still holding and tries to hook it through the steering wheel of the bus. For a moment it holds and his eyes turn, horribly, towards me (my stomach churned like Jenny's after a curry, Tom, I can tell you) before the Vortex grabs at his legs and snatches him out of the window and into the killer void.

He was gone in the time it takes to blink and suddenly everything was moving at normal speed again.

Iris – all business again – stood up and pushed the loose hair behind her ears. 'Everyone OK?' she asked briskly. 'Panda? Are you alright?'

I nodded yes, and closed the window. With my face so close to the vortex I had a damn fine view of it fading away, to be replaced by a thin slice of blue sky and, from my position wedged awkwardly against the window frame, a portion of green grass and what seemed to be a stone wall.

'This is where the General asked to go,' said Iris to the remaining cats. 'I said no but now that he's gone, perhaps you do want to be here after all.'

I'll be honest Tom, I was expecting a period of quiet reflection, a time to consider what we'd all (especially me!) been through and come to terms with it. Which only goes to show how poorly I know cats.

The damn animals were out of the Bus as soon as they could get the door open, the shower of shallow sods. I could see them through the windows, running across a green lawn and playing tag round a beautiful marble water fountain – the stone wall I thought I'd seen a moment previously.

I stuck my head round Iris' leg where she stood in the doorway. 'Shouldn't we go after them?' I asked.

Iris shook her head. 'No, let them explore' she said, 'They'll be fine. We need to get out of here quick sharp though.'

She pushed the door shut and made sure it was securely locked. 'Come on' she said as she made her way back to the driver's seat, 'It's time to get back to our own Universe.'

'What about the cats, Iris?' I said, quite annoyed at her seeming lack of concern regarding my own terrifying ordeal. I mean I was delighted that they'd turned on their brutish leader, but still – I had been kidnapped, when all was said and done; kidnapped and imprisoned in fact. And if that weren't awful enough, I'd then been manhandled, assaulted and nearly thrown into the deadly interstitial void which separates universes.

Yet Iris seemed inclined to let bygones be bygones and simply allow the swines who had mistreated and nearly killed me get off scot-free. Instead of hatching wonderful plans to bring them to justice, she was gently nudging the bus into the air and whistling under her breath.

'Do those cats get away with everything they've done?' I snapped. 'Iris! Aren't we going to do *anything*?'

Looking back on it now Tom, I can't remember ever having seen Iris looking quite so vexed as at that moment, when she turned round in her seat and faced me.

'They're in a whole new universe Panda. An entire cosmos away from their homes. And they can't go back – not today, not ever. They'll never see their home again, the planet they all grew up on, the only one they've ever known.' She grinned and poked me in the tummy. 'And you don't look much the worse for the experience in any case. A bit slimmer, if anything.'

'Harrumph' I said, or a noise very like that and, determined not to snap out of my bad mood quite so easily, I stomped over to the back window and peered out.

We were hovering about fifty feet off the ground. The city – because it was a city – we had landed beside was laid out beneath me like a rather unimaginative model, all straight white walls and long, thin streets. I could see the cats already exploring the meadow we'd landed in, chasing one another round the grass and over the fountain.

Then, off to one side, I saw dark figures moving through the shadows of the streets, converging on the playful pussies. I was swithering whether to warn the cats or not and was shamefully undecided even when I realised that the dark figures were actually massive dogs, cloaked in shining silver coats.

'The Ogg' Iris breathed behind me (she can be very light on her toes Tom, as I'm sure you remember!). 'Cybernetically enhanced canines descended from domestic pets run wild. Absolute honeys so long as you're from what they consider animal stock. They've allowed no-one human to land on the planet since their masters up and left them millennia ago but they welcome all kinds of non-human waifs and strays.'

'So there are other cats, like you told that one earlier? I asked.

'Oh yes, plenty. The General's troops will be fine here. Trust me, Panda.'

She sighed and shook her head sadly. She looked old, did Iris, and that frightened me a lot more than the cats ever had.

'It's...funny being so near to home,' she said.

She started flicking switches and turning dials distractedly, almost randomly it seemed to me. 'It's dangerous here,' she said, 'Everything gets watched and recorded from the Clockworks, Panda, but the Obverse isn't a safe place for strangers. And I'm not sure if even I'm not a stranger here now.'

She gave the Segment a flick with her finger and then, as it started up, stood up and gave herself a hard shake, like a dog coming out of the water.

'Time for gin,' she said, 'Fancy one, Panda my lad? There's tonic water in the cabinet.'

Battleship Anathema

Philip Purser-Hallard

I

It begins with flares, in space.

Each burst of light burns for a moment against the empty starfield, each heralding the emergence of a spaceship. One upon another, these vessels with their freight of humanity flare into their tiny existence, until the entire Cardinal Flotilla is visible.

Now some thirty craft drift steadily across the void, their shapes and configurations overwriting it like an alphabet, bringing their cargo of context and meaning. What was mere vacuum now becomes, in human presence, an abyss, an abandonment, a loneliness.

However: these spaceships are not the kind a kiddie would be thrilled to find inside their Christmas stocking. A motley ragbag of designs, they manage to be uniformly neither bright nor sleek. Most of them show signs of hasty repair, of burning or of blast damage. Some are asymmetric, sections missing from them like bites from a bagel or a chocolate bar. The Flotilla has been travelling for a long, long time.

In the centre of them, largest and most sharklike, cruises the Battleship *Anathema*. Crusted with armaments, it must have once been a magnificent sight, the flagship of an awesome power. Now it is shabby, greying, patched with metalwork and industrial rivets.

It expands suddenly – altogether too abruptly, in fact – until a single baleful gunport fills our vision. Then shrinks, until the *Anathema* is just one dot among the many. Then it expands once more.

'Bugger,' says Iris, fiddling with her camcorder's viewfinder. 'I nearly had it then.'

II

'What the throck is it, Dan?'

A grizzled, weathered face above a starched uniform collar stares down towards the light of a console screen. 'Talk to me,' Rex Halidom, Admiral of the Flotilla, the senior military officer of this bedraggled, theoretical remnant of the Seven Cardinal Worlds, adds redundantly.

Around him, the gloom of the *Anathema*'s bridge, metallic and functional as its exterior, is crammed with blocky workstations like ancient arcade games. Crewmen and women in drab uniforms stand at them looking tense.

'Throcked if I know, Admiral,' growls Captain Daniel Stela. He is grim, black, unevenly-shaved and in a perennially foul mood. 'We just came out of interspace and there it was.'

Iris Wildthyme says: 'Ooh, you'll love these people, Panda. They're always such fun! Everything's so bright and cheerful and gay with them, and they're always having such adventures! Aliens and time-travel and princesses and all sorts. Their leaders are always very stately and wear togas, and their pilots have colourful flying-jackets with funny badges, and give each other silly nicknames like Mule and Pixie and Nero. And they have robots – cute little things who go chukka-chukka-chukka and fall over.

'What's that, lovey? Oh yes, one of them was called Pixie. They don't take themselves too seriously, that's the point I'm making. I can't stand military men who take themselves too seriously. And they were fighting a proper war, mind – their enemies were great slavering dinosaur things, Cyclopes or Cyclones or something of that, with this heavy robotic body-armour that they never took off. Except they must have sometimes, 'cause they also had humaniform body-suits for infiltration.

'Very scary, they were. They'd blown up these poor people's home system a few years before. They captured me once, and would have done God-knows-what to me if Rex Halidom – Uriel, they called him – hadn't rescued me from their diabolical clutches.

'Ooh, he was very handsome, was Lieutenant Halidom. He had a real thing for me, you know!

'You look sceptical, lovey, but back then I was all leggy and bosomy and honey-blonde. No, really. It's amazing how much more colourful and cheery that makes the rest of the universe look. And Rex had an eye for the ladies all right – just like the rest of them. They're all men's men here. Real traditional space-pilot types. And such adventures we all had! There was this one planet we visited where everybody was a pirate – *or so it seemed at first*. Well...

'What? Oh, don't be such an old misery, Panda. You'll love it here. The costumes, the lights, the hair... I wasn't always so sure about the hair, I have to admit. Some shades of purple don't look so well on a man.

'I can't have been hereabouts for – ooh, it must be nearly thirty years. I wonder how long it's been for them?

'I'm much loved round these parts, though, that's the point. They'll lay out the red carpet for me, you'll soon see.'

A smaller spaceship is hastily dispatched, one of the Flotilla's battered Starvixens. 'Coming up on the object now,' says Nero, the pilot, as it approaches the intruder at speed.

'Watch your throcking ass near that thing,' warns Stela over the command channel. 'We don't know what weapons the throcker has.'

'Throcking right I'll watch my ass, sir,' says Nero. 'But it don't look like no throcking Cyrene.'

On Rex Halidom's screen, the image of the interloper grows larger and more distinct. 'Throck me...' he whispers to himself.

It has wheels. It's red. It is, not to put too fine a point on it, a double-decked, internally-combusting public transport vehicle from a century so distant that Halidom would be hard pressed to name a single figure or event from it.

He recognises it nonetheless. 'My God, it's *her*,' he says.

'Her who?' says Stela. 'You mean you've seen that throcking thing before?'

'We both have,' Halidom groans.

Inside the alien object, Iris – a scrawny, raddled, ageing bag-lady who lives in a bus and whose best friend in the universe is a fraying stuffed panda – waves excitedly, the camcorder dangling from her wrist, as Nero's Starvixen makes its first pass.

'Ooh-ooh! Hello, chuck! Cooeee!' she calls inanely through the vacuum.

'It's Iris, Dan,' says Halidom. 'It's Iris Wildthyme. She's come back.'

Captain Stela stares at him aghast. 'Oh fuck,' he says quietly.

III

Iris says coldly, 'I have nothing to say to you, Rex Halidom.'

She sits in state in the brig of the Battleship *Anathema*, like a family matriarch at Christmas. The brig is supposedly a sparse, bleak place, designed for intimidation – even more so than the rest of the great battleship's interior. Iris' cell has been, at her insistence, decked out with a well-stuffed armchair, lamp, occasional table and magazine rack taken from her bus. It looks almost homely.

She contradicts herself immediately, of course. Dignified silence was never Iris' forte. 'Where's my friend Panda? What have you done to him?' she asks.

Her vehicle itself has been impounded and is sitting, surrounded by Starvixens, on the *Anathema*'s hangar deck. The engineers are repairing the doors through which the boarding-party of Cardinal marines burned their way in, shortly before knocking the stuffing (quite literally, it seems) out of Iris' friend Panda.

Admiral Halidom shifts uncomfortably on the metal chair he's carried with him into the brig. 'He'll be fine,' he says. 'Doc Zero's looking him over now.'

'Well, that's... acceptable, I suppose,' Iris concedes grudgingly. 'Wait a minute – Doc Zero? You mean little Billy Zero? Ooh, he must be all grown up now. He was a wee slip of a child genius last time his Auntie Iris saw him. And don't think you're going to win me round that way, either,' she snaps, 'talking about old times like that. Why have you got me locked up in here?'

'What is he, Iris?' Halidom asks, meaning Panda. 'Some kind of artificial life form? We've never seen anything like him before.'

'He's a stuffed panda, of course,' she retorts. 'An unusually pompous and conceited one. Didn't you have pandas in the Seven Worlds?'

'Not... that I'm aware of,' he says. Three decades after their disintegration by the Cyrenes, Rex Halidom remembers very little of the Seven Cardinal Worlds: not Sapientas, not Fideon, not even his own home planet of Carita. He is, however, reasonably sure that the indigenous fauna were made from flesh and bone, not cloth and cotton wool.

He's seen strange things during his subsequent travels, but nothing like Iris' walking, talking, swearing, pontificating... whatever-it-is.

'As far as we're concerned he's a wildcard,' Halidom tells her. 'Just like you, Iris. You don't fit any of our categories – I learned that when you were here with us before. Even if I hadn't, the change in your appearance now...'

'The change in my *what*?' Iris looks indignant. 'You're on thin enough ground already, buster.'

'I just mean...' Halidom surreptitiously moves his buttocks on the uncomfortable seat. Women's looks aren't really his area of expertise. 'I mean, you look great. I like it, honestly. That last look, with the long legs and the big... the big, well... they didn't really suit... not that... But that's not what I came to talk to you about,' he concludes hurriedly. 'I'm interested in your vehicle, your...'

'Bus,' Iris supplies crisply.

'Your bus,' he agrees, relieved at the successful change of subject. 'We know it's not just a spacecraft. It doesn't even travel through interspace as we know it.'

'It bloody does if I want it to,' Iris huffs.

'The first time you were here with the Flotilla, you drove it out of nowhere, straight into the *Anathema*'s Council Chamber.' He smiles now, just for a moment, at the thought of those dignified, robed Representatives and their aides – most of them long dead now – scattering in panic. 'It's revolutionary technology.' *In every sense*, he thinks. 'We've nothing like it, and nor have the Cyrenes. It could give our forces an invaluable strategic advantage.'

Iris gawps at him. 'What are you talking about?'

'A stealth insertion,' he suggests, realising immediately that this was an unwise phrase to use. He waits for Iris to finish cackling, then continues.

'We use your bus to establish a bridgehead on the Cyrene Queenship. Don't worry, you'll be in no danger. Just show us how to pilot your craft, and you won't need to be involved. You and your... animal will be quite safe here.'

'You want,' Iris repeats, 'to use my bus – *my bus* in some kind of suicide mission against those cyber-dinosaur things?' Her voice rises to a shriek. 'And why should I help you after you've banged me up like this? What's happened to you, Rex Halidom?' she shouts. 'We used to be friends! Just think of all those adventures we had together! You were such *fun*! And now you're just a humourless, macho, military... bully! Is that what you want to be?'

'It's what I need to be,' he tells her curtly.

There is a long silence.

Then, 'I want to see Nero,' says Iris. 'The real one, not that potty-mouthed slip of a girl. The right smooth charmer, with the nice smile and the twinkly eyes. The handsome one. The *fella*.'

Halidom takes a packet of tobaccellos from his uniform pocket. He sighs. 'He died, Iris. A Cyrene patrol cornered his Starvixen and blew it out of the sky. There weren't enough ashes left to scatter.'

'Oh, dear.' Iris seems genuinely taken aback. 'Oh, dearie me. He was your friend, wasn't he? Oh Rex, I'm sorry.'

'It was a long time ago,' says Halidom. 'Almost twenty years. Five years back we gave his callsign to young Kylie Pontus. She's earned it.'

Iris sniffs. 'Jumped-up little trollop. She should have been given a good spanking. *As a kiddie I mean*, so you can wipe that smirk off your face right now, Rex Halidom.'

Halidom isn't smirking.

Iris goes on. 'And where's your little robot? Chukka-chukka-chukka, he used to go. What was his name?'

Pain clouds the Admiral's face. 'It was Chukka,' he admits.

'That's the fella!' Iris seems caught up in her reminiscences now, her indignation at being banged up placed temporarily on hold. 'Dear little chappie. Where is he now?'

Halidom offers a tobaccello to Iris, ignites both with the lighter given to him by his alien friend, Feathers the Aquilian, shortly before his slow and agonising death in a Cyrene bioweapons assault.

He takes a long and welcome breath of peppery smoke, breathes out again.

'Chukka died too,' he tells her. 'The Cyrenes captured him, reprogrammed him as an assassin. He tried to kill the Viceroy, put her in a coma for six months. Her bodyguards melted him to slag.'

'Oh heck.' Iris is shocked.

'It was for the best,' says Halidom. 'He was quite insane, at the end.'

Iris' eyes are teary. 'Poor little scrap-metal scamp... What about Pixie?' she asks, tentative now. 'And Feathers? And what-was-his-name, with the moustache and the Hawaiian shirts?'

'It was Butch,' Halidom says. 'He's dead. They're all dead, Iris. The Cyrenes killed all our pilots from those days, except for Dan Stela. Mule. And myself, of course. We both got lucky.'

'Dearie me,' Iris says again. 'You have been in the wars.'

They sit in silence for a while, smoking their tobaccellos.

At length, Halidom says, 'You have to understand, old friend. We've been fighting these throcking canned lizards for a generation. A handful of us have left the Flotilla, to found their own colonies or settle down on neutral worlds, but the Cyrenes have a habit of tracking them down and massacring them. Most of us understand why it's important that we fight on.

'It's thirty-three years since the Seven Worlds were blown to gehenna. When you visited us before... well, it hadn't really sunk in. Those of us who were young then – it was all a big adventure to us. We weren't taking it seriously. The elders were just doing their best to hold things together. Hanging on to the old traditions – the togas, the religious symbolism... None of us understood then what the enemy was really capable of.'

'I'll bet,' she says dismissively. 'We had some fun though, back then, didn't we? Hey, do you remember that cat-woman nightclub-singer who Mule fell for, and it turned out she was really a dog-woman who'd had plastic surgery? And Pyras, the Planet of the Pirates, who all turned out to be automata controlled by their sentient parrots? What about that time we were trapped in the historical theme park, eh, and all the robots went berserk and made us sing karaoke versions of Abba hits until we managed to escape? Or when we were kidnapped by mad Duke Anubis and put in his menagerie, and forced to have passionate, steamy –'

'Yes, *all right*, Iris!' Halidom barks. 'I remember those times. And they were stupid! They were silly and garish and... just throcking ridiculous.'

'I don't think they were,' says Iris stubbornly. 'I think they were fabulous.'

He shakes his head. 'In any case, they ended long ago. We were so young – so naïve. Small wonder the Cyrenes were able to pick us off. When the Seven Worlds fell we were already decadent.

'We've all had to reinvent ourselves. After Princess Celestia died of leukaemia brought on by radioactive fallout, our royal line was finished. We had to build a new constitution. We had no option but to re-examine everything – our politics, our laws, our principles... The old leaders died off, and their successors didn't see the point of the old ways. We in the military tightened up on uniform discipline. Our ships became old and dilapidated. All that glitter wore off, all the cheery veneer you so enjoyed, and left... despair.'

Iris is silent for some time, while they finish their tobaccellos.

Then she asks, 'How did it all start, Rex? I don't mean the attack on the Seven Worlds. Why were the Cyrenes your enemies in the first place?'

'It happened a long time ago now,' Halidom tells her. 'At the Ecumenical Council on Temperas.'

'Ecumenical Council?' Iris is confused.

He fumbles for another smoke. 'The Cyrenes are Apollinarians, Iris. They believe that Christ had only the one nature, God's nature, and that his human body was just a peripheral. A plug-in. The Seven Worlds' founders were

Nestorians. We believe that Christ's body was a vessel for two persons, a melting-pot for the human and the divine.'

He waits for Iris to finish boggling. 'Come again?' she screeches. 'You've been fighting for decades over some tiny discrepancy in your christological small print?'

Halidom shrugs. 'They're very different viewpoints. It's not a trivial disagreement to us. The Cyrenes are heretics, which is exactly how they see us. Why do you think our flagship's called the *Anathema*?'

'Then I was wrong,' she says. 'You haven't turned into fascist Germany after all. You've turned into the Spanish Inquisition. At least I brought my own comfy chair,' she adds obscurely. 'And now you're happy to lock up an innocent woman – your *friend*, Rex – just in case she comes in useful later? What'll you to do to me if I won't help you, torture me? Oh, I saw what you've got out there, when your Sergeant Hadrian frogmarched me into this cell. The equipment. The *instruments*. Use them on your Cyrene prisoners, do you? Your heretics? Or on your own people when they start making trouble?'

She is shouting now, but Halidom is just as angry. 'Our way of life is under constant threat!' he bellows. 'We've learned what the universe is like now! When a society's survival is in the balance, it can't afford the *luxury* of your kind of scruples!'

'You listen to me, my lad!' she shouts. 'If this is what you're doing to your *enemies*, never mind your friends, then your way of life's not under threat. It's gone completely! And it wasn't those lizard things who took it away from you!'

He takes a breath, then another. He remembers his discipline. He forces himself to be calm. 'Everything I stood for is long gone, Iris. Nearly all the people I loved. Our entire culture. After you left, I began to really understand that. We'd lost our churches, our museums, our libraries ...'

'You still had that Jane Austen book,' Iris reminds him. '*Persuasion*, remember? You used to read it, over and over...' she stops.

'Over and over,' Halidom agrees. 'It was the only book I owned, back then. It still is. I've not been able to bear looking at it for twenty years.'

'Oh Rex, chuck,' she says. The fight's gone out of her now, and she's sympathetic again. 'I know all this stuff is important to you. Your war, your politics, your religion. But still, you take it all so *seriously*. I know you're refugees with no home. I know you're forever battling with an implacable foe. I know you have enemies without and within and that your most sacred principles are forever under threat – but does that have to mean you can't have a bit of *fun* now and again?'

'Fun,' says Halidom flatly. 'I can't remember the last time I had any fun.'

IV

Subsequently...

The Cyrene Queenship is darker inside even than the *Anathema*, filled with a roiling, sticky steam through which half-cybernetic, half-reptilian figures lumber. Each is at least eight feet tall, their metal chameleon-eyes constantly swivelling. They carry gigantic side-arms, the size and texture of alligators.

A swirl of fog becomes a sudden gale, a vortex, spitting out the blocky scarlet shape of Iris' bus...

As Iris, Panda, Nero and the Cardinal marines watch in horror, Sergeant Hadrian's skin begins to unpeel, revealing an underside composed of sparking circuitry. Where the cyber-skin comes away, the sergeant's true flesh is revealed, glistening and scaly...

'Unhand me, madam!' Panda cries.

'Little creature,' croons the Cyrene Queen, naked and whole unlike her subjects. Her forked tongue flickers as her wicked talons turns the toy bear this way and that. 'How soft and tiny you are, little creature. How helpless...'

'Throck you, you motherthrockers!' Nero yells, her machine-pistol juddering frantically. 'Throck you and throck your throcking spies and infiltrators and throck your motherthrocking Queen and throck your mothers!'

She sprays bullets across wave upon advancing wave of cybernetic reptile flesh...

'Iris,' the Admiral gasps with relief. 'Nero. You made it.'

'And *me*,' Panda points out indignantly.

'I thought I'd sent you out to...' says Halidom. 'Well, to... never mind.'

'With respect, sir,' says Nero, 'all the others *did* 'never mind'. The rest of the men you sent are throcked to gehenna. *Sir*.'

'You did all right in there, our Kylie, I'll give you that,' Iris concedes. 'I'll tell you something odd, though,' she muses...

Panda stares, utterly aghast at the figure facing him. 'And what in heaven's name are *you*?' he demands rudely.

'I could ask the same of *you*,' his double replies. 'Imitation's the sincerest form of flattery, I suppose, but really, you could have made the effort not to look so *scruffy*...'

'But Iris,' Panda whispers theatrically (as if he were capable of whispering in any other way), 'this gentleman-safecracker friend of yours lived in the early twentieth century. Whatever makes you think the lockpicks he gave you can get us into a high-security laboratory on a seventy-ninth-century spaceship?'

The lab door clicks once, decisively...

'What are you doing here?' The Cyrene sentry hisses his demands. 'Who are you? And why are you so small? And... cute?'

The diminutive, white-and-black-furred figure blinks his button eyes. 'Do you know,' he declaims, 'I'm not altogether sure...'

'Oh come on, Mule, just a little kiss!' Iris cackles. 'You never used to be this uptight.'

'Wildthyme, you're drunk!' accuses Captain Dan Stela.

'So what? You never used to worry about having a little drinkie, either.'

'You're drunk and you're a goddamn civilian,' Stela bellows. 'Get this goddamn drunk civilian woman the gehenna off my bridge!' he thunders to the Flotilla at large...

'This is *Cardinal Voices*, speaking to you from across the Cardinal Flotilla. And joining me today are author and political commentator Trey Chomsky, Commodore Lydia Philemon of the military vessel *Christotokos*, and Panda, celebrity companion of Iris Wildthyme. Welcome, friends. First up for discussion, the proposed laws restricting freedom of association for religious dissidents. Panda, any thoughts?'

'Well Sonia, the Viceroy and I are *close friends*, as you know...'

V

Archdeacon Barnaby says: 'So let's see if I've got this straight, Ms Wildthyme.

'First Admiral Halidom captures you, and keeps you locked up till you let him use your transport as his bridgehead in a last-ditch assault on the Cyrene Queenship. Provided you and your toy panda – I'm sorry, of course I mean your *associate* Panda – get to go along and see the action, am I right?

'The attack fails because your sergeant turns out to be a Cyrene spy in a humaniform body-suit – dozens of marines die, you barely get out with your lives, etcetera – but you've noticed the Cyrenes getting obsessed with Panda.

'Among the people the Admiral briefs about this is Doc Zero. Now Zero knows that the canned lizards can't have children of their own – that armour they wear isn't just a suit, they have to amputate lots of their body-parts to bond with it. Let's face it, the Doc's obsessed with body-parts. He guesses that seeing somebody ten inches tall, furry and cute – yeah, sorry Panda, I guess I do mean 'distinguished' – woke up the Cyrenes' dormant parental instincts.

'So Zero then decides that Panda's form's ideal for these sentient A.I. nukes he's been working on, so they can infiltrate the lizard fleet and bomb the throckers to gehenna. So he makes himself a Panda lookalike robot and uses it to house the bomb.

'But then you and Panda – feeling some parental responsibility of your own, maybe? – break into the Doc's lab, sabotage the prototype pandroid so his trigger mechanism won't operate, and set him loose among the Cyrenes where he'll be looked after properly. Meaning the lizards are able to back-engineer more pandroids, which become exactly as popular with them as Zero had hoped – only without those all-important bomb components.

'Then later still, some of the Cyrene-manufactured pandroids get recaptured by the *Anathema*, and turn out to be just as appealing to *us*. While you've been hanging around the *Anathema* annoying people, your little pal's become a celeb in the Flotilla. We used to live with ecosystems full of animals, these days all we've got's a few scrawny dogs and cats. So now Doc Zero's mass-producing pandroids to make a quick denarius, Panda's suing him over the unauthorised use of his likeness and our ever-thriving lawyers are having a field day.

'Meanwhile, every kid in the Flotilla's nagging mommy and daddy for a pandroid of their very own and – well, it seems that ultimately a love for cybernetic duplicates of your pet – sorry, *confederate* – is one of the few things Cardinal and Cyrene society now have in common.

'Have I left anything out, Ms Wildthyme?'

The chaplain's office on the *Malabar* is a poky closet, offset from the scarcely larger chapel area. Iris sits cramped in a small swivel chair, almost knee-to-knee with Archdeacon Barnaby. Panda sits – following extravagant and violent protest – on Iris' lap.

'No,' Iris says. 'I reckon that's about the size of it, your archdeaconry.'

'Please don't keep trying to get my title right,' the cleric says. 'I told you, call me Barnaby. Well, it's a great story, sure, but I can't see why you're telling me.'

'The thing is –' Iris begins to reply.

'We need your help,' blurts Panda. 'In fact we *demand* your help. We want to hold a convention for pandroid-lovers – h'rrmm, perhaps that could be better phrased – a convention for pandroid *devotees*, on a neutral planet. Bringing together those who admire my personal charisma, even in such a debased and commercialised form. Uniting parents and children, men and women, Temperans and Fideans and Caritans and Speons and –'

'And most importantly,' Iris interrupts him, regaining control of the conversation's flow, 'humans and Cyrenes.'

'I was *getting* to that,' snaps Panda.

But the Archdeacon is busy exploding. 'Say *what?* You want *me* to get involved with this shifnal-for-brains scheme? Why the throck would I want peace with those murdering scaly apostates?'

'Well, your archdiaconate,' Iris says softly, 'I would have thought that was obvious. You see, Archie,' she wheedles, 'we *know*.'

The Archdeacon goes pale. He stands, walks over and closes the chapel door. 'You do?' he says. 'I mean – you're not just bluffing?'

'We're deadly serious,' Iris confirms.

'Ah well,' says Barnaby. 'I guess you can't fool all of the people all of the time. Not even the unaugmented mammalian heretics.'

He peels his cybernetic skin away. As it sloughs to the floor he stands, expanding to his full, eight-foot height. Yellow-green scales and metallic prostheses gleam in the pale candlelight.

'Jesus uncompounded Christ,' the Cyrene sleeper agent swears. 'You would not believe how stuffy it gets in that thing. So – I help you out, I get to cuddle the original Panda, yeah?'

VI

Rex Halidom returns to his quarters after directing his pilots in their latest, particularly harrowing battle against the Cyrenes. One of their basecraft came out of nowhere, then sat there – not attacking, just defending itself – for twenty minutes, during which he lost two of his best pilots.

Not Nero, thank God, but Subway and Cougar. He'll have to tell their families.

Shortly before he came off duty a message came through from the hangar deck that Wildthyme's bus had gone. Iris has left the Flotilla, along with Panda and – for some reason – a cleric from one of the civilian transports. Rex has lost her again.

He should have kept her in the brig. He never should have allowed her her freedom. He should have –

He should have said goodbye to her. He should have tried to patch things up between them, before she left.

On Halidom's desk is an unfamiliar object. He stares at it, unwilling even to contemplate the existence of such an article: a thick, fat leatherbound book, sitting at a jaunty angle as if deliberately placed for maximum disruption to the military austerity of his rooms. The gold-tooled title on the cover reads *Jane Austen – Complete Works*.

Scarcely daring to touch, he reaches out and runs his hands across its leathery surface – the texture of a Cyrene scout whom he was forced once to kill with his bare hands, on a desert world.

Admiral Rex Halidom stares at the book without opening it, for a long time, alone in his quarters.

Iris and Panda watch from where the bus is parked, on a high crag overlooking the colonists' domes on Gongen. Gongen is a neutral world, a colony of Buddhist orang-utan people. Sublimely uninterested in the factional divisions of eighth-millennium Christianity, the Gongens have certainly never been party to the war between the Cyrenes and their adversaries.

One of their larger domes displays a banner reading 'WELCOME TO PANDACON 7883'.

Two of the atmosphere-capable ships from the Flotilla, the *Thomas* and the *Ossuary*, are parked nearby. They look rather like large office buildings constructed in cubist imitation of, respectively, a nut-and-bolt and a pestle-and-mortar. Ten minutes ago they disgorged some six hundred Cardinal citizens, six hundred tame pandroids in their arms. All have now filed into the dome.

Panda sulks as Iris ushers him into the bus. 'But *why* shouldn't we stay?,' he insists. 'They asked me to be guest of honour. If I don't do it, they'll only have that jumped-up little tit Zero. I owe my public better than that.'

Iris sits in the driver's seat. She seems nervous. 'I'm just not sure it's a good idea, Panda lovey. Even if all goes well – which it will, of course – people don't take kindly to being tricked into making peace with their mortal enemies. And if things *did* take a nasty turn – which obviously they won't – they might start blaming us. I find it's often better not to stick around after a good deed of quite this magnitude.'

'You mean,' says Panda acidly, 'you're not sure that this will work?'

'Oh, it'll work,' says Iris, airily. She turns the ignition key, and sets the engine idling. 'Prefect Barnaby's invited all his Cyrene chums. They're all very excited. Once they're in there with the humans, all showing off their little pandroid pals, they'll bond straight away, you'll see. Well, you would see, if we were staying. They'll be fine with Rex to look after them, anyway,' she adds, wistful suddenly.

Panda preens. 'So in essence, a generation of war will have been brought to an end by these people's collective admiration of *me*?'

'I'm not surprised you lot are endangered, you know,' Iris mutters under her breath. 'Oh yes,' she breezes, 'once this little war's behind them, I'm sure they'll get straight back to the good old ways. All colourful and bright, with fabulous clothes and long hair. Time-travel and robots and princesses. Big muscles and disco dancing and inappropriate cultural assumptions.'

'And you consider this a good thing because – ?' Panda begins, but is interrupted by the arrival of a Cyrene basecraft.

Spiny and crablike, and heavy as an iron island, it drops directly out of the sky to come to rest, as gentle as an air-kiss, next to the Cardinal ships. 'Ooh look,' says Iris. 'Here comes Barnaby.'

'So it would seem,' Panda agrees, as armoured Cyrenes begin to file from the new arrival. Nestled gently on the shoulder of each is the black smudge of one of his own cybernetic brothers.

'Time we were going then, I think,' says Iris. 'Let's find some fab new adventures of our own.'

The bus trundles across the outcrop, picking up speed – until a flare of magnesium runs along its length, unzipping it into unreality.

Beneath the suddenly empty clifftop, the convention-goers fall in together and begin to march towards the dome.

The Dreadful Flap

Paul Magrs

They were having Bellinis mid-afternoon in a café bar and Iris had come to the conclusion that life on Earth suited Jenny much better than a life racketing about the universe. Jenny was lean, tanned and fit. Back in the day, travelling aboard Iris' transdimensional bus, the ex-traffic warden had always looked peaky, and a lot less happy.

'For one thing,' Iris suddenly laughed. 'You used to get the runs, didn't you? Every time we flew through time and space. Bit inconvenient that, eh, lovey?'

Jenny smiled. She was determined not to let Iris aggravate her. Not yet, anyway. But they were only about an hour into their reunion and already the strains were showing.

It was twelve years since Jenny had said goodbye to Iris, here in the North East in the mid-Nineties, during that strange affair with the jellyfish creatures, their hidden moonbase and the cast of a daytime soap opera Iris was partial to. Now here was her old friend, back in Darlington, looking quite different again, and accompanied by a small, stuffed, talking Panda. Panda hadn't said much for the last little while. He was content to sit back on the leather sofa and guzzle his second champagne cocktail. He scowled at Iris' unfortunate mention of her ex-companion's tribulations.

'Don't embarrass the girl, Iris,' he said sharply.

Iris cackled and started hunting around in her clutch bag for her black Sobranies. 'Ha! It'll take much more than that to make our Jenny blush, won't it, lovey?' She sighed happily as she lit her ciggy, surrounding herself in a blue haze of reminiscence.

Jenny wondered whether she should warn Iris that she couldn't smoke indoors. Not here and certainly not where they were going next. But there was no changing Iris, was there? The old ratbag would smoke where she wanted, say the wrong things, and insist on generally messing everything up. That's what she always did.

A shiver of perturbation went through Jenny.

Things were different now. Since Iris had left her here on Earth, things had indeed changed.

Panda smiled at her politely. 'So, my dear. Do you miss life with old Aunty Iris at all, hmm?'

Iris rolled her eyes. Panda was sending her up, as usual. To her surprise, Jenny swept into this nostalgic rhapsody: 'Oh, it was dangerous and downright horrifying at times. But I wouldn't have missed it for the world! Any of it! We saw the whole Multiverse, it seemed like. Oooh, I saw such things. Iris showed me such marvellous things in outer space and all through history...'

She trailed off and there was an embarrassed pause. Iris reached forward and patted her hand. 'All right, lovey. Don't get carried away.' As far as she recalled, her journeys with Jenny hadn't been that joyous at all. Jenny had stumbled aboard whilst trying to slap a ticket on the bus in a side street in Sunderland in 1991. It had taken Iris four years to get her back anywhere near home. Jenny had been pretty mardy and gyppy the whole time.

'Go on, lovey,' Iris said, changing the subject before they could revisit the past in too much detail. 'Tell us all about your life here. This outfit you're working for. This secret organisation...'

Jenny smiled. She looked very pleased with herself, Iris thought.

'Well, it isn't secret to you, is it, Iris?' she said.

It was true. The Ministry of Incursions and Other Alien Wonders – MIAOW – was a shady government body that Iris had worked for, sometimes reluctantly, during the period she had been trapped on Earth. 'I worked for the South Kensington branch of MIAOW,' she said now. 'I have no idea what the Darlington branch is like. And it's what, nearly forty years later? I imagine things have moved on a bit, eh lovey?'

Jenny smiled and hoiked her trench coat off the back of her chair. 'We'll go and see, shall we?'

Panda scooted forward on the settee, getting Iris to help him with his tall, empty glass. 'Oh! Are we going to your secret headquarters now? Marvellous! Oh, erm, Iris, would you mind popping me in your carpet bag when we go outside? Sitting in swanky wine bars is one thing, but I'm not sure Darlington is quite ready for the sight of me toddling about...'

Iris grinned and held her carpet bag ready for him to hop in.

Jenny watched them, shaking her head. Where had Iris met this strange creature? What was she up to? Jenny waited impatiently as Iris made a great palaver pulling on her leopardskin coat and her ludicrous, shapeless hat, and paying the young waiter with a variety of not very current currencies. Suddenly Jenny was struck by an awful thought. She felt embarrassed by Iris. She was used to blending into the crowd. Slipping between places like a shadow. Stalking about surreptitiously. But walking through the streets with Iris – she remembered – was like the circus had arrived in town.

When they hit the streets of the bustling market town, however, it was as if Iris picked up on Jenny's discomfort. She scuttled along in her wake, clutching her various bags and clamping her hat to her head. She was trying not to draw any more attention to their small party than was strictly necessary. Which was unusual for her.

It was a blustery, grey day in Darlington as they hurried across Skinnergate and down the narrow cobbled lane of Posthouse Wynd. They were making towards the marketplace, in the very centre of town.

Jenny was explaining how the local branch of MIAOW had considered naming themselves after Iris herself, in recognition of all her good work for the organisation.

'Oh no, lovey,' Iris said, secretly pleased, as they tried to cross the busy main road. 'It's best if I keep my presence on Earth quiet. I don't like people to know where and when I've been.'

Jenny nodded tersely. 'Exactly. So we were going to name ourselves after an anagram of your name.'

'Oh yes?' Iris frowned, as they stepped inside the indoor market, which rang with the cries of vendors.

'We came up with three possibilities,' Jenny went on. '*Mis Drily White* or *Him Dies Twirly.*'

'Oh!' said Iris.

Jenny went on, 'And then there was, *I'm Weirdly Shit*.'

In Iris' carpet bag, Panda let out a great guffaw.

'So we just stuck with MIAOW in the end,' Jenny said.

'I should cocoa,' Iris frowned, and saw that her friend was pointing to a small remainder bookshop in the furthest, dowdiest corner of the indoor market.

'Here we are,' Jenny said. 'We go in through here...'

Several hundred metres below the tripe stall, the fruiterers and the fishmongers, lay the gloomy recesses of MIAOW's secret base of operations for the whole of the North of England. It was a grand place, teeming with electronic gadgetry and computer consoles, which were all ticking, hissing and fizzing with activity as Jenny led her small party proudly from the secret elevator shaft into her den.

'Very nice,' Iris nodded. 'Very nice equipment.'

'What's it all for?' demanded Panda gruffly. 'Are you MIAOW people doing the same stuff as you were back in the early Seventies, hm? Watch the Skies and all that?'

Jenny led them on a quick tour around the base and sat them down in a kind of coffee lounge area, hemmed in by glowing maps of Tyne and Wear, the Lake District and County Durham. 'Almost the same, Panda, yes,' Jenny said. 'Back then it was a simpler world, and an easier job.'

'I don't remember it being easy!' Iris chuckled. 'No coffee for me, lovey. How are you fixed for gin?' She shook her head wheezily. 'I remember there was an alien invasion to foil or a weird interdimensional incursion to put a stop to just about every week, back when I was scientific advisor! Eeeh, we were run off our feet, weren't we Panda?'

'Hmph,' said Panda, remembering. 'What was more, *I* was also reviewing ballet and opera for several broadsheets and august organs of culture – at the same time! Oh yes. The nineteen-seventies were a devil of a time for us. But now! You seem to have enough technological gubbins down here to help you with just about everything!'

Jenny shrugged and smiled and looked – Iris suddenly thought, as she accepted a Bombay Sapphire on ice –rather shifty. The ex-traffic warden was hiding something from her erstwhile mentor. As Iris knew of old, MIAOW could be a pretty nefarious outfit when they chose to. In fact, that had been the reason she had stormed off and left them back in 1978. But it looked to her that Jenny had fallen for their hardline rhetoric hook, line and sinker.

'Surely you don't do all the work by yourself, lovey?' she asked pleasantly.

Jenny introduced her visitors to various operatives and helpers who sat at computers, welcoming Iris and Panda blandly. Panda pulled a face, 'What a dull bunch!' he hissed to Iris as they were led on a tour round the laboratories and the emergency prison cells. 'It doesn't look like much fun, does it?'

Iris had to agree. 'Who do you keep in your cells?' she asked Jenny sharply.

'Oh, you know what it's like,' Jenny smiled. 'There's always someone. Aliens who've lost their way. Creatures and villains. People it isn't safe to let roam the streets. We keep them here until we can decide the best thing to do with them.'

'Hmmm,' said Iris. To her the place looked horrible. Like being in torture chambers. At least back in the Seventies MIAOW had made more of an effort with the décor and everything.

They met a few other colleagues of Jenny's: an elderly Eastern European Woman who sat knitting in front of a series of computer screens, absorbing raw data with her limpid sea-green eyes. Panda drew sly attention to the fact that her lower half terminated in a mermaid's tail only partially concealed by a tartan rug. There were several other, more conventional-looking MIAOW operatives. A rather sexy young man that Iris liked the look of. But Jenny saved the best till last

'My boss,' she said, with a nervous flinch. She nodded towards the main entrance of the base, where a very tall and dapper figure had slipped in and was making his way, almost silently, up the gantry towards them.

Iris swallowed involuntarily. Her throat had gone dry and Panda was clutching at the left leg of her trouser suit.

'Welcome, welcome,' said Jenny's boss, in a velvety, cultured sort of voice. Now he was upon them they could study the fish belly white of his flesh, and the boot polish black of his slicked back hair. He was ageless and suave, bowing to kiss Iris' hand with chilly lips. 'I am Kristoff Alucard,' he purred. 'And I am at your service. Welcome back to MIAOW, Ms Wildthyme. The organisation has not been the same, deprived of your unique talents.'

Iris narrowed her eyes for a moment, and then gave in to his flattery. 'Alucard. I'd heard you'd been recruited by this lot. How very interesting.'

'Has Jenny opened the gin?' he asked.

'She's made us very comfortable, yes.'

He hung up his cloak and swept off to examine a series of print-outs. 'Forgive me if I catch up with my emails and so on, my dears. Then, perhaps later, you will join me on a little mission, hmm?'

'Mission?' frowned Iris.

Jenny put in, 'Kristoff, they are only here for a visit...'

'Nonsense,' Alucard grinned wolfishly. 'Iris' help would be invaluable to us this evening. She is an old hand at incursions such as these.'

'I am indeed,' said Iris. 'Has this something to do with the interstitial gap my bus's instruments detected here?'

Panda looked surprised. 'Did they?'

'Ooh yes, lovey,' Iris said. 'Didn't I mention it? That's what drew us to this place in the first place. There's something here in Darlington. Something that goes right through this whole market place above this base of theirs. Some kind of savage gash through the Very Fabric of Time and Space.'

Panda sipped his gin and fiddled with some Japanese rice snacks Jenny had put out. 'Oh, that's very interesting.' Inside him though, his heart had sunk a little. Iris had found them something to investigate, hadn't she? This wasn't just a social call, after all.

Alucard stepped a little closer to Iris and studied her face calmly. 'Oh, you've lost none of your sharpness, have you?' He chuckled. 'You're quite right. We call it the Dreadful Flap. And, occasionally, things come through it. And that is why our base is here. To collect those things when they come through from other dimensions.'

Iris frowned. 'What sort of things?'

Alucard laughed playfully and swished off to his office. 'You will just have to see, my dear, this evening...'

Jenny shrugged helplessly at them. Iris wasn't at all amused. 'What are you doing hanging around with the likes of *him*, lovey?' she hissed.

But Jenny didn't have an answer for her.

Later on it snowed in the marketplace above their heads. Darlington was coated lightly but firmly by a frosty blanket as the shops and stalls closed down and people started heading home. The MIAOW operatives watched this all from the cool seclusion of their hidden base.

'I'd rather have gone round the shops,' said Panda glumly. 'It's not much fun down here.'

'What's that, lovey?' Iris grinned. She had whiled away the hours tapping into MIAOW's databanks and surreptitiously uploading their files into the memory crystal concealed in her cigarette case. Jenny had let them be for several hours, leaving Iris to make free with the gin and nibbles.

'I'm getting itchy feet,' sighed Panda, waggling his chunky, furry legs. 'I also feel like a prisoner here.'

'I know what you mean,' Iris murmured, staring intently at the info whizzing across the tiny screen in her cigarette case. 'Look at this, lovey. It's about tonight. This intervention Alucard is planning to make. The Dreadful Flap opens up at eight p.m tonight and they are expecting some awful kind of evil warlord robot to come out of it. From the far future and from right across the other end of the cosmos. They seem very well informed...'

'What would an evil robot want with coming to Darlington?' Panda frowned. 'I mean, it's very nice, especially since they did the town centre up.'

'Looks to me like this robot thingy is trying to escape from somewhere,' Iris said. 'Its original coordinates are given as a space station. Antelope Slash Nitelite. Anyway, it's given itself up to the vagaries of the vortex. And it's heading here. Where it'll fall straight into the hands of MIAOW.'

'Poor thing,' Panda said. 'Even if it is an evil warlord. I wouldn't want to end up at the mercy of this lot. Especially that Alucard.'

'They want to cannibalise it,' Iris said, closing her cigarette case quickly as she saw Jenny making their way towards them across the base. 'That's what they do. Salvage alien tech and try to make best use of it.'

Panda was wearing a very dark look. What if MIAOW suddenly decided that they wanted to make best use out of Iris and himself? He just knew these people weren't to be trusted.

'It's time to go upstairs,' Jenny told them gently. She was all tooled up in a catsuit under her trenchcoat. 'It's almost eight o'clock, and time for our rendezvous with this alien creature.'

'Oh?' Iris smiled, looking and sounding more drunk than she actually was.

'Come on, Iris,' Jenny said, with just a hint of impatience showing through. 'You said you wanted to see what we were up to these days.'

'Pop me in your bag again,' said Panda, scooping the last of the nibbles into a handkerchief in case he got peckish during their adventure upstairs.

Alucard joined them again as they stepped out of the elevator and into the remainder bookshop. Beyond the glass doors the whole of the high-ceilinged marketplace was empty by now. The lights were out and there was an air of desolation and a whiff of spoiled meat about the place.

'What we will face tonight,' said Alucard softly, as they made their way down the aisles, 'will be nothing like the kind of thing you faced back in the Seventies.' He smiled at Iris.

She found herself scowling back at him. 'Don't flatter me, Alucard. I've had blandishments off better men than you.'

'I bet you have,' he chuckled.

Panda was listening from inside Iris' bag, and he was chuntering away to himself. Like Iris he had taken an instant dislike to Jenny's elegant boss.

'The gash always opens up here,' Jenny said, glancing at them nervously. 'Outside the wool shop.'

'It's almost eight p.m,' Alucard said tersely.

Iris watched them draw out very large, clunky weapons. Far too advanced for this period in Earth's history. 'What are you going to do? Shoot it to pieces as soon as it sets foot in Darlington?'

'What a waste that would be,' Alucard said. A curious fizzing, whooshing noise was starting up all around them. 'No, we will immobilize the creature and take it to our secure unit.'

Iris hated weapons of any kind. She used to have a rather neat pink pistol thing that she toted around and strapped to her thigh, back in the old days. But that had been mostly for show and delivered a blast that gave its victims the equivalent of a nasty hangover. These guns of Jenny's and Alucard's, they were of a different order altogether.

There came a shocking screech of pain then, as lightning descended through the glass roof of the Victorian building. It slashed and crashed to the concrete floor and every hair stood up on Iris' head.

She had seen transdimensional phenomena before, of course, but they always fazed her a little. Wormholes, gateways, all that stuff. They gave her the willies, really. This was a particularly fine specimen. A very sharp gap in the Very Fabric. It really was quite impressive and... as she gazed blinking at the tidy edges and the twinkling miasma beyond, she found that it was actually reminding her of something. A phenomenon she had seen before... perhaps in another life, another reality...

But there was no more time to think. A squat and bulky shape had materialised in the gash. It teetered at the very brink as it hoved into view, warping gradually into proper substance and shrieking in panic at the sight of its welcoming committee.

A very unwelcoming committee we make, thought Iris unhappily.

Jenny and Alucard had gone straight for their weapons and were waving them about. They're enjoying this, thought Iris.

And her next thought was: that's no warrior robot. That's a Servo-furnishing.

'Ohhh! Help! Help me! Where am I?' came the high, warbling voice of the new arrival.

Panda thrust his head out of Iris' bag. 'What's going on?'

Iris frowned. 'Well, lovey. The two of them are in the process of arresting what looks like... a vending machine.'

'I don't mean any harm! Please don't shoot me! Oh, no! Where have I ended up?' Two clunky arms went up in the air in surrender.

'What's your name?' snapped Jenny, her aim unwavering. 'What is your mission here?'

'I-I'm Barbara,' sang the servo-furnishing uncertainly. 'And I have no mission. I don't even know where I am!'

Alucard snarled. 'A likely tale.'

'Honestly, sir. I exist only to serve humankind. I am fully stocked with crisps and fizzy drinks and...'

Alucard drew back from the beseeching creature. 'Winterleaf – take it down to the cells.'

'Aye, sir,' clipped Jenny. She stepped forward to attach a transmat disc to the robot's body. It shimmered and vanished mid-sentence, just as it was explaining about how it had only just managed to escape before the destruction of the space station Antelope-slash-Nitelite in the thirty fifth century.

'Where have you sent her?' Iris demanded.

'The cells,' said Jenny. 'So it can be stripped down and made use of.'

Alucard watched until the Dreadful Flap closed up again, and then he decided there was nothing more to see. He slipped away, into the shadows.

'But she was NICE!' Panda burst out, swinging round in Iris' bag to shout in Jenny's face. 'She seemed like such a nice person!'

Jenny shrugged and walked away, back to the secret lift.

They followed, leaving the indoor market looking as if nothing had even happened. There was a slightly singed aroma to the air, and maybe an odd tingle in the atmosphere. But no sense, really, that anything cosmic or untoward had transpired here.

All that night the snow tumbled down over Darlington.

Iris and Panda insisted on braving the cold and the ice and leaving the MIAOW base. They wanted to go back to their bus, which they had left beside a park near the Arts Centre in Vane Terrace. It was important to them to get away and spend the night at home, in their usual beds. In the past few hours they had really started to feel like they were prisoners of Jenny and her team. Indeed, Jenny looked very unwilling to let them go.

Once on board the bus Panda set to, mixing them a nightcap, and Iris put on an old Cilla Black album. She claimed that Cilla's voice helped her think, though Panda couldn't see how that could possibly be.

'They seem very self-important,' she sniffed. 'Defending the Earth against possible alien visitors, and so on.' She flung herself down on her lumpy chaise longue. 'I suppose MIAOW was always a bit like that.'

'I don't like them,' Panda said severely. 'And it looks to me as if young Jenny has had her head turned by that cadaverous fop, Alucard.'

'Oh dear,' said Iris worriedly. 'Something else that bothers me is the nature of that... Dreadful Flap, thing. I've seen one very like it before. It isn't a natural phenomenon. Someone has manufactured it.'

'Alucard?'

She shook her head. 'He couldn't do anything like that.' Then she was opening her cigarette case, sparking up a pink and gold Russian fag, and glaring intently at the information she had gleaned from the MIAOW database. 'According to what I can make out, that tear in the fabric of time and space has been there for forty three years. Before that, nothing.'

'So, who tore it?' wondered Panda. He stared out at the snow tumbling past and lying thickly now under the evergreens of the park. He'd have to dig out his hat and scarf if they were going out in all that tomorrow.

Iris said, 'There's only one man I know of who could create a rent in time-space like that.'

Panda sat up interestedly. 'Who?'

She made a rueful face. 'But I may be completely wrong. I don't even know if he ever travelled this way. I'll have to find out. Tomorrow.' She was up on her feet again, drawing thick curtains against the blustery night. 'I hope we don't get a ticket, parking here.'

Panda found himself drifting off. 'It's all right,' he heard himself say. 'Jenny's not a traffic warden anymore.'

They were up at first light. Iris was clattering about in the kitchen at the back of the bus, whipping up some steaming hot porridge and thick black coffee. Panda joined her blearily at the breakfast bar and she told him, 'I've written down their security codes on a post-it note, here, lovey.' She stuck the yellow scrap to his paw. 'So I want you to get into their base and down into the cells. I want you to free poor Barbara, the vending machine.'

'Hurray!' said Panda.

'It isn't right they should keep her captive, poor old moo,' said Iris. 'And in the meantime, I'm off to do some research. I need dates and times and details...' She went off muttering mysteriously, slamming all their dishes in the washer, and lighting herself a ciggie. 'But I'd say we've got time, first, for a run around in the snowy park, don't you? We could make a snowman or something.'

Panda nodded thoughtfully. 'I'd say that was an excellent plan, Ms Wildthyme. A spot of running about is just what I need!'

'Barbara? Barbara, are you there? Oh. Blast it. Where are you? Which one did they put you in..?'

Panda had found it pretty easy to slip past the alarms and security features of the MIAOW base. He was an old paw at this kind of thing, and he found that his enemies weren't often expecting their infiltrators to be a mere ten inches tall and as light on their feet as Panda could be. He shimmied and sashayed his way under the laser beams and hidden cameras and soon found himself in the dungeons beneath the base, deep below the ground.

'Barbara?' he called again, suddenly acutely aware of curious snufflings and snortings from the cells that lined the chamber. He was disturbing the other alien creatures that MIAOW were holding captive. For a moment he was tempted to free the whole lot. What right did Jenny have to clap aliens in irons like this? But then he thought again. There might be allsorts of bother if he set monsters loose in Darlington. Best just do what he came here to do...

He found her in the very furthest cell. She looked desolate, with her arms hanging down loosely at her sides. Panda didn't know exactly how he could read so much pathos into just the way a vending machine was holding itself. But he was left in no doubt about how delighted she was to see him as he pressed up to the bars of her cell.

'My dear!' he called. 'I am here to rescue you!'

Barbara's castors squealed with glee. She teetered towards the bars. 'Oh! Oh! It's you! You were there last night when I stepped out of the Gap in the Fabric! You were with the people who took me prisoner.'

'It was nothing to do with me, my dear,' Panda said. He studied the sticky note Iris had given him. Which were the correct codes to open this dratted door? 'I was a mere witness to your plight.'

Barbara gasped. There was a new gleam of optimism in her glass frontage all of a sudden. Something whirred and clunked happily inside her. 'Oh, my shining prince! My knight!'

Panda growled, impatient with himself. 'Well, I will be, if I can just...' He jabbed at the control panel. Right first time! The cage flew open. 'Let's be off!' he beamed.

Barbara paused. 'But how? I've no idea where I am. They transmatted me here from above ground. I don't even know... I mean, is this Earth?'

'Twenty first century,' Panda nodded. 'The north of England.'

'Oh good,' Barbara said. 'That's rather what I hoped for. I come from the far future, but I had to escape. And I'm fashioned rather retro in style. I thought I might fit in better here, in the past.'

'Indeed,' said Panda, turning to lead the way out. He'd chosen to rescue a very garrulous robot, he realised.

'What about some nice crisps, hm, Panda? As a reward? Or I've some very pleasant fizzy pop. Hardly flat at all. What do you think?'

'Hm?' Panda was wondering already if she was going to chunter on like this all day. 'No thank you, my dear. Iris and I have just had breakfast.'

'Oh, Iris is the lady whose handbag you were in last night?' Barbara asked.

'She's no lady!' Panda laughed.

Barbara frowned at him. 'That's not very nice, Panda. She looked like a very respectable kind of person to me.'

Oh god, but she was earnest. Panda felt impatience prickling through his fur. 'Look, come on, Barbara, please! We don't have long before the MIAOW people discover that I have sprang you out of—'

And just at that moment the klaxons started wailing, the red lights went flashing like mad, and Barbara got such a shock that three cans of fizz popped out of her front slot without her even knowing.

Iris spent the morning in the town library. Searching the internet didn't help her at all. She was looking for a particular man, in a particular time and place... as she told the receptionist at the desk. 'Story of my life, chuck,' she added ruefully, examining a lovely spray of lilies set out on the desk. 'Would you direct me to the local history room? I'm interested in the theatre and who might have been playing in any given week...'

So then she whiled away several hours with bound dusty volumes and spools of microfiche. Peering at theatre bills and programmes, alert for the slightest mention of that particular name.

As it happened, Iris quite enjoyed this kind of spadework. Everyone seemed to think it was the dashing around and the punch-ups that she liked most about the various adventures that she got into. But she loved doing actual detective work, too, and getting her fingers grubby with long-buried evidence.

By lunch-time she was snoozing face-down on a heap of ancient Northern Echoes. The librarian shook her – none too gently – awake, and with a shrivelling look, stopped her lighting a ciggie. Iris looked down shame-facedly – and saw straight away what she had come here to find. 'He's here! I've found him!'

There, in the December of 1962. Noel Coward guest starring as the Genie of the Lamp in Aladdin. Darlington Civic Theatre's Glitziest Panto Ever. There was a photo of the playwright in his most sumptuous dressing gown, clutching his lamp rather fiercely, a furious glint in his eye. Iris was shocked. 'Noel did panto? In Darlington?'

But she had found him, at any rate. Just as she had expected to.

She went hunting through her bag for change and copied the relevant pages. Then she was hurrying out of the Victorian building, heels clipping loudly on the marble flooring, gasping for a fag as soon as she was outside. Now she knew where she was going. Same place. Same season. But forty six years earlier.

Now the wind and snow were barrelling along Queen Street. She was buffeted backwards as the snow plastered itself all down her thick fur coat. The tide of Christmas shoppers got on her nerves, too. She nipped through the arcade and into a nice-looking pub for a quick snifter of gin.

Sitting in the window she scanned through the articles she had clipped. There was something queer here. Noel had surely been far too successful in 1962 to play a Genie twice a day for two months in Darlington. Something had happened to the timelines again.

Buggery bollocks.

It was Jenny who waylaid them as the klaxons sounded and they tried to leave the MIAOW secret base. She looked scandalized at the sight of Panda urging the frantic Barbara into the lift.

'What are you doing?'

Panda growled at the ex-traffic warden. 'I'm not holding a reasoned argument with a woman levelling a gun at my head!'

'Oh my!' Barbara cried, jogging her pneumatic feet up and down, making her insides rattle like mad.

'I asked you, Panda,' said Jenny grimly, 'to explain to me what you're up to.'

'I'm taking Barbara away from here,' he snapped. 'To Iris' bus. She doesn't deserve to be locked up in here. She's done nothing wrong.'

'She's an alien interloper,' Jenny said. 'She needs to be studied. Broken down.'

'Yes! Cannibalised! So you said!' cried Panda. 'How callous of you, Jenny.'

'Oooohh!' Barbara shrilled. Panda nudged her to stop. She'd have all of the MIAOW people swarming round if she carried on like this.

'Callous?' frowned Jenny.

'Yes, indeed,' said Panda. 'I'd have thought better of you, Jenny Winterleaf. Iris has told me so many wonderful things about you. About your compassion and sense of justice. How interested you were in other life forms and places when you went travelling with her on board the bus...'

'That was a different lifetime,' said Jenny, still levelling her weapon at him. 'Things are different now. More complicated. We can't afford to be naïve anymore. We have to look at... these things, these alien things... with much more suspicion. With less hopeful eyes.'

'I don't see why that's true,' said Panda. 'I don't see what's so complicated about this age you're living in. I think you've just gone to the bad, Jenny. You're hanging around with ghastly people and, quite frankly, I think your attitude stinks.'

'Oh my,' breathed Barbara, fully expecting to be shot to pieces at any moment. Why was Panda baiting the woman like this?

'I...' Jenny wavered. She lowered her gun.

'It's that Alucard!' Panda went on, his voice ringing with triumph. He was winning! He was getting through to her! 'He has perverted everything here. He's turned MIAOW into something paranoid and hateful like he is.'

'But...' Jenny said. 'I love him!'

'What?' Panda boggled. 'You're a flaming lesbian, Jenny! You always were.'

'I know!' cried Jenny helplessly.

'And what's more, that satanic fop is *Dracula*! You *know* that! You're in thrall to the most wicked being mankind has ever known!'

Jenny's face fell. 'Hang on. Dracula, you say?'

Panda stamped on the ground. 'What's the matter with you? Didn't his *cape* give it away? Can't you do anagrams, girl?'

'W-who's Dracula?' asked Barbara.

'It doesn't matter now,' Panda said. 'We just need to get out of this awful place ASAP. And Jenny here will be coming with us. You're going to help us escape, aren't you, dear?'

'I... I...' Jenny wavered and staggered slightly. Her hand flew to her neck, reaching under her collar.

'See!' Panda cried. 'You've got bite-marks, haven't you? He's been having a nibble of you down here in his stinky catacombs!'

There was no time to fetch Panda. Iris lurched onto her bus and jumped into the driver's cab. With a bit of luck – if she got her sums right – she would be back here in this spot almost before she left, anyway. She was pretty smart at these short trip things, as it happened.

She gunned the engine. Now... 1962...

Zero visibility outside. The blizzard (for that's what it was by now) whirled and whipped and thrashed at the windows of the bus. The streets had been clearing of shoppers as Iris had hurried home. Premature night had set over Darlington. In a way it would be a relief to nip off and spend some few hours in a different winter.

She felt in her pockets for the photocopy. The cold and wet had almost obliterated the pages. But there was Noel's face, glaring at her from under his ludicrous genie's hat: looking affronted at her across the gap of years. Soon be seeing you again, lovey! She grinned and set about dialling up the co-ordinates. Easy-peasy. Piece of piss. Then she chomped down on her ciggy and flung the final dematerialisation switch.

She was ready to get to the bottom of this. She was going to the root cause. She was determined to find out what had caused this Dreadful Flap in Darlington in the first place.

But she had left her friends behind.

Seconds after the solid shape of her double decker had faded away from its parking spot, a large mini cab rounded the corner. It ploughed through the deepening snow, and pulled up at the edge of the park. It was a mini bus big enough to get Barbara on board, and it had taken a little longer to find.

By the time that Panda and Jenny had paid, and helped the confused vending machine out of the back, they were far too late. There was no bus here. Panda ran up and down a little in the snow, horrified at what he had found.

'Where is it, Panda?' Jenny shouted, over the rising noise of the blizzard. 'Where has she gone?'

The taxi pulled away. Too late, Jenny realised that she should have told the driver to wait. Now they were stuck out here, alone.

Panda was standing by the gap in the slush where the bus had been, until a matter of seconds ago. Already the space was filling with fresh snow. He looked up bleakly at his two companions. 'She's left us behind, Jenny! She's gone and left us behind!'

'I have no idea who this woman is,' the Genie sighed. 'I'm sorry, but I have never seen you before in my life.'

'Yes, you have!' Iris laughed. 'But I looked quite different back then. Oh, come on, lovey! Look harder!'

Noel rolled his eyes and peered a little closer at the woman, shuddering at the gin on her breath. He was exhausted and he could do without this kind of nonsense. The matinee was over and he had a couple of hours to rest in his dressing room with a cold flannel across his overheated brow. It wasn't even worth popping back to his hotel for the afternoon, the gap between performances was so tight.

Noel felt enslaved in this production as much as any genie ever had in its lamp. And now, to make matters worse, there was some crazily raffish baglady propping open the stage door. Mr Cripps the Manager was looking distinctly annoyed.

'For goodness sake,' clipped Noel irritably, 'You might as well let her in. There's a terrible draft whooshing in behind her.'

'I've brought the blizzard with me, it seems,' Iris cackled. 'All the way from 2008!'

Noel blinked at her. 'I beg your pardon?'

She gazed at him in delighted appreciation. 'Ooh, look at you! Even in your genie cossie you're still every inch *him*, aren't you!'

'Of course,' Noel tutted. 'Every inch.'

He led her crossly to his dressing room, hidden deep in the labyrinth of dirty white passageways behind the stage area. He sat primly at his dressing table mirror and invited Iris to slump on a shabby settee.

'Cigarette?'

'Go on, then, chuck. Do you know, in the future, they don't let you smoke indoors at all, anywhere?'

'How dreadful,' he said, toying with his lighter. 'I imagine the future is just as Mr Wells once predicted. Frightfully commonplace.'

'Don't give me that,' Iris smirked. 'You know just what the future's like. On this and many others worlds.'

Noel pursed his lips. 'Indeed?'

Iris made a very deliberate mime of someone snipping through the air with a large pair of scissors. 'Eh? Eh?'

Noel frowned at her. Several rather dark lines appeared on his forehead. 'You seem to know rather a lot about me, Ms...?'

Iris gasped. 'You mean you still don't recognise me?'

He narrowed his eyes at her. There was a whine from the dog basket in the corner of the dingy room. Iris turned to see a large red poodle curled up and mumbling in its sleep. 'Aha! Still with the poodles, then,' she grinned.

'They are very loyal companions,' he said. Then his eyes widened slightly in surprise. 'You're Iris Wildthyme.'

'Mistress of the Magical Bus and Transtemporal Adventuress Extraordinaire!' Iris sat back on the lumpy sofa and curled her toes in pleasure at his shocked face. 'I haven't seen you since that affair in Las Vegas with the singing goblins, have I? When was that? Centuries ago!' She nodded appreciatively as Noel moved to the art deco drinks cabinet in the corner. 'Ooh, cheers, chuck. I think we could both do with a drink.'

'I could do with a very stiff one,' Noel muttered, and then cursed himself. Just a few minutes with the blousy old bag and he was descending to horrid double entendres! In his experience Iris had a very cheapening effect on his humour. 'What are you doing here, Iris? Pursuing me to the ends of the Earth?'

She smiled and watched him whiz up a couple of Martinis. 'Well, first of all, I wouldn't call Darlington the ends of the Earth, lovey. It might seem like that to you, here in 1962. But in the future, you know, it's quite a desirable destination for creatures from space and other dimensions and whatnot. They tend to break through and stop off here quite often.'

'How very interesting,' Noel said, rattling the metal shaker busily. 'Rather like the aristocracy staying at Scotch Corner in the nineteenth century, on their way up to the Highlands. That's rather near here, as a matter of fact.'

'Perhaps Darlington has always been a kind of nexus point,' mused Iris, 'for intradimensional wayfarers and also people making their way to Scotland. Hmmm.' She frowned at him. 'Be that as it may, Mr Coward. I have examined the interstitial gap that exists in Darlington in the future and it seems to me to be the work of one particular human being.'

'Oh yes?' Noel poured their drinks and popped an olive into each glass. He handed one to Iris, and one to the poodle. 'Who would this particular human being happen to be?'

'You,' she said, very pointedly.

'Me?' he smiled, playing for time.

'Don't give me that,' she said, almost snarling. She hated it when men went recalcitrant. 'I know exactly what you're capable of. With those pinking shears of yours.'

'I don't know what you're talking about,' he said.

'They're magical pinking shears,' she said. 'And you've used them for years, zipping hither and thither through the cosmos. You and that German tart you used to knock about with.'

'If you're referring to Marlene...'

'That's the one,' Iris nodded, sipping her poisonously strong Martini. 'She was no better than she ought to be. Where's she now, eh?'

'Marlene's in semi-retirement in Paris,' he said sadly. 'And our days of – as you put it – merrily zipping about in time and space with the magical pinking shears are, I assure you, Miss Wildthyme, well behind us.'

'I'm glad to hear it,' snapped Iris. 'Because the pair of you caused your fair share of damage to the flaming timelines, you know.' She glared at him beadily. 'Tourists! Amateurs! Nincompoops!'

'How dare you,' thundered Noel. 'You come in here, demanding entrance to my...'

'That's a point,' Iris broke in. 'Why are you here? In Darlington? Shouldn't you be more successful and famous than this? Shouldn't you be living it up in Jamaica, or wherever it was you had your posh estate? Shouldn't you be hanging out with the Queen Mother and Ian Fleming, rather than playing the Genie in Aladdin twice daily at Darlington Civic?'

Noel sat down heavily. 'I... I...'

'Come on, lovey. You can tell your Aunty Iris.'

He stared at her dolefully. Ooh, those clever, hooded eyes of his, she shivered. He said, 'You were right about those timelines. About my buggering up my own personal history. I've... I think I've messed up my own life, Iris.'

Ha! she thought. Haven't we all?

Poor Barbara, thought Panda, who had come rather quickly to admire the vending machine's doughty moral fibre. But she was finding it difficult ambling down the narrow cobbled streets of the market town. The sleet and snow, dropping thick and fast and slicking their route didn't make it any easier. Thank god the streets were clearing of people, though, and so there were fewer souls about to point and stare at the ambulatory drinks-and-snacks machine and the panda plodding alongside her.

Jenny Winterleaf strode ahead, as if pretending she wasn't with them. Panda was rather disappointed by Jenny. Not only was she involved in kidnapping splendid sorts like Barbara, but she had left herself open to being fingered – only figuratively, he hoped – by the nefarious Alucard.

'We must watch out for him,' Jenny had warned. 'He knows we've taken Barbara. My bleeper's been going off all day. He'll be on the lookout for us.

Panda didn't know what to do for the best. His instinct was to get Barbara as far away from MIAOW headquarters as possible. He couldn't sit back and allow them to wrench his new friend's back off and poke around in her innards. But at the same time there was nowhere else in this time and place that he could take her. He didn't belong anywhere, did he? There was Tom of course, down in London, but he wasn't sure if Tom would be any use, or whether he would even talk to his former Panda friend. Maybe not.

Panda stood in the snowy street and felt like weeping. Where have you gone, you flaky old tart? He shouted at the sky, shaking his fist. He tried to reason it out. She couldn't have just abandoned them, could she? Had she got herself tanked up and simply slipped away, forgetting all about them? That wasn't unheard of, in the course of her very long and very boozy life.

It was Jenny who had proposed their current course of action. She knew that there was no use hanging around waiting for the bus to reappear. She had been caught out that way before. She merely pointed out that they couldn't stand around in this kind of weather. They had to get into shelter.

'It's true,' Barbara complained. 'My parts are freezing together. All my pop is turning to ice!'

'Quite,' said Panda, whose fur was standing in frosty tufts.

'I'll take you to my place,' Jenny said.

Her flat turned out to be a very nice one in a newly-developed part of town, not that very from the market place.

'Very handy for work,' Panda commented as Jenny led them into the compound and the lift and at last into her fourth storey apartment. From her living room window they could see the whole vista of Darlington market place, howling with wind and snow. Jenny had the radio on and was crouching to hear the forecast.

'It's all to do with the Dreadful Flap, isn't it?' asked Panda. 'This weather is all a part of it? It's causing atmospheric disturbances...'

'And temporal ones,' Jenny nodded worriedly. 'That's one of the things MIAOW has been looking into. The Flap leads directly into another universe. One that keeps seeping into our world. A whole other kind of universe, about which we know very little.'

'How very interesting,' said Panda, hopping onto a bean bag. 'Is it the Obverse, maybe?'

Jenny's jaw dropped open. 'How do you...?'

Barbara was a dab hand at interrupting at the right moment to avoid awkward scenes. She went THUNK WHIRR KLUNK and dropped some cans of pop and bags of crisps into her front tray. 'Hungry, anyone?' she beamed.

Just then Jenny's intercom buzzed.

Panda took a bag of crisps and opened them happily. 'Krispies, excellent, Barbara, thank you! Oh, Wombat and Spring Onion. My favourite.' He started munching and didn't like to tell her that they were slightly soggy. Barbara just looked pleased.

Jenny turned to them. 'That was Magda on the intercom.'

'Who?' frowned Panda.

'You've met her,' Jenny snapped. 'Mermaid in the wheelchair. Our all-terrain operative who's a whiz with any kind of extra-sensory phenomena. Anyway, she also runs the remainder bookshop above the base. She says she's been instructed to bring something very important to us...'

'Not from that awful Alucard man, is it?' Barbara quavered. '*He* hasn't sent her, has he?'

'No,' said Jenny, though she couldn't be sure. Anyway, it was too late, Magda was coming up in the lift.

Panda thought she was a stunner. At least, for a mermaid. She wheeled herself quickly into the flat and barely stopped to greet them all before handing Jenny a book from her shop, wrapped in brown paper.

'What's this?' frowned Jenny.

'I cannot stay long,' said Magda, quickly and urgently – just like a spy, Panda thought. 'Alucard will know I am gone. He is very suspicious of everyone today. Ever since...' the mermaid nodded in Barbara's direction. 'He is determined to steal you back, my dear.'

'Well, he can't have me!' exclaimed Barbara hotly. 'You'll fight him off won't you, Panda?'

'Yes, erm, of course,' said Panda. 'What's in the parcel, Jenny?'

'I don't know yet... there's a note with it. A very old note...'

'It was given to me this afternoon,' said Magda. 'It was the strangest thing. A very old solicitor came into my shop and handed me this note, which he said his firm have been waiting over forty years to deliver! As you see, it instructs me to bring you a copy of the enclosed book and to get you, Jenny and Panda and Barbara, to open it to page three hundred and thirty six.'

'WHAT?' gasped Barbara. 'But how can that be?'

Jenny pursed her lips. 'You're saying that someone forty years ago knew that you'd be stocking a certain book in your shop, and that we three would be here in this flat this afternoon, in December 2008?'

Magda nodded and swished her tail excitedly under her tartan rug. 'I am!'

Panda narrowed his eyes. 'I know who this sounds like...' he growled.

Jenny ripped the brown paper off the book. '*Noel Coward's Collected Quips.*'

'I've got a dozen copies in my front window display,' Magda said. 'But how did someone back in the Sixties even know I'd have a shop there, let alone which books I'd have in stock?'

'There are ways and means,' said Panda darkly. 'What does it say on page three hundred and thirty six, Jenny...?'

Jenny flicked through.

'Ooh, it's like being a detective, this!' Barbara cooed.

Jenny said, 'Well, it appears to be an account, by Noel Coward, of Pantomime season in 1962, here in Darlington. And — oh. Right in the middle of the page, look. Printed in a different font.'

She put the thick book on the glass coffee table so they could all have a look. Here was a message written by a hand other than Noel's:

Dear Panda (and Jenny and Barbara) –

This won't make sense to anyone else – but who cares? – so long as it gets to you. Well, here I am back in the past! And there's a right to-do back here. I'm at the theatre and Noel's off doing his second stint of the day as the Genie-in-the-Lamp. He's absolutely furious with me. The thing is, I came back here because I strongly suspect that it was all down to him with his magic pinking shears, cutting a hole in the Very Fabric of Time and Space – it was this that caused the Dreadful Flap in Darlington.'

Jenny broke off from reading. 'Is she saying Noel Coward is responsible for our Dreadful Flap?'

'That she is,' said Panda. 'Let's read the rest.'

'Anyway, loveys, I'm a bit worse for wear now, what with finishing off the gin and everything while Noel's out on the stage, doing his bit with Aladdin. The thing is... Can you come back and help me? I wouldn't normally ask. Jenny, have you still got that special time ring-thing I gave you years ago? The one that was specially disguised? Would you mind using it to come back to 1962 – on the evening of the day before Christmas Eve? It's just that – I think there's bound to be a barney when I try to change history... well, there always is. And I could do with back-up. Okay. That's all I've time for. Come and help me!! I'm going to pop this note in with Noel's special diary in his drawer and hope that it somehow gets to you lot... '

'This is madness!' Jenny said.

'I think it's wonderful,' Barbara said, in her gushing contralto. 'What a fabulously resourceful woman!'

'Oh, she's that alright,' muttered Panda, thinking of her sitting alone and drunk in Noel Coward's dressing room. He noticed that there were a few more words as a PS before the text resumed in Noel's style. 'What's this she added at the end...?' he said.

Jenny read the smaller print aloud to them: 'It says: *'ALUCARD! HE IS HERE!!'*

The bus was parked near the railway station, just a couple of streets from the Civic Theatre. As the snow came down and the evening shadows lengthened, nobody noticed when the bus's doors shunted open a tiny way and a small, dark body fluttered out.

Alucard had always been slightly disappointed by his bat-self. He wanted to be sleek and vicious-looking, with jagged teeth and long, long ears. Instead, his bat-self was rather portly and fluttery, like a kind of daemonic robin. But, no matter. The form of the bat could get him into the places he wanted to be. Like, here for example – time-travelling with Iris, unbeknownst to that mistress of the celestial omnibus.

He was used to various forms of travel – even moving about in time like this. It took a lot to discombobulate Alucard.

He sniffed the air and listened hard. There, ahead. She was at the theatre, for some reason. He could hear the laughter and the singing and the resounding kerfuffle from within the building. All lit up it looked like a birthday cake someone had sat on.

He fluttered and swooped round the back. The narrow windows at ground level, by the bins. One was left ajar and, sure enough, Iris was sitting inside at a dressing table mirror, knocking back the gin, smoking ferociously and scribbling some kind of elaborate note.

Alucard slipped into the room and turned back to his more usual form. 'Iris...'

She squawked and almost dropped her glass. Swinging round, her eyes just about popped out of her head when she saw him. 'What the buggery are you doing here?'

A burst of laughter threw him. Then he saw that there was a loudspeaker, relaying sound from the main house.

'No matter,' Alucard snapped. 'I have pursued you across time and space itself, Iris. I have come all the way back to the Sixties.'

She shrugged. 'So?'

'You have betrayed me! You have let your... Panda friend steal something of great value to me.'

'What Panda gets up to is his business, buster,' she growled. 'It's got nothing to do with me.'

'I want Barbara back,' he snarled, stepping towards her, menacingly.

'I don't have her,' she said. 'And you keep your distance from me. I'm not having you mesmerizing and biting chunks out of me!'

He grinned at her and licked his lips. 'How I want you, Iris.'

She jerked her head. 'What did you say?'

'Can't you tell?' He shivered deliciously. 'Ooh, I can taste your blood right now. A pure distillation of time itself. All stirred up with the spirits of ages past and spiced with eternity. You're a knockout, Iris. Let's get it together.'

She picked up a chair to fend him off. 'Get thee back, Satan!'

Had they been listening, they would have heard thunderous applause from the speaker. Act One of Aladdin had clearly finished and the curtain come down with a velvety thump. And so it should have been no surprise that the door flew open a few seconds later and Noel came bursting into the room, in full Genie ensemble.

He was greeted by the sight of his dressing room in terrible disarray and Iris wrestling on the ground with Alucard. The cocktail glasses were smashed on the floor and the two figures were wound about with Alucard's cape. Princess the poodle was sitting up in her basket, barking crossly.

Noel cried out: 'Would someone mind telling me what this grotesque performance is in aid of?'

Iris started shrieking. Alucard's breath was hot on her tender neck. She could feel his teeth, cold against her flesh.

'NOEL!!' she howled, writhing under the slight weight of the triumphant vamp. 'DO SOMETHING!!'

Panda fell about laughing. 'That's not a Time Ring-Thing, Jenny,' he said, wiping his eyes with both paws. 'That's a vibrator!'

Jenny went beetroot. 'It still does the job,' she said.

'I'll bet it does,' Magda frowned, peering at the monstrous dildo Jenny had unearthed from her hall closet. Jenny was busying wiping dust off the controls.

'I've hardly ever used it,' she frowned. She looked at the others. 'I mean, for travelling in time. Iris insisted it was only for the gravest of emergencies. There's a setting here that will take us to wherever and whenever she is, in a flash.'

Panda's eyes boggled. 'It's a *homing* dildo?'

'I don't understand,' said Barbara, 'What's a dildo?'

'It doesn't matter,' said Jenny. 'Magda – you stay here. Keep tabs on what's going on at MIAOW HQ.'

'What do I tell Alucard?' said Magda worriedly.

'I don't know,' said Jenny. 'But I think things are going to change for MIAOW Darlington. Alucard's going too far. Iris is right.' She held the jet black Time Cock aloft in both hands. 'Okay you lot. I'm off now – to the Sixties. To rescue Iris!'

Panda was up on his stubby feet in a flash. 'You're not going without me, young lady!'

Barbara trundled forward. 'Me, too. You might... need some snacks or fizzy pop...'

'Panda, yes, Barbara – no,' said Jenny tersely. She grabbed Panda's paw and activated the curious time device. It juddered and glowed and everything started to whirl around...

'Back to the Sixties!' cried Panda, 'Yet again!'

Noel did the only thing he could do, under the circumstances.

He set his poodle onto Iris' attacker.

'Princess – kill!'

In a livid rush of scarlet the dog was upon the struggling pair. Iris who had never been good with pets – gave a great yell as the creature snarled and slobbered over her. Alucard got by far the worst of it. Princess had him by the scruff of the neck.

'Good girl,' cried Noel. 'Iris, get yourself up off the floor at once and explain yourself. Who is this ghastly person?'

She scrambled up hastily and none too elegantly, screaming: 'It's Dracula! Stake him! Stake him through the bloody heart!'

In that instant, however, Alucard managed to gather the strength of will to transform himself. Next thing they knew there was a huge, slavering hound in his stead. Princess squealed in shock and leapt away, but not before the black dog could nip her nastily. Then he bayed once at them all, and bounded out of the room. They heard various squeals from backstage as the hound darted past dancers and other panto performers.

'After him!' Iris roared. 'We can't just let him run about in the past!'

Noel looked at her helplessly. 'You'll make me miss the beginning of Act Two.' Then he was aware of Princess whimpering, loping back to her basket.

'Oh crikey,' said Iris. 'Did he bite her?'

Noel was examining his ailing poodle. 'Yes, but... do you mean that...?'

Iris looked grim. 'We'll just have to deal with that later. For the moment, we need to get rid of Alucard. You wouldn't believe the havoc he's been causing in the future. And now he'll do even worse things in the past. If we don't stop him. Now, lovey. Do you have something you could use as a stake?'

Noel thought for a second. His inscrutable eyes narrowed suddenly. Iris knew that look. He was having an epiphany. He told her, 'I have just the thing.'

'Panda! You held her hand, damn you!' cursed Jenny.

They had come out of the coruscating, scintillating maw of the time vortex and now the three of them were standing in the snow of a dark Darlington street at night.

Rather shame-facedly Barbara took a step backwards.

Panda defended her hotly, 'Why shouldn't she come along? At least she wouldn't sell us out to some cadaverous dandy!'

'What's that supposed to mean?' snarled Jenny, stowing her Time Cock back in her trench coat.

'It means that I trust lovely Barbara a great deal more than I do some bloody traffic warden.'

'Erm,' put in Barbara. 'Where are we? Are we sure that we're in the right place?'

'Just look at her!' Jenny pointed out. 'We're supposed to go incognito. Don't you think she's going to stand out? She's a frigging robot!'

Panda ignored her. 'This is definitely the right place,' he said, sniffing the snowy air. 'I can feel it in my fur. There's definitely a Sixties vibe.' He turned around, nose twitching. 'And – what's more – there's Iris' bus!'

His heart swelled with pride and joy as he stared at the lit up windows of the bus.

'That's something, I suppose,' grumbled Jenny. 'Come on. Let's see if she's aboard...'

'But shouldn't we find this theatre?' said Barbara. 'Remember, the last thing we heard was that she was being menaced in the dressing room by...'

'AAAggghhhHHH!' Panda yelled.

They whirled about in time to see a huge black dog bounding towards them through the snow. Its eyes glowed a ferocious red and slobber was dripping from its jaws, pink and frothy with someone's blood.

'That's him,' Jenny breathed. 'My master...!'

Barbara balked. 'What? Your what?'

Jenny wasn't herself. She became passive and limp. She took a step forwards, into the path of the great, ravening beast. 'Master... I have brought them to you...'

'Pick me up! Pick me up!' Panda gibbered at Barbara. He didn't fancy his chances against the great hound.

But the dog stopped in its tracks, sending up a huge plume of snow. It stood there snarling at them and howled once. Then it shimmered and turned back into Alucard.

Barbara gasped and her innards thunked with fear.

'I have brought them to you, Master, across the barrier of time,' said Jenny – rather sententiously, Panda thought, even for a mesmerized lackey.

'Well done, daughter,' Alucard grinned. 'The Servo-furnishing is all mine..!' He approached and reached out to touch Barbara. The poor robot found she couldn't move an inch. Even she was powerless before his balefully seductive eyes. Her insides quivered as his cold hands stroked her glass panels.

'Iris knew you were up to no good, Alucard,' Panda boggled at him. 'But we'll stop you, you see if we don't!'

Alucard's face darkened. 'Why should I listen to you? Just some bear. Just some stuffed toy.'

Panda stood up to his fullest extent. '*Bear*?' he thundered. '*Stuffed toy*?!'

Alucard grinned, and bent to pick him up off the ground...

Oh fuck, thought Panda.

During the interval, those audience members in the foyer, or taking a breath of night air outside the theatre were rather startled to see the star of the show flying past, in full costume, at full pelt. Also, he was brandishing a pair of sparkling pinking shears before him. Behind him, breathing raggedly, was an extraordinary-looking woman in a large hat and unhelpfully spiky shoes.

Noel kept his head down and tried to ignore them. Best get this ludicrous escapade finished with as soon as possible, and get back to the show and start

Act Two. He couldn't afford to mess up another show, now that he was getting his life back on the rails again...

But Iris was right. He had to see to Alucard.

Why was she shouting at him, though?

The frozen wind was too fierce. The snow was rushing down in stinging flurries.

'Don't use the pinking shears!' Iris bellowed. 'Use something else! Anything else!'

He couldn't understand why she was shouting this.

Ah, there was the dog, bounding ahead. They weren't far behind. They could get him still.

He shouted back to Iris, 'What's wrong with the shears?' They were marvellous. They were magical. They had taken him into such wonderful adventures in the past and the future. Even into other dimensions. Back in the Thirties, when Marlene had given them to him, claiming they had come out of Old Russia and she'd been given them by an Old Russian Count in Berlin and—

No! There was no time for this now!!

Here was Alucard, turned back to his relatively-human form. And he was standing in the snowy street, arguing the toss with three figures... a girl, a machine of some kind, and a small bear...

Iris skidded into the back of him, shrieking: 'Pandaaaaaaa!'

Like dominos they went down, into the snow, one against and on top of the other. It was utterly undignified, as usual for one of Iris' do's, as Noel remembered from all his earlier dealings with the woman. Everyone was shouting at once, calling out each other's names and dreadful insults.

There was only one way to put an end to this nonsense.

Noel extricated his shears and waved them aloft. What had nanny always said about running with scissors?

Ah yes. Don't do it.

Unless, of course, you're setting out to stake a bothersome member of the Undead and also open up a neat gash in the Very Fabric of—

'Noooooooo!' Iris screeched right in his ear. 'Don't do that, Noel! You'll--!'

Of course, it was much too late.

Alucard looked startled and outraged as the pinking shears plunged heartily into his immaculate shirt front. As the blood spurted darkly like blackcurrant jam he swore very loudly in Noel's face.

'What have you done?' Iris shouted.

Jenny reeled backwards as her Master shrivelled and dessicated before her eyes...

But the pinking shears hadn't yet finished their work.

The gap was opening up before their very eyes.

Panda, Barbara, Jenny and Iris drew back at the sight of it. Like a great fuschia zigzag of metaphysical lightning. Cracking open unstoppably in the middle of Darlington.

'Oh no!' cried Barbara.

'Stand back everybody!' yelled Panda.

'Would someone please explain to me...' began Noel, feeling like he had gone too far.

Dazedly, coming to her senses, Jenny intoned: 'It's the gap! It's the gap! It's the Dreadful Flap!'

Iris nodded sadly as they watched the zig zag shudder and terminate somewhere across the town centre. Somewhere in the middle of the market place. 'This is where it all starts,' she sighed. Then she looked at the others. 'Does one of you have something we could put Alucard's ashes in? We can't leave them hanging around here.'

Barbara leapt into action, giving Iris a choice of pop can or crisp packet. As it turned out, the remains of the undead smoothie filled both.

They watched the Dreadful Flap seethe and glow. Then it faded gradually out of sight.

'It hasn't gone though, has it?' said Panda.

Iris shook her head. 'Nope. It's here for good now. And that's why we need MIAOW, and Jenny here, to watch over what comes through the interstitial gash from now on.'

'Well,' said Noel, feeling rather uneasy, and hiding the pinking shears back in his genie's robes. 'I really must get back to the second half of the show. You're all welcome to come and watch, by the way. It's a remarkably good panto, as it happens.'

'Fab!' grinned Iris, picking up Panda and dusting some of the snow off him. Maybe a nice pantomime might cheer them all, and make them feel better for having started this whole Dreadful Flap in the first place.

Before they went home again that evening Iris guided the bus gently to a certain town on the north east coast, not so far from Darlington. She felt she ought to drop Alucard's ashes somewhere they would be safe from interference. She parked the bus at midnight outside St Mary's church high atop the cliffs in Whitby. It was here that Alucard had first come to England, over a hundred years earlier, bursting onto these shores in the form of that same slobbery great hound.

The others stood about in the graveyard, shivering under the snowy moon, as Iris nipped down into the church's crypt to stow away the can of pop and the crisp packet.

She returned, dusting herself down. 'Now, Jenny,' she told her former companion sternly. 'You're free of the old dandy's control now. But no more vampires, all right, lovey? You never know where they've been.'

Jenny nodded, a little shame-facedly.

'Ooh, that reminds me. Noel could well have a vampire poodle on his hands. I should have warned him to watch out.' Iris tutted. 'But I can't do everything, can I, gang? Anyway. Let's get you all back to Darlington, eh?'

She hustled them aboard the bright, welcoming interior of the bus.

'That is, of course, unless either of you would rather join Panda and me on our travels, eh? Jenny, Barbara?'

Jenny smilingly declined, already anticipating another bumpy ride through the vortex.

Panda looked keenly at Barbara. 'What do you say?' he said, patting her metal arm fondly. 'We have a marvellous time racketing about the cosmos!'

Barbara looked perplexed. 'I think I've seen quite enough of the cosmos just for now, Panda dear. Darlington will probably be quite exciting enough for me. At least for the time being.'

'Ha!' Iris swooshed the doors closed and jammed one of her compilation cds in the player. 'Panda, crack the drinks cabinet open! This'll only be a short hop! Hang onto your hats everyone! It's time to go home!'

And Not A Drop To Drink...

Steven Wickham

The story of Mr Panda-Wanda
A tale for tiny tots By Peatrix Blotter

Once upon a time there was a nice big black and white bear. His name was Mr Panda-Wanda. He lived in a lovely quiet forest, where no other creatures lived.

Except for his best friend of course. His best friend was called Samuel Snake. He was a serpent who lived curled up in the trees above Mr Panda-Wanda's cave.

'Now, Mr Panda-Wanda', said Samuel Snake one fine morning, 'You are running out of your favourite bamboo shoots, and soon you will have nothing left to eat.'

'Oh dear, said Mr Panda-Wanda. 'What shall I do?'

Samuel said 'You must go into the forest to look for more. But don't go into Mr Chee Woo Lin's garden as he is not very nice.'

'Oh my God!!!!'

Panda jumped, the piercing voice of Iris Wildthyme sending a shudder through his recumbent form. Thrusting the rather tatty and dog-eared edition of his favourite childhood work of fiction down the side of the driver's seat, and swiftly grabbing a week old copy of *The Times*, he sat bolt up right, and waited for more signs of life from the top floor of the bus.

Iris had earlier decided on a little 'quality time'. She had retreated upstairs with a bottle of Bombay Sapphire, yelling from underneath her new favourite feathered monstrosity of a hat – 'I do not want to be disturbed. I'm gonna do me nails, and have a relax. I am not at home to anyone, anything, or any time. Got it?'

'Oh yes, Iris, I have indeed got it. While you are off primping and preening, and no doubt imbibing heavily, I shall also have a little 'Me' time. Enjoy.' With an imperious wave of the paw he smiled as much as pandas can smile and headed for the front of the bus, pulling the grubby beige curtain across, sealing off the driver's cabin from prying eyes. With a gentle claw he switched on the in-bus stereo system, and some highly pleasing music began to play. The best of Barry Manilow. Such a favourite.

The ambience was perfect. Panda reached under the seat for his favourite book in times of need. A gentle look at the life of a fictional panda, which always made him feel good. It calmed him and the generally happy existence of its hero always made the worst times seem better.

He had hardly finished the first page when Iris' voice came screeching down the stairs. 'Oh my God! Panda...Panda! It's a disaster... OH MY GOD!'

Knowing that to ignore his travelling companion's cries would only lead to arguments, recriminations and tears, Panda rolled his eyes, and creaked to his feet, padding down the aisle to the foot of the stairs. 'What is it now?' He watched as a pair of leopard skin mules clumped down the staircase, behind them a disconsolate Iris.

'What have you done? Painted your nails the wrong shade of black?' Panda crossed his arms and waited.

'It's worse than that...' she gulped, biting back tears, her lower lip quivering slightly. 'I've just finished the last bottle of gin.' With a huge shudder she sank onto the bottom step, upturning the bottle in her hand, squeezing the neck of it, as though trying to wring out the very last drop of that sacred liquid.

'Oh Iris,' Panda sighed, an amused grin twitching up the corners of his mouth. 'We have the whole of the universe at our feet, worlds to explore and rescue and devastate and you are upset at having finished your umpteenth bottle of booze? What is that?' He cocked his head on one side as if listening to something unexpected.

An anguished wail escaped Iris' lips. 'But it's a Sunday, and where will I get some gin on a Sunday? Everywhere will be closed.'

'Shhh.' Putting a claw to his own lips, Panda strode forward, and pointed at an orange light on the bus control panel, which was flashing intermittently with an annoying beep. 'Listen, listen. Can't you hear that?'

'Hear what?' Iris ran her slippery nose along her sleeve, and looked up at Panda with the slightest hint of contempt. 'The strained caterwauling of Mr Big Nose?'

'No... that beeping. It's a distress call.'

The bus screeched to a halt, sending gravel flying in all possible directions, Panda's foot pressed firmly on the brake, a silent oath of prayer and thanks formed in his throat.

Descending the steps, Panda and a sniffling Iris looked around them with difficulty. The night was dark, even though a brilliant canopy of sparkling stars filled the sky.

'Where are we then?'

'How should I know?' Panda sometimes wondered how this woman ever did anything, her general incompetence seemed astonishing. 'Have you got that torch?'

Reaching into the capacious pockets of her coat, Iris pulled out a small silver tube. 'Here you are love. Oh, and a signal scanner... you might as well take that too.'

'Thank you.' The beam of light shone out quite fiercely and illuminated a grand castle, complete with gothic turrets, flying buttresses, gargoyles and a big friendly notice.

WELCOME TO GLEN GORBALS DISTILLERY
Home of Scotland's best whisky, gin and liqueurs.

Iris grabbed hold of Panda's arm and he winced as her newly painted nails dug in deep. 'I have never been a religious woman you know Panda, but at times like this I think there might be a God after all... and *He'll* be the sort of bloke who loves a good piss-up...'

Leaving her companion standing Iris hitched up her skirt and headed off around the side of the imposing building, bits of gravel path shooting out from under her feet. With no choice but to follow, Panda aimed the beam of the torch at Iris' rapidly disappearing back, the gentle humming of the signal scanner vibrating slightly in his paw.

Even though she always wore what Panda considered extremely unsuitable footwear, Iris could still move with quite surprising speed. As he rounded the corner of the building there was no sign of the sozzled adventuress.

'Now where has she gone?' Panda shone the torch back and forth, the beam illuminating a large brass-studded door in a far wall, which stood half open. 'Through there, presumably...'

As he approached a tingle of dread coursed through his fur, making the ends stand up and shiver in the night breeze. 'Oh dear.' The sign on the door read 'Distillery – No Entry for Unauthorised Persons'. That could only mean one thing. Alcohol. And lots of it. With an extended claw he gingerly pushed the door and shone the torch through, noting that the signal scanner was vibrating with a little more urgency than before. Gripping the device tightly he entered and surveyed the scene.

There was no sign of Iris, and indeed no sound of her either, which was odd. A short exclamation of surprise escaped him as he saw what lay ahead. A large cavernous passageway, lined with huge oaken barrels, each nearly 20 feet high, brass bound, with a ladder allowing access to the top. The atmosphere was heady with the aroma of brewing and fermenting liquor. It filled his nostrils and immediately gave a slight uneasiness to his steps, and a giddiness to his vision. It brought back an overwhelming memory of the time they had both got intoxicated after an evening of throwing back shots of Minoran Worm Juice.

A familiar voice made him jump. Iris stepped out from between two of the barrels, her arms outstretched in a position of prayer. 'Look Panda... isn't it beautiful? I have seen some sights in my times, but nothing has ever matched this. I feel like someone has put a hand in my chest and is squeezing my hearts, making them beat faster.'

The blank expression on Panda's face seemed to energise Iris and she whirled around, her voice growing louder and more passionate. 'It's a temple. A temple to one of life's great glories. Alcohol... That wonderful organic, flammable compound, synthesized from fermenting sugars and starches, and saturated hydrocarbons. Booze. Hooch. Slug. Rotgut. Firewater. John Barleycorn. Dutch Courage. Call it what you will my black and white friend. It is the only thing that can give one's ordinary existence a sense of extraordinary clarity. The universe always looks sparkly through a bottle of gin.'

Panda stood immobile, and completely amazed. Iris was never really one to eulogise, preferring short sharp action in favour of words. But something seemed to have inspired her to greatness. Perhaps those all-pervading odours had affected her head too, he thought. There was something rather great about her. After all the time they had spent together she still had the power to surprise him.

'Iris... I really don't know what to say to that.'

'Don't say anything, Panda. Just stand still and listen. Open your fluffy ears and listen to sounds of alcohol in its rawest sense. The drip and plop and bubble of Whisky and Gin and Vodka and Ale being made. And it's all for me.'

'Er... What did you say?'

'It's all for me. I am going back to the bus. I must be able to find some kind of gadget that will help me to transport as much of this fabulous stuff as I can. I'll be quids in for weeks!' She spun on her heel and with a flurry of feathers and leopard-skin raced for the door. Before Panda could even put out a claw to stop her she was gone.

Panda sighed, so loudly it echoed around the room. 'Was there ever a time when I didn't sigh so much?' he asked rhetorically. No-one answered.

The hum of the signal scanner was becoming more insistent, and Panda looked down at the small metal instrument in his paw. Time to get back to the matter in hand. Someone was in trouble and needed their help. If Iris wasn't going to do anything about it then he certainly was. 'Hello...?' Panda gave a tentative call. The scanner gave a shudder. He was on the right track. Whatever it was that had sent the distress call wasn't too far away. Hoping it wasn't going to be some ferocious, ten-legged, bear eating space monster, Panda padded slowly down the central pathway, the barrels of fermenting alcohol throwing large, imposing shadows across the vaulted ceiling. 'Come on now... be a brave boy,' said Panda to himself. 'And stop talking to yourself...'

It took two or three minutes to reach the far end of the brewing room, in which time the hum of the scanner had settled into a fairly rigorous pattern. It meant that he was very close to its source. But why was it proving so difficult to find? In Panda's experience most crashed life-forms who have had the capacity to send a distress call out into the void usually want to be found and helped to safety. They don't tend to cower in the darkness, playing hide and seek. Unless it liked playing games and was waiting for the right moment to pounce and devour any passing friendly black and white Tibetan Ailuropoda Melanoleuca.

'Er... hello? Look I have come to help you. I am a nice, jolly, unarmed Panda. If I can give you any assistance I certainly will.' Silence. He tried again. 'We received your distress call. Are you hurt? Hello.....?'

Nothing. Just the constant groans and drips from the towering barrels.

A sharp bang from the direction of the door made him jump and drop the torch. The light went out leaving him, a small, rather nervous figure alone in the semi-gloom. Thank goodness his other paw still had a tight grip on the scanner. Looking up towards the entrance, he saw the figure of Iris staggering towards him, clutching a strange melange of instruments and gizmos, her large hat tipped over her eyes.

'PANDA!!' Her voice, shrill and piercing, rang out.

'Shhh.' He put a claw to his lips and swiftly started towards her. 'We must be as quiet a possible. We don't want to wake whoever lives here, and we certainly don't want to scare our distressed alien.'

Iris looked up with an almost fanatical gleam in her eyes. 'Whatever you say love.' And with an ear-shattering clang she dropped the bundle of equipment on the stone floor, fell to her knees and started rummaging through it, muttering to herself. Panda rolled his eyes and eased himself down beside her.

'Can't we try and be a little more... er... subdued, Iris? If the owners of this place find us here, they will throw us out, more likely call the authorities, and we will end up incarcerated, and you'll be without any kind of stimulants for days probably.'

Gasping, as if she had just made a discovery of national importance Iris looked up into her companion's big, round eyes. 'You're right, Panda. I wasn't thinking straight. The lack of drink must have addled my brain. Now have a *quiet* look in that tool box, I need a *quiet* spatial displacement unit. But do it *quietly*.'

'What are you trying to do?'

With a big smile, eyes aglow, beaming at Panda through the drooping feathers of her millinery, Iris leaned forward and whispered conspiratorially. 'I want to make a mini version of the Bus. See this?' She pulled a small plastic bottle from her pocket, which was already encrusted with various circuits and wires. 'If I can make it bigger on the inside then I can get all of that booze over there *in here*!'

There was a strange logic to what she had said, but sighing again, for probably the hundredth time since bringing the bus in to land, Panda couldn't see it working. Iris had never been the most creative person he'd met. She once had trouble changing a plug on her hair straighteners, and the memory of the bad language that had filled the upper deck of the bus still made him blush.

He reached into the overflowing tool box and started pulling items to and fro. 'What have you got in here?'

'All sorts of handy things that could come in useful for the trans-temporal explorer. Ouch.' Dropping a screwdriver, she sucked on her thumb and stifled the urge to shout out some loud obscenity.

'A torque wrench. A bottle opener. A spark plug. Three AAA batteries. A cuddly toy...' Iris was deep in thought and this failed to get a reaction. Panda dipped into the box again. 'A drill bit. A neutron flow reversalometer. A magnifying glass. A cigarette lighter. A tea spoon. Ahhh!!' Sitting back on his haunches with an expression of pure delight, he held out a rather tatty paperback book. '*'The Galactic Observer Book of Alien Distress Signals'.* Now that is what I call serendipity. Look at this Iris. Iris?'

The trans-temporal explorer was pulling a very strange face indeed, her tongue lolling from the side of her mouth in deep concentration. 'Hmmm?'

'This will come in very useful. Help us to work out exactly who we are dealing with. Excuse me for a moment.' Getting to his feet, Panda strolled away to a small crate, nestled against the wall, empty of bottles and conveniently up-ended. Settling his considerable bulk down on it, he flicked the cigarette lighter from the tool box and opened the book to page one.

'Amoeboids... Animus... Atlantean Fish People... Axo... ah. Wait a minute what's this?' The import of what he had just found took a moment to sink in. Then the horrible truth dawned and the equally horrible possible consequences.

'Ah... Iris. I think you should come and take a look at this. Iris?' He looked up and at the spot where she had been squatting. Apart from a colossal amount of electronic clutter she was nowhere to be seen. 'Oh dear, where is she now? Iris...?'

Dropping the book and the lighter, but still holding tight to the signal scanner Panda started to look around the barrels nearest to him, whilst calling out in a strangled voice, 'Iris... for heaven's sake, where are you? We have to talk...before you do something you'll regret. I mean it. Where are you?'

There were times in his long and usually fruitful relationship with Iris Wildthyme that Panda laughed. Sometimes he laughed a lot. Sometimes even until something unpleasant snorted out of his nose. There were times when he got angry, and lost his temper, once even letting out a snarled *'knickers'* at Iris' startled face. There were times when he was completely dumbfounded, stunned by her actions and words. There were times when he thrilled at her audacity, the way in which she found an escape from some unexplainably dangerous situation. There were times when they had sat together, arm in arm, she with a large cocktail, he with some tasty bamboo shoots, gazing with wonder at the alien vista that lay before them, exploding sunsets, mountains that seemed to stretch into forever, strange wheeling creatures which circled in the air, a myriad of beautiful planetoids and shooting stars. And there were times when he gave up. When there was nothing to do but wait and see what she did next. This was one of those.

The sound of metal being moved knocked him from his reverie. It came from nearby. Scooting round the barrel, Panda saw Iris, gadget in hand, skirt hitched up, carefully climbing one of the ladders, heading for the top of one of the barrels.

'Oh dear, I'm not good on heights,' Panda muttered darkly, and grasping tightly, began to follow upwards. As he climbed he noted with vague apprehensions a brass plaque screwed to the side of the barrel.

'FINEST GIN'

Around the top of each barrel was a narrow walkway, and halfway round this walkway there was a strange contraption seemingly a mixture of a clock, and a thermometer. By the side of this was another ladder leading down into the inside of the barrel where the precious and expensive brew could be seen glistening just below the rim.

'Perfect. Now how can I do this?' Iris was talking to herself, kneeling at the top of the inner ladder. She held onto the top rung, and unsteadily leaned forward, plastic bottle in hand.

Puffing slightly as he reached the top of the ladder, and vowing to himself to do a little more exercise rather than sit reading magazines all day, Panda put out a steadying hand.

'Careful Iris. You don't want to fall in...'

'Ooh there you are Panda, me old mate, me old mucker. Well don't just stand there give us a hand.'

Sensing danger, Panda gritted his teeth but continued. 'What do you want me to do?'

'Grab hold of me ankles, tight now, and don't let go 'til I say so. I just want to...reach...the...aaaaaargh!'

The splash was loud and resonated round the room. Wondering why Iris had leant forward before he had even managed to get a firm grip on her ankles, Panda bent over the edge of the barrel. 'Are you alright? Can you grab hold of the ladder? Iris?'

There was no need to worry. Iris was in her element. Eyes wide in amazement and disgust, Panda watched as she seemed to be indulging some weird kind of solo synchronised swimming routine, back strokes, forward kicks, all the while gulping down large mouthfuls of the clear liquid, and occasionally throwing out an excited cry of delight.

'WEEEEEEEEEEEEEEE!'

'Iris, come out of there at once. There is something you have to know... Iris!'

With an extravagant back flip, Iris appeared to jump out of the water, a spout of the glorious fluid fountaining from her mouth. 'Look at me Panda, I'm a mermaid! I'm Esther Williams... no, I'm Duncan Goodhew... No, I've got more hair than him... I'm Moby Dick!' With a large gulp she was gone again.

'I have a bad feeling about this,' said Panda out loud, to nobody in particular. This was definitely one of those times when he would have to just wait for Iris. But how long could she continue? Five minutes? Five hours? Who knows? He looked down at the signal scanner which had begun to vibrate in a strange, uncoordinated manner, completely unlike the regular humming of before.

Leaning over the edge again, Panda was about to shout out one more time, when a bedraggled figure appeared out of the barrel. Grasping the top of the ladder and unsteadily heaving herself up onto the platform, sodden and blindingly drunk, Iris held aloft the small, blue plastic bottle. She opened her mouth and tried to form some cohesive words, and failed dismally. 'B... bottle... Bu... haha! Worked... Got the gin... Bingo!! Bingo... dingo... lingo........'

'Iris you are becoming incoherent. I think we had better leave.'

Looking down into the now empty barrel, Panda had to grin. The gall and audacity of this woman took his breath away. Every single drop of gin had gone, and all that was left was Iris' feathered hat, on the bottom of the barrel looking like a drowned bird of paradise.

Gripping the signal scanner gently between his teeth and hoisting the comatose and limp body over his shoulder he timidly began to descend.

'Here you are, black coffee. Try and sip some of this.' Panda held the mug to Iris' lips, and watched, concerned, as she downed the steaming liquid. They were back on the bus, doors shut tight, controls activated and except for an empty barrel of gin, and some skid marks on the drive, no-one would have known they had ever been at the distillery. The magic dimensionally transcendental bottle was lying on the seat beside Iris.

'Thanks Panda. Sometimes I don't know what I'd do without you.' Iris gave a wan smile, and scooped a clump of matted hair out of her face.

'Neither do I,' chuckled Panda. 'Are you feeling any better?'

'Yes... a little bit. I think for the first time in my life I actually over-indulged.'

'Is that actually possible?'

Snorting with an amused but wry grin, Iris put down the mug. 'Apparently it is. I got kind of mad I think, when I saw we had run out of gin and I suppose I over-reacted.'

Panda gave a fruity chuckle. 'Over-reacted is a mild understatement for what you did.'

Sheepishly Iris looked up at her furry friend, silenced and slightly shamed of her actions.

'More coffee?'

'Not right now Panda.' Iris shuffled and pulled the blanket tighter around her shoulders. 'But there was something I had to ask you, and I can't think what on earth it was. Something to do with aliens was it?'

Raising one eyebrow, in what he thought was a rather debonair fashion, Panda sat down opposite Iris and took one of her hands. 'Yes. There is a small matter we have to discuss. Do you remember why we landed at the distillery in the first place?'

'No... not really.'

'Well... we were answering a distress call. Somebody or something was in trouble and we had gone to help. Now while you were busying yourself with your contraption, I was also busying myself. Finding out exactly who or what had crash landed. As I walked about there were faint traces of a signal, but it was hard to pinpoint, and after I had gotten you out of the barrel it changed.'

Iris took another swig of coffee. 'Go on... so what was it?'

'An odd life form actually. A tiny liquid based creature called an Aquaform, highly intelligent and extremely telepathic. It must have been in trouble and honed in on the distillery as somewhere safe for itself to hide. But then we came along.'

'And I was in the same barrel as a strange aqua creature? What if it had tried to kill me?'

Panda raised his eyebrow again, and let go of her hand. 'It's a little more complicated than that. I believe that it uses its telepathic abilities to draw someone in, and as we were in the approximate spatial vicinity it latched onto you. The fact that you were on a gin hunt was an added bonus for it, making the telepathic link even stronger than usual. But...'

Iris looked puzzled and perched herself on the edge of her seat. 'But what...?'

'I assumed that after you'd drained the barrel that it would be inside the blue bottle. But the scan shows nothing there...'

'So...?'

'So... we have to assume that whilst you were frolicking in the barrel you swallowed it.'

Iris groaned. 'I swallowed it? But what if..? I mean...what do I do now?'

Panda realised that this was becoming one of those times when he was about to laugh. Laugh until something unpleasant came out of his nose.

'You'll just have to wait until nature takes its usual and functional course. Just remember not to flush afterwards.'

Iris Wildthyme y Señor Cientocinco contra Los Monstruos del Fiesta

Cody Quijano-Schell

Iris was always somewhat unsettled by the way Panda slept with his eyes open. Usually it didn't bother her unduly, but this time he had fallen asleep in the middle of one of her yarns. Whilst driving the bus, she liked to entertain Panda with tales of yesteryear. And tomorrowyear for that matter!

Initially, she didn't realise he *had* fallen asleep. Whenever she looked back to emphasize a point, he had seemed to be listening in rapt attention.

Panda's gentle rhythmic breathing and vocal unresponsiveness made it clear, however, just how fascinating he thought her story was. She finished telling the story out of spite...

'...and so once we finally got out of there without leaving any evidence or damaging the time lines, I realised I'd mislaid my half-eaten ham sandwich somewhere. So in the end, we just decided to leave it and hope for the best!'

...but the ensuing silence annoyed Iris.

Panda's unwavering stare began to turn annoyance into uneasiness. Goose pimples formed on the admittedly already somewhat-chicken-like skin of her neck.

She forced herself to ignore Panda and concentrate on driving. The swirling fractals of the vortex were fascinating. 'It's easy to lose ones self in this entrancing vista!', she told herself, unconvincingly if she was honest. She tried to let her attention be consumed by their flight through the vortex.

The expanding and collapsing fields of temporal potentiality hitting the windscreen made a barely audible sound as the bus ploughed through them. A sound like snow hitting warm glass and melting into nothingness, in reverse. Like an Eno album played backwards.

Backwards. Reverse. Behind her. Tiny panda eyes staring blankly at her. Tiny unblinking panda eyes burning into the back of her unkempt head of hair. Tiny unrelenting, unblinking, glassy panda eyes examining everything she did!

Infuriated, Iris whipped her head around so suddenly that her large feathery hat almost remained facing the front of the bus. Panda's eyes were still wide open, staring forward. Straight at her. She could hear a diminutive wheeze and an intake of air. Not enough to be a snore, but clear signs that Panda was deeply asleep.

It drove her batty! Why did he have to do that? She briefly wondered if Panda even had eyelids.

Ignoring the path of the bus for long enough to reach over and grab a lace doily doubling as a seat cover, Iris held her breath and prepared to gingerly toss it across the aisle to cover his face. Panda's shallow breathing and the low hum of the bus' engines were the only sounds she could hear. In Panda's toylike eyes, Iris could see the reflection of the hypnotic whorls of the vortex. She held her breath, and prepared to throw the doily with utmost precision.

Panda suddenly bellowed 'PLACE AT THE CENTER OF THE LAKE MOON!'.

Iris jolted, and fell halfway out of her seat, doily still in hand.

Panda made a smacky noise and turned over, still asleep.

Pulse racing, Iris just stared at the back of his fuzzy little head trying to understand. She felt a warm dampness spread across her crotch, but thankfully it was just the melted ice dribbling out of her overturned tumbler.

Out of the corner of her eye, Iris saw something in the swirling mists outside the bus. With a tiny 'eep!', she hopped fully back into her seat and slammed on the brakes.

Panda and half the objects in the bus hurtled to the left like some sort of knick-knack tsunami as the bus went spiralling out of control.

Iris didn't know it yet, but the bus was not only about to crash, it was about to crash a party.

The bus had a rough landing, but Iris was surprised she'd blacked out. As surprised as one can be, hovering on the cusp of consciousness. She was finally brought back to full awareness by furry Panda feet running directly across her face and out of the bus.

'Panda?'

Panda was snarling and drooling as if possessed. He *was* possessed! Iris chased after him. Despite now having an unusually large amount of energy for a Panda of his type, he still had trouble scaling a small stone wall.

Iris grabbed him with both hands. He growled murderously as a mass of tacky bracelets slid down her wrists towards him.

'Lovey! This isn't the Panda I know! What's gotten into you, chuck?' Iris almost would have laughed at the sight of his fuzzy muzzle, thirsty for human blood, if this wasn't her best friend gone out of his mind.

Like a cloud passing, the madness was gone.

'Iris? For god's sake woman, you're squeezing me too hard! Where are we? What are we doing here? Where is the sound of that horrid horn combo coming from?'

For the first time Iris had a moment to look around her. The bus had landed in a rather run down residential area. She could see skyscrapers in the distance, and beyond that some hills. Nothing familiar. No, wait!

'Look at those hills Panda!'

'You'll have to unhand me if you want me to look. Honestly!' As usual, neither of them realised how loudly they were talking.

'I don't know the city, but those hills... I'd recognize them anywhere! I've been here before!' Panda surveyed the seedy, muddy alleyway and was somehow not surprised.

'This is Tenochtitlan! But this must be the city that was eventually built on top of it. This is Mexico City! Remember? I told you about that business with Montezuma.'

Panda coughed, 'Ah yes! If I recall correctly, it was Jenny's first trip with you. You arrived in ancient Mexico, became embroiled in local politics.'

'Aye, you didn't sleep through that one, did you.' Iris took a flask out of her handbag but it was empty.

Panda ignored her and continued. 'You stole an important ceremonial bracelet, and Jenny got blamed for it. Montezuma swore he would have his revenge.'

'And he did *that,* all right. But just to clarify, I didn't steal it. It just got stuck on my arm. Sort of. Besides, I lost it. I'm always losing bracelets.' huffed Iris.

'Iris, what happened to me? The last thing I recall is being on the bus. You were talking about hitting your friend Ellen about the head and shoulders with a copper pipe or something.' Iris knew he was ridiculing her story, but his little amber eyes suddenly seemed incredibly vulnerable and sweet. He was worried.

Iris was solemn. 'Panda, you were possessed, love. There's something influencing you, and through you, my bus. Something brought us here.'

'Montezuma?'

'No, he's long gone. Something else. Something... evil.'

'Would that explain my uncontrollable desire to find the source of that horn combo? Iris, it's actually sounding catchy to me now, and that chills me to the bone.'

Iris reflected briefly that Panda didn't have any bones. However, she knew she had to distract her friend from what was happening.

'That music sounds like a swinging party! Free booze! The best kind of booze!' She elbowed him in the area where ribs would be if he had them. 'You know what they say, Panda. Don't drink the water! So it'll have to be ALL gin this time!'

Panda sighed a huffy little sigh. 'At least one of us is acting normally. Let's find this party. I need to regain my refined sense of taste. Perhaps we can find a television set and wait for a reality programme to appear on it and then shoot the screen with a pistol!'

Iris cackled.

Iris and Panda hadn't walked far when Panda's right ear started to twitch. 'Iris, something is coming over me. That house.. birthday party.. we mussst.. sslluurrRRSST!'

Panda had gone all slobbery and savage again. Iris held on to his legs like a divining rod as he somehow dragged her along behind him, jutting out like an arrow.

She could hear a lively party going on in the back yard as Panda pulled her along the side of the house. It was increasing in intensity, with music, laughter and occasional flashes of light.

Panda was in a blind rage.

'Panda! Wait!' Iris saw more flashes of light and felt a stinging sensation on her skin like a sunburn. She noticed that the plants at the edge of the back yard were withering quickly. There was a mighty boom of light followed by a sudden silence. Panda passed out.

Iris peeked around the corner. What she mistook for party streamers were bloody gauze bandages, hanging across the courtyard. They clung stickily to everything in the yard, like shed skin. Skeletons were scattered around. Some were holding bottles, some wearing party hats and candy necklaces. One skeleton had another, that of a small dog, on its lap.

Iris found the remnants of a birthday cake. 'I think someone left this one out in the rain!' The frosting was covered in gouges as if it had been attacked by an eagle. There, intermixed with the buttercream, in claw-mark shaped puddles: blood. Her heart sank. She had to conclude this wasn't some weird sort of performance art. These party goers had been murdered just moments before she'd arrived. She saw bottles of booze in a cooler, but for once she wasn't in the mood.

Iris squinted and pushed some hat feathers away from her eyes. She thought she'd seen something through the bandages! A metallic face. Metallic, but at the same time... cloth? Hadn't she met some rubbishy cloth-faced robots or cyborgs somewhere? The ones she remembered didn't have numbers on their heads like this one did. A Number 10 right on the forehead that glowed like a neon sign.

Clutching her handbag close to her, she did a strange shimmy, trying to see through the forest of gauze. 'Panda, I think we'd better quietly slip away from this party.'

But Panda had vanished from the little chair where she had set him down.

In the alley, she saw the figure she'd seen earlier. Number 10! And wrapped up tightly in the robot's cape was Panda! His mouth was gagged by the fabric and she could only see his imploring eyes. The figure tucked Panda under his arm and leapt into the air, flipping over the fence with inhuman agility.

'Kidnap my best friend, will you!!' She gave chase, but knew instantly she'd never catch up. Not in these heels!

Iris didn't know what to do. She approached people on the street to see if they'd seen anything. But once she started babbling about robots and they smelled the drink on her breath, they walked away laughing, blissfully unaware of the grim scene going on in their neighbour's garden.

Eventually she found someone who would listen to her. A boy named Rodrigo selling small packets of gum called chicle, knew instantly what she was talking about.

'Señora! That is not a robot! That is Señor Cientocinco!! Mr. 105! You must know who he is! Everyone knows!'

Iris shook her head. 'Tell your Auntie.. your *Tía* Iris about him!'

He is Luchador! A Mexican wrestler with the finest physique, as well as the finest mind, the world has to offer. The man of more than 100 masks! One for each element! Some say he draws his power from these masks. Some say he's simply a man–a remarkable man, but a man nonetheless. Others say he controls the building blocks of creation!' Rodrigo recited this information as if it were something he'd memorised after hearing it on the playground.

'Is he known for kidnapping pandas?'

'He would not kidnap anyone. He is a hero, a Técnico! He is very kind and always buys some of my chicle!'

Iris perked her ears at this information. 'You know him personally! Do you know where I can find him? It's very important, love!'

Rodrigo grinned. 'Just *how* important, Señora?' holding out his merchandise to her.

Iris harrumphed and started sifting through her purse.

Iris couldn't believe her luck sneaking into the grounds of 105's house. She was sure that shrieking as she fell off the brick wall was going to attract some sort of attention, even if the subsequent swearing didn't. Upending the birdbath onto her face as she tried to get to her feet wasn't the most subtle of actions either.

The house and grounds were beautiful. The house had a tiled roof and was surrounded by exotic plants. As Iris slipped through an unattended entrance, she found dark hallways with shiny wood floors, walls painted pink and turquoise, wrought iron and intricate glassware. She could hear Panda talking loudly from another part of the house and followed his resonant voice to what appeared to be a clinical laboratory.

Hiding behind an ornate wall partition she could see Panda lying on a table. 105 had his back to both of them. He was intently examining some X-rays on the wall.

Señor 105 had changed his outfit. He now wore a dull grey mask and bulky overalls with extra padding. As before, he was wearing a cape. 'You realise I allowed you to enter my grounds and house?' He didn't look up from his notes.

Iris grabbed a heavy iron candlestick holder.

'Put that down,' commanded 105 over his shoulder.

She gripped it tighter. 'Listen up, buster! What are you doing to my best friend?'

He put down his notes and turned to her, and for the first time Iris had his full attention. He looked her up and down, admiringly. 'Señora! Let me apologize. What I've done is incredibly rude. This is no way for me to treat a lady. I am.. Señor Cientocinco, or Mister one-oh-five.' Before she knew it, he was holding her hand and kissing the back of it.

This was the perfect opportunity to club him, grab Panda and run, but there was something about this man.

'Ms. Iris Wildthyme.' she replied icily. It was hard to read his face through the openings in his ornate leather mask, but she felt she could trust him. He stood fully upright, towering over her. She looked up at the black 82 on his forehead.

'Lead.' he said. 'I was conducting some tests on your little friend here. I'm afraid the X-rays are far from conclusive. Despite his behaviour, I don't think he has anything in common with the... party monsters.'

'Please excuse me, Señora, make yourself comfortable. This ensemble is.. utilitarian and not made for long term use. *Un momento.*' He turned and Iris saw his cape had the alchemical symbol for lead stitched into it. The cape ended just above his waist. As he disappeared through a white door further into the interior of the house, Iris couldn't help looking down at his muscular spandex covered frame.

'Oh my!' Iris blushed.

Panda stirred. 'Iris! Thank God!'

Iris ran to him and gave him a big hug. 'You gave me a quite the scare there! You are okay, aren't you, chuck?'

'Iris, he used that barbaric ray on me. I didn't even have an opportunity to close my eyes!'

'I don't think he means us any harm. He may even be able to help us remove this evil influence from you. And I think we can help him stop any more parties from going so horribly wrong.'

'Iris, I can tell you're already smitten with him! Honestly. You really are so predictably shallow! All it takes is the body of an Olympian God, the mind of a Nobel Prize Winner, and the intrigue of a mysterious masked hero and you're all agog. Don't you have any standards? You probably like his accent too.'

Iris hushed Panda. Señor 105 had re-entered the room and was wearing a new combination. His leather mask now read the proper '105'. This uniform was all orange and black, all spandex and leather. He was bare chested and wearing black tights and blue boots. Iris couldn't help but notice his little outer-underpants were also a matching blue.

'Ahh! Much better. I feel like myself again' he said, stretching.

Now that Iris could see him better, she realised he was older than she'd previously thought. He certainly had the physique of a 20 year old, but there were tell-tale signs that he was probably in his early 50s. A roughness about the knuckles of his large hairy hands. A glimpse of salt and pepper in his jet black beard. She was dying to see what he looked like under that mask!

He threw back his cape and she could see alchemical symbols were tattooed up and down his arms. Tearing her eyes away from his broad barrel chest, she looked back up at his mask. 'So, 105..' she fiddled with the buttons on her cardigan, concentrating... 'Let me think... that's Dubnium!'

'No, this new element is being called Hahnium.' He chuckled. 'I wouldn't expect you to be up to date on recent developments.'

'Listen here, bucko! I know more about eka-tantalum than you ever will! You just wait. You'll be eating that mask in 30 years when you find out I was right'. Eye level with his shiny chest, she failed miserably to tower over him.

He put a meaty hand on one of her shoulder pads. 'Señora, I apologize. It seems I've been rude again. I saw you arrive in your bus. I already know you and your *osito* friend here have had many experiences and have many tales to tell.'

'Osito?' inquired Panda.

'Let me show you around. I will tell you more about the problem, and perhaps we can work together to bring this situation to a climax.'

Iris took her hands off her hips and softened slightly. 'Well, if you put it that way...'

105 showed Iris further into the house. In one room, a large wall was covered in framed photos.

'Ooooh! I love me some snaps! Who's this then?'

'These are photos of my friends, to remind me of previous adventures.' There were several photos of 105 in a fine cut suit shaking hands with Mexican presidents, local officials, and colourful folk. There were photos of him visiting the Eiffel Tower, and one of him sitting in a rowboat with Einstein. In another, he was wearing pilots' goggles over his mask. Yet another showed him decked out in a full western outfit, with a broad white cowboy hat covering the number on his mask. There were also some sepia-toned photos from the turn of the century of some masked Luchadors named 'Tierra, Viento y Fuego.' Viento was a lady wrestler, a *luchadora*. There was even a photo of Rodrigo.

'You've travelled widely I see! A man after my own heart.'

'Indeed. I've had many adventures all over the world. I've tried to help wherever I go, but I always come back to Mexico, my home. It seems like it needs special help. It has it's own particular vulnerabilities.'

'Vulnerable to what?' Iris started to get excited, scanning more photos. 'UFOs! Witches! Wolf-women! Purple midgets!' She pointed at one photo that appeared to be a pair of thick-framed black glasses floating in the air. 'What's this one?'

'El Hombre Invisible.'

Iris grinned toothily. 'Interesante!'

A second wall was dominated by a large map of Mexico. 105 indicated an area with a blue-gloved hand. 'You are familiar with recent geological findings about the extinction of the dinosaurs? Some of my colleagues and I believe it may have been caused by something from space impacting the Earth. Here. The Chicxulub Crater' He pointed to an area of water off the south-eastern point of Mexico.

'That's the Yucatán Peninsula. I was there once,' said Iris, looking slightly shifty.

'Sí. Something from space hit here, bringing alien influences with it, laying dormant until now. Periodically these influences reawaken, reaching all throughout Mexico, as well as New Orleans and the Bermuda Triangle. Creatures, technology, spirits, strange doorways, all unearthly. And other materials located here seem to attract even more unwanted attention.'

He indicated photos of groups of men wearing reptilian inspired leather masks. 'This is a family of Luchadors who call themselves the Terrible Kings. They believe they are the inheritors of the power of the extinct great lizards. Each of them has chosen an identity. Snakes, lizards, amphibians.'

'They look like an untrustworthy lot, a bunch of thugs!'

'Indeed. And worse, they're also politicians. They're obsessed with power. The power of the unearthly material, the alien technology and supernatural powers deep within the Earth. I've battled them often. They must be monitored at all times.'

'I'm sure they do! Monitored! Get it? You know... lizards?' Iris joked, but 105 seemed lost in thought.

Against another wall was a clunky looking upright piano with a simple potted cactus on top of it. Next to the cactus was a bottle and some glasses. 105 offered her a drink, which she tried not to accept too quickly. 'Gracías, Señor!'

'So, Spanish is not your first language, Señora Wildthyme?'

'Oh no, chuck, it's not even my third or fourth language!'

'You speak it quite well.'

Iris blushed. 'What can I say? It's a gift'. She threw the tequila down her throat and set her empty glass down loudly on an ornate mahogany end table.

105 picked up the glass and wiped at the moisture ring with a corner of his cape.

Iris was digging furiously through her handbag like a cat in its litter box. 'Where *are* my ciggies??' She lost balance slightly, teetering on her heels and mashing a handful of piano keys.

She gasped as an automated panel slid swiftly apart revealing row upon row of recessed cubbyholes.

'You've discovered my collection of masks.'

Now that the panel was completely open, Iris could see that the cubbyholes were arranged to resemble the Periodic Table. Each cubbyhole was numbered and housed a mannequins head. Each head was wearing a mask and each mask had a number. Folded neatly next to each head was the rest of the outfit.

105 walked over to the piano and started hitting different keys. The corresponding mask would mechanically slide out and a small bell would ring once it emerged.

'ORO! PLOMO! COBRE!' thundered 105 as the corresponding elements slid out, each with an accompanying 'ding!'

'JET black velvet! PURPLE capes with houndstooth lining!' Iris was amazed. 'LEMON yellow boots! Beautiful!'

'The spectrum of elements is my inspiration. However, science is only one of my passions. I am open to all possibilities.' He flexed his arms, showing Iris his alchemical tattoos. 'These symbols seems superstitious now, but they were the science of their day. And I want to be open to the science of tomorrow. I welcome anything that can help me do what I do.'

Iris gazed back at the wall. 'There's an element missing. Number 47.'

'Silver. Out of respect for one of my colleagues, I do not wear *una máscara de plata.* A professional courtesy. Otherwise, I have a different identity for each element. And I expect to gain more in the future. This is an exciting time to be a scientist.'

'It always is, chuck!'

In a shadowy corner of the room Iris noticed a blocky Wurlitzer Zodiac jukebox. The front panel glowed weakly. She considered punching in a letter/number combination but 105 stopped her. 'It's not quite working yet. This is just another hobby of mine, working on fixing this machine. I'll have to show it to you another time.' He draped a cloth over it.

She clapped her hands together suddenly and the gust of air made the oversized feathers in her hat bobble up and down. 'So, why don't we get down to business! Let's figure out what's sucking the life out of all these parties and ruining otherwise jolly times! Nobody likes a party pooper, eh?'

Iris' hands held her hat tight to the top of her head – partially to keep it from flying off, partially to force it down far enough to hide her eyes. She couldn't remember the last time she rode in the sidecar of a motorcycle.

Panda was euphoric, leaning forward and enjoying the ride with exclamations of 'GLORIOUS!' and 'MARVELOUS!'.

105 was wearing his goggles over his mask, but no helmet. His gloved hands firmly gripped the handlebars, his ultramarine blue leather boots resting in the riding position.

Iris closed her eyes for just a moment. They had just pulled an all-nighter in their research. After analyzing samples of bandages and other debris in 105's state of the art lab, they discovered that the creatures were made of bandages and paper mache that had been altered at a sub-molecular level. The material had been altered at a sub-molecular level by an unknown force.. They were now on their way to a nearby piñateria to see if the owner has noticed anything strange.

Panda spoke in his normal voice which was more than loud enough for Iris to hear over the revving motorcycle engine. 'You know, I was thinking about why these creatures have been able to affect me so. Perhaps it's something to do with the fact I'm a time and space traveling panda, and thus more sympathetic to etheric vibrations and such. In the same way horses react to earthquakes before humans do. I'm obviously too cultured to be totally controlled.'

Iris didn't respond. She knew that the theory she and 105 had postulated would not go down well with Panda. The fact that Panda was of the inanimatus variety of *ailuropoda melanoleuca* was probably more of a factor than his animal nature. Simply put, Panda was stuffed. These creatures were able to inhabit and influence him to a degree.

She clutched him closer as they ripped around a corner. 105 was talking to a small screen on his bike's instrument panel. 'No, Gustavo! You know I am not happy with recent events, but I have not been avoiding you for that reason.' Iris hoped 105 was watching where he was going. He seemed very angry with the person on the other end of the video link. Video link? Sometimes the sixties weren't quite like she remembered them.

'Despite what happened at Tlatelolco, I still hoped to honour your request. However, I have other obligations. Lives are at stake. I'm not sure I should expect you to understand that. May I suggest Norma as my replacement.' Iris heard indistinct protests. 'Yes, a woman! Why not? Women take part in the games, why not let one light the Olympic cauldron? This is the first time the games have been in Latin America, let it also be the first time a woman has this honour. It's your decision, Gustavo. Adios.' Iris heard 105 grumble something about 'Inteligencia militar'.

The bike came screeching to a halt and 105 leapt off the bike, cape billowing, boots planted firmly on the cobblestones. He offered a gloved hand to Iris and helped her out of the sidecar. 'It's still early, but the store will open soon.'

105 reached into the blue lining of his cape and offered a handful of something to Iris. 'Chicle?'

She thanked him but politely declined. 'Thanks, but I'll have to pass on the chuggy while I'm smoking.' She blew the smoke out of her mouth sideways in the way that smokers often ineffectually try to keep smoke away from non-smokers.

105 popped some of the gum in his mouth. Iris grinned at the way his mask slightly shifted as he chewed. He was very pensive, upset about something. 'What's wrong, chuck?'

105 absent-mindedly traced the numbers on the forehead of his mask with the tips of his fingers. 'Señora, as you know, today are the opening ceremonies of

the Olympics. The proximity of the recent violence at Tlatelcolco, these disturbing party monsters, and the Olympic ceremonies makes me nervous.'

'Heaven forbid that I admit this, but I was eavesdropping. You were supposed to be the one to light the cauldron today. That's quite an honour!'

'Sí, Señora Wildthyme. I even had a special Olympics themed mask made for the occasion. But this is more important. If we can find anything out, we may be able to save lives.'

Panda fidgeted. 'Shouldn't this place be open by now?'

Iris sifted through the bracelets on her wrists to see if she was wearing a watch, but she wasn't. She shrugged. 105 snapped into position, facing due north and checked the sun's position in the sky. 'It's past opening time, they're late'.

Iris almost broke her neck walking across the uneven ground in her heels. Sometimes a broken neck is the price you pay to look fabulous, she told herself. She rattled the door, which was secured tightly. But something stirred inside. Something emitting a guttural moan.

105 rushed to the window *'Híjole!* The shopkeeper is on the floor... it's horrible! The creatures are on top of him!'

Iris rushed to 105's side, her fingernails digging in to his hairy forearms as she steadied herself. She could see the paper mache creatures inside jumping around, knocking over displays. Adorable donkeys, cartoon dogs, and strange 9 pointed stars were sniffing around like a pack of wolves. 'It's like a nest of them! A restless swarm of hand-crafted evil!'

Panda suddenly leapt out of Iris' handbag, smacking the glass with a hard plastic tube of Iris' blue mascara. 'BRETHREN! THIS WAY'

'Panda, no! Give me that mascara!'

105 looked down at her hands *'Máscara?'*

'Not a mask... makeup! I always knew my makeup was going to get me noticed, but this isn't what I had in mind!'

The piñata monsters had indeed noticed them. At the front of about forty of the creatures was a tiny grey paper mache donkey, striking the shop floor with his hoof, snorting murderously.

'They're going to charge!' shrieked Iris.

105 shoved everyone to the ground, throwing himself on top of them. His cape covered them just as the quaint storefront window with hand-painted lettering exploded outwards. Iris could hear what sounded like a stampede of creatures rushing out of the store, and felt strange feet traveling up her body. But it was over amazingly quickly. Her hat shed feathers from the stress as she jerked her head from left to right looking for the creatures. They were retreating into the distance.

'Where are they going?'

105 pulled Panda out from underneath him. For once Panda was grateful for

105's presence. 'Iris, I could feel their minds. They're leaving to feed off the living energies of a party.. no.. not just a party.. a celebration!'

Iris and 105 glanced at one another. 'The Opening Ceremonies!'

The trio were back on the bike, racing back the way they came.

'My house lies between the piñateria and the site of the ceremonies... I think we can assume Panda is correct.'.

Panda piped in. 'They can sense the anticipation! They're going to be there when the ceremony reaches its frenzy'.

Iris put her blue mascara away. Perhaps while riding in a motorcycle sidecar chasing strange alien creatures wasn't the time to apply makeup to her lashes. 'Now we know what the creatures are... but what about those sunburn flashes... and the bandages?'

'105 look out!' yelled Panda. 'They've spotted us! They don't want us chasing them!'

A nine-starred piñata hung back from the crowd, hovering in the air in the middle of the road.

Panda sensed instantly this was not good. 'Stop the bike! That piñata's gone kamikaze!!!'

The piñata suddenly exploded, sending searing red-hot pieces of candy whizzing through the air in every direction. Most of the pieces missed them, but one hit the front tyre of the bike. It exploded and 105 lost control. A few more stars hung back, but seeing the bike was disabled, zipped off after the caravan.

105 helped Iris and Panda out of the sidecar again. 'We're not far from my house. We can get my other bike. Or my convertible. Or jet packs!' Iris could tell he was eager to show his vehicles off, but she had other ideas.

'Or my bus! I have a feeling I'm going to need something out of it to deal with these creatures!'

They ran. Feathers, fur and cape flying.

Fortunately it hadn't been far to 105's house. Iris' bus was parked along the stone wall where she'd left it. Out of breath, she hurried everyone inside. 'Welcome aboard my bus, my home, my castle! My bus *es su casa!*' 105 stared around him in incredulity at the interior of Iris' time and space machine. He was shocked. She *lived* in these conditions?

'What a mess! What happened in here?'

Iris plopped into the drivers seat. 'Never mind the mess! We had a bit of turbulence on the way here. Be a dear and just clear yourself a spot to sit.' The bus started with a roar, various objects jangled, jingled and shuddered. 'Panda, you'll have to help guide me to these creatures'

'Perhaps you ought to lash me to a post, like Odysseus hearing the sirens call! Turn left at that fruit stand.'

105 picked up a framed photo of Iris from the floor. 'Who is this lady with you?'

'Lady? Oh, that's Jenny! I'm impressed, most people don't realise she's a woman right off the bat. It takes most people some awkward guessing.'

105 grinned cockily. 'Oh, Señora, I can always tell a woman.'

'So could Jenny, lovey! So could Jenny!'

105 leaned into the drivers cab. 'Look! They're turning left, away from a direct path towards the ceremonies. I don't understand.'

Panda started drooling slightly. 'A party. they've found another party in full swing... the draw to it is stronger and more immediate. They're going to... feeeed! FEED! FEED NOW. THEN CONSUME THE PLACE AT THE CENTER OF THE LAKE MOON!'

'Hold on! Panda said that before, in the vortex! The Place at the Lake Moon! Where's that?'

'It's Mexico City, Señora. Tenochtitlan. These creatures must intend to consume the city! They must be tied somehow to one of the forces that arrived in the ancient collision.'

'You know, I had a mess of New York club kids on my bus once, I know the destruction that can happen when a party goes out of bounds! The psychic anticipation of the Olympic celebrations must be pulling the monsters out of hiding, drawing them here! Ruining small parties at first, but now larger ones!'

'Yes, Señora, and from what I've seen is that it doesn't take much for these creatures to gain hold. A small party can be influenced by them, getting more and more crazy. The party goers don't even realise what's happening to them. Games are played, drinks are drunk...'

'Carpets are stained! The shenanigans gaining momentum! Come on, chuck! It's up to Auntie Iris to *ruin* a party for once! Well, intentionally anyway!'

105 pointed out the window at piles of trash and empty bottles. 'Aquí! It looks like this party has already been going on since last night, these creatures are just joining the others!'

Panda was now wearing Señor 105's red-lensed *infrarojo* goggles. Iris had correctly surmised they would help strain out the hypnotic effect. He still felt an unnatural vitality running through him, energising him. He was pacing about like a caged animal, but was still in control of himself.

Iris jerked on the brakes and opened the doors. 'Panda, you better stay here. Come any closer and you'll lose control again.' Iris and 105 rushed out of the bus and into the backyard of the house. It was dark like night-time. Something was soaking up all the light like gravy.

In the dim light, Iris could see men and women in various states of distress, even though they appeared to be perfectly happy about what was happening to them. A young man grinned maniacally as his turn on the Twister wheel indicated his left hand should go on yellow. He promptly broke his arm in order to reach it. Other people had engorged themselves with so much food they were literally bursting open. As with many parties, there were couples discreetly disappearing into the shadows. However, Iris wasn't sure if those two moustachioed cowboys would have felt so amorous were the circumstances different. Who knows? Iris shrugged and grinned. 'Look at the size of those belt buckles!'

Everyone looked exhausted, but showed no signs of slowing down. Meanwhile, a dozen or so star shaped piñatas hovered over the barbeque grill, spinning slowly, as if absorbing the life of the party.

Iris and 105 came upon another set of party goers who were gesturing wildly, playing charades with bloody stumps.

'What are you trying to tell us, amigo?' 105 was distraught, not knowing what to do. The man, a disturbing sight, gestured. 'I think he wants us to put him out of his misery... is that right, is that what your gestures mean?'

'105, no! Don't get involved in their games! You'll be drawn in!'

He couldn't hear Iris. 'You want us to hang you? Something involving a cord.. is that a rope? Three words.'

'NO, 105!' She tugged at his cape but it was like trying to move a redwood tree. She couldn't get him to stop trying to guess the gestures. This was going to require more extreme measures. She positioned herself squarely in front of him, stood on an overturned ice bucket and slapped his face as hard as she could.

For a moment his face filled with anger and he snarled at Iris. Then he had a moment of recognition 'Iris!' She teetered on the edge of the ice bucket as he lunged for her. He pulled her close to him and his mask was inches from her face. 'You enchantress! You are mine!'

Iris melted a bit, but quickly realised she had replaced one symptom with another. One she couldn't fall victim to herself. She had to do the one thing that would trigger a defence mechanism in Señor 105. She gave him a giant slobbery snog and reached behind his head and started to unlace his mask. Maybe it was the kiss, maybe it was 105's deeply rooted instinct to keep his mask on at all costs, but he jerked away from her, and snapped out of the trance. 'Iris!'

Iris scolded him 'You have to concentrate, you mustn't let yourself join in again.' He nodded and swallowed hard.

Iris inserted her thumb and index finger between her teeth. 'Here's your gum back, love.'

Embarrassed, he took it from her and tossed it.

105 threw a new batch of chicle into his mouth and pointed. 'The piñatas aren't paying us much attention now.' The star shaped piñatas were rotating and revolving high above the party, and below the animal shaped ones were performing strange circular dances congruent with each other.

Iris took some opera glasses out of her handbag and peered through them.

'Looks like they're busy absorbing the power of all the activity. Can't you feel it, like a cold flame sucking away all the heat?' It was starting to get deathly quiet. Iris shrieked as a nearby group playing Mexican bingo imploded into a plume of dust, leaving their seated skeletons behind. The scorecards were covered in ash. 'Sorry about that, I'm not usually given to screaming like a little girl.' At that exact moment the couples at the edge of the party started combusting explosively, sending detritus and objects into the air. Iris bit her finger and was able to keep herself from screaming.

105 pulled Iris closer, protectively. 'Señora, it is not shameful for a woman to express her natural feminine fear in a situation such as this.' Iris was about ready to jab him hard in the ribs when a belt buckle returned to Earth and slammed into the lid of the barbeque grill. It was 105's turn to yell out in surprise.

'We've got to calm down and do something! These people are dying. How can we stop them? This is your home, what do you know about these piñatas? Anything you think of could be important!'

105 traced the number on his forehead, popping bubbles in concentration. 'There was a song about Piñatas... how does it go? *Ya le diste una, ya le diste dos; Ya le diste tres, y tu tiempo se acabo.'*

He gestured excitedly. 'Don't you see? Hit it once, hit it twice, three times! A count of three! I have to wrestle these creatures!'

A voice echoed from deep within the bowels of the barbeque grill: 'By the rules, I must accept your challenge.' One of the spinning star piñatas lowered to ground level, circling faster and faster. At the end of its' cones, razor sharp tassels blurred the air. The blurring formed a doorway and out of it stepped a figure wrapped in wet, seeping bandages. A two metre tall mummy! It stretched its arms out in front of it, lumbering like a zombie.

Iris recognized a crackle in the air. 'Watch out! It's not as slow and clumsy as it seems. It's walking like that because it's pushing its way through the potentiality of dimensions, ripping through each layer, skin by skin, like my bus does.' Bloody bandages flashed out of the doorway, encircling the party, absorbing even more energy.

The creature's eyes, a pair of horrible green lights, shone through the gauze. In response, four victims from each side of the party were drawn into position, hanging in the air in agony. They were enveloped by a dark purple glow and the snakelike bandages whipped around them forming a rudimentary wrestling ring. A flash of light burst out and the four corner post victims turned into skeletal totem poles. The mummy creature absorbed their strength and his tall frame filled out with muscle. With a final step, it ripped through the final dimensional skin and was now fully solid.

'I am Axixmiqui. Throughout the centuries, I have faced your kind before. Masked ones.' Iris and 105 made eye contact, both confused. 'I will not be defeated again. It has taken me this long to regain my strength.' One of the paper mache stars exploded and golden fizzing blobs hung in the air in its place. The mummy outstretched his hand. A bandage snaked out and snatched the glowing globules out of the air like a frog catching a fly, absorbing the power.

Iris leaned in close to 105. 'Does that name mean anything to you?'

'I have never heard it as a name, but it is the Nahuatl word for 'having the need to go to the bathroom'.'

Iris swallowed hard. 'Maybe he knows Montezuma!'

'We are the Brethren, and I am their champion. I am again on the verge of returning and opening the way for all my kind. Your challenge is the only thing standing in my way. I will win and I will consume the Place at the Center of the Lake Moon.' He pointed towards Iris. 'We will need an impartial judge.'

'Impartial? There's nothing impartial about me in this affair, bucko! I'm about as partial as I can possibly be!'

'Not you. The one who hovers between black and white, between good and evil, life and death, this world and the next.' Iris heard the doors to her bus swoosh open.

'Oh my stars and garters!' Panda boomed as he flew through the air and stopped, hovering between 105 and the Mummy.

'This being, garbed in black and white, has been chosen to be the referee for our confrontation.'

'*Moi*?' Panda was almost flattered by the appointment.

'Yes, Panda. You have been selected for many reasons. Your unblinking stare misses no action. Part of your aspect is like the creatures on this plane, part of you is like my brethren. There must be no doubt that I have won this plane utterly and completely. You will judge.'

'Iris, what should I do?'

'I think we have no choice but to go along with this, love.' Iris looked to 105 for confirmation.

He nodded. 'Señor Panda, I accept you as an impartial judge.' He removed his cape and handed it to Iris and rubbed his oily chest, limbering himself.

Iris took a step forward. 'And what I am supposed to be, the scorecard girl in a bikini?'

'You are irrelevant, old woman. You have no place in the ring of battle.' Slithering bandages encircled Iris' shoulders and yanked her out of the ring. She squawked like an angry hen, her feet kicking.

Panda found he could harness the ambient energy to levitate around the ring, but not out of it. He floated to the centre where 105 was standing face to face with the bandaged giant. 'Right, then.' He cleared his throat slightly, then again more theatrically. 'Keep it clean.' His paw karate-chopped the air between the two luchadors, indicating the fight could begin. The two opponents circled each other like bobcats.

Outside of the ring Iris noticed that the partygoers were all very still. She quickly checked them, they were alive, and no longer being drained. They were, however, all exhausted from their unwilling celebrations. 'Lightweights!'

Iris reasoned that if they were no longer being drained, then the mummy must believe he had all the power he needed, stored in his piñata creatures. She peered into the ring through the horizontal bandages.

Watching 105 fight, Iris could see a whole new side of him and was impressed all over again. The night before, she'd had spent some time getting to know 105. He was a master of modern scientific principles, familiar with a variety of literary and historical texts and could play the piano like a virtuoso, but he was born to wrestle! The Man of 100 Masks was now in his element.

As judge, Panda was given a knowledge of the moves employed by the wrestlers. Flying cross body presses, spin kicking, submission holds, drop kicks, jackknife holds. 105 was almost a blur around the lumbering giant.

The mummy had mentioned he was also a champion fighter. Iris could see his strength ebb and flow through him, even if he didn't share 105's agility. A strength he drew from the poor saps at the party, she thought angrily. This creature had taken advantage of innocents and dismissed her because she was an old woman.

Iris raced to the bus, certain she could do something to help.

Panda found he had to scramble to stay out of the way of the luchadors. They exchanged blows, bouncing off the ropes, leaping into the air. The occasional exploding piñata unnerved him. Periodically, he had to separate them and the opponents would start again.

105 was good at getting his opponent to expend energy, then strike when the mummy was weakened. However, at that point the mummy would burst another of his reservoirs, restoring his vitality and gain the upper hand again. 105 had no such method to replenish his reserves. He didn't lose his energy as quickly, but once it was gone, it would be gone for good. The mummy would win and consume Mexico City.

Panda could see 105 slowing, doing more delaying in order to recover. He felt in his heart that if 105 lost, he would be compelled by the ancient powers to call the competition honestly. Hope seemed lost.

There was a loud clang from outside the ring as Iris kicked over the barbeque grill. 'Irrelevant eh?'

Panda saw Iris was holding an ornate hookah that had been given to her by Kublai Khan when they visited Xanadu. Khan had allowed Panda to keep a tiny pair of custom made emerald roller skates, which he had never used since. Iris, on the other hand, loved that hookah. She and Tom had used it many times, talking and laughing about ridiculous things. He wondered what she could be doing with it now. 105 and the mummy had also both paused and turned to watch. The Mummy beckoned for a few piñatas break out of formation and attack her.

'I had to rip parts out of my engine to lash this up, so I'm really brassed off!' Iris threw a switch on some electronics taped to the side of the hookah and quickly pointed the hoses at the creatures rushing towards her. The hoses came to life like a mass of snakes, and from the mouthpieces bolted pink lasers blasted the piñatas to smithereens! Those taken care of, she started on the ones hovering near the ring.

'When I saw you pushing through the dimensional skins, I knew I had a way to push you back! My bus does the same thing.'

'Cursed hag! You force my hand.' The mummy gestured and the remaining piñatas exploded and the golden spheres surged into him. The explosion threw Iris off her feet and the hookah smashed to pieces against a stone.

The Mummy was almost three metres tall now, bloated with power and clumsier than ever. However, it would now only take one blow for him to pulverize Señor 105, who was at this point exhausted.

'It's all in your hands now, ducky!' cheered Iris from the ringside.

105 dodged and darted, and executed a back flip off the ropes. The Mummy's meaty fist grazed 105's temple as he flew by and 105 landed with his back against one of the ring's grotesque corner posts.

He couldn't get up, it was no use. Suddenly, he heard whispering. The corner post, it was speaking to him!

'Avenge us! Avenge our lives. Don't let our life force be used for evil! Avenge our deaths! Avenge all the time, effort and money we spent planning this party!' The spirits of the dead were somewhat unfocused, angry and irrational, but they were right. Justice must be served.

105 could see the lumbering Mummy closing in on him. He had to plan this just right. The giant struggled to lift its oversized hands above its head, ready to crush 105. 105 feigned defeat. At the last second, with the last vestige of his spirit, 105 threw himself out of the way. The wet, glowing, bandaged fist bounced off the soft ground and back into the giant's face, knocking him flat on his back. Stunned for a moment, the mummy struggled to upright itself, like a turtle upside down on the road.

Panda hovered over to 105 and touched a paw to the number on his mask. 'Get over there and pin him, you lummox!' The energy drained out of Panda and into 105. No longer able to levitate, Panda fell into 105's hands who set him down gently, facing the action.

105 was barely able to drag himself up onto the mummy's bandaged chest.

Panda beat the ground with his paw and thundered the count. 'ONE!'

Iris cheered and waved a wine bottle from the sidelines.

Panda beat the ground again. 'TWO!'

The mummy roared in anger and threatened to lift its shoulders from the ground, but it was no use. His strength was also his weakness. He had been forced to absorb too much at once, all because of that Wildthyme woman.

'THREE!' He was defeated, fair and square.

'No! I refuse to admit defeat!'

105 panted on the ground. 'Where's your honour now, creature?'

'We refuse to remain trapped. Any ancients who would punish us for breaking the rules are by now long gone. This was our last attempt to do this by the prescribed rules. Now we will take this world by force.'

Panda and 105 were both drained by the wrestling match. Panda managed to lift a paw. 'Iris... it's up to you. Oh, dear lord! Behind you, woman!'

Iris spun in place. The creature raised itself to its full height. It outstretched its arms and bandages extended in every direction, weaving a cat's cradle. The decaying stench was overpowering.

Iris felt like a very tiny fly at the centre of a very large spider's web.

105 called to Iris. 'Señora... the bandages are forming a mathematical ratio.'

She could see it too. 'I'm way ahead of you. He's going to use it to open the doorway of dimensions. I've got to stop him.' Steeling herself, she ran straight towards Axixmiqui.

'Iris, no!' cried Panda.

He laughed. 'Foolish woman. You think you can succeed where this masked warrior has failed?'

Pushing her handbag strap more securely over her shoulder, she dove between the mummy's legs and slid through. 'Couldn't catch a pig in an alleyway!'

'I don't need to catch you, Wildthyme. You cannot escape from me. My web of bandages will ignite and drain the entire continent of its life force. There is nowhere to run.'

Iris pulled some of the bus' electronics out of her purse. 'Oh, I'm not running anywhere.' A click, a high pitched whine, and Iris planted the pile of junk at a juncture of five bandages. 'I just wanted to reach the dimensional sweet spot!' Then she neatly dove back under him and back to the other side.

With a boom, the bandages ignited, burning and unravelling.

'Nooooooo!' moaned the mummy. He quickly realised that all the flaming bandages eventually converged back on him. He struggled to yank himself free, but it was too late. The ratio was collapsing and feeding on the mummy's power. His muscles shrivelled and disappeared.

The corner posts giggled and cheered and burst into dust which swirled around Axixmiqui in a whirlwind. Beneath a pile of fallen gauze, the barbeque collapsed inwards and formed a dark purple mini-singularity. It started sucking the mummy into it, along with all bandages and the remains of the piñatas.

Iris rushed to catch Panda just as he started to be sucked in as well. Iris, in turn, was caught by 105. The three of them clung tightly together as all the unearthly material cleaned itself up in a cyclone of human ash. With a 'blip!', the purple hole blinked out of existence.

'Señora! We did it! Everything is going to be alright!'

Iris smiled bittersweetly. 'Not quite everything love.' She scanned the ground, searching for something. Once she found it, she scooped everything into her hat. Nestled as if in a birds nest, was a mass of smashed and scorched electronics. 'My poor bus!' Her face pinched up as she tried not to cry. From each side, she was hugged by one of her friends.

Iris was under the bus, checking the petrol line. She crawled out from underneath and then extinguished her cigarette. 'That looks fine, so we'll just have to go over everything again.'

'Don't worry, Señora, we'll find the source of the problem. Sit here and relax. I brought us some drinks from inside the house.' He was still wearing the same mask he'd worn to the Olympics that morning. Number 68 to represent the 1968 Olympics, green, white and red, mimicking the Mexican flag.

'Did you enjoy watching the boxing events today, lovey?'

'Sí! Although I could tell it wasn't Panda's cup of tea. I swear he fell asleep, but it looked like his eyes were wide open.'

Iris cackled and rested her head on 105's muscular shoulder.

'Are you talking about me?' Panda was on top of the bus, sunning himself.

Iris waved her hand in the air. 'You better just go back to relaxing and enjoying it while you can, Panda! Soon the bus will be fixed and we'll be off again, getting into trouble and causing mischief!'

105 took Iris' hand. 'I see you're wearing your new bracelet!'

'That's right! An official commemorative bracelet of the 1968 Mexico Olympics, see?' She indicated some lettering with a sloppily painted red nail. It read 'Mexico Olympiad'. 'It's a tacky faux-Aztec piece of junk, but I love it! I'm going to wear it everywhere! Venus, ancient Pangea, the planet Zwen... absolutely everywhere!'

Panda's voice drifted down from above. 'Just don't lose this one!'

'I never lose jewellery!' she countered. 'Anyway, I really am eager to go. You know me, never stopping for anything, always on my way to a new adventure, new horizons and new dimensions!'

105 stood up and adjusted his cape. 'Señora, I admit I don't understand how your bus works, but it seems as if we've checked and rechecked everything countless times. The Olympics are almost over and it seems we're no closer to getting your bus working than before.' He stood and looked at the engine again.

'It's only a matter of time. I've imposed on you for long enough.'

105 met her gaze. 'I wouldn't call it an imposition.'

They both quickly looked away. 105's eyes settled on a glass tube sticking out of the engine. He tugged at his goatee with his fingers. 'Señora... what is this? It looks as if it should contain fluid, but the end has come out of position.'

Iris looked uneasy. 'Ah, I'm not sure, let me take a look at that, love.' she laughed nervously and looked at the tube for half a second. 'You scamp! That's it! You found it!' she said, a little too quickly.

'This just needs refilling and everything should work again! I don't know how I overlooked that! You must think Iris is a silly old bag!' Iris took her flask and filled the tube with brandy and slotted it into position. The bus hummed happily and lights blinked into action. 'Eureka! My bus is back and better than ever!' She gritted her teeth angrily and slammed the engine casing as hard as she could. 'I'm so happy we can be on our way now!'

It was hard for Iris to read 105's face. 'I guess this means you'll be wanting to getting back to your adventures, then.'

'Of course I do, lovey! I'm just itching to get out of here!' Iris turned her back to 105 and dabbed at her cheek. 'Oops, must have splashed some brandy, my... my mascara is running.'

105 wasn't sure what to say. 'Señora... Iris. Before you go, I have a surprise for you. Don't move.' He ran into the house.

Iris watched him disappear inside and then hastily threw things into the bus. She quickly climbed up the ladder to where Panda was resting. 'Come on Panda, time to load up, we've got to go! Snap to it!'

'What? You've finally repaired the bus? But I'm catching some rays up here, and stirring my mint mojito with a fresh stick of bamboo! Aren't we going to say goodbye to Mr. 105?'

Panda in hand, Iris hurriedly descended the ladder. 'No time! I've just remembered we've got to be somewhere. Can't dawdle in one place too long, you wear out your welcome!' Iris pushed Panda inside the bus.

Iris turned around to grab her last bag of souvenirs and saw 105's boots next to it. 'You could never wear out your welcome, Señora.'

Iris laughed a little too loud. 'Oh, you must not know me very well, just wait, soon I'll be breaking dishes and staining your hardwood floors. You're lucky to be rid of loud, old, annoying Iris Wildthyme!'

105 knew he wouldn't be able to stop her from leaving. 'Please, Iris. I have something to show you before you leave.' He lead her by the elbows around to the back of the bus where Panda wouldn't see. 'First, I show you as I truly am'. Iris gasped. He reached behind his head and unlaced his mask, removing it completely.

This is a totally private moment for both Señor 105 and Iris Wildthyme, and even the drunken diaries of the shameless hussy say nothing about it. Nor does any story in any format give the details of what happened once 105 removed his mask and a few short minutes later donned a different one.

'Second, a gift.' He reached behind his head and started lacing his new mask up tightly. Iris saw this mask was number 22: Titanium. It was a shiny metallic red that matched the bus exactly. The trim around the eyes, mouth, nose and neck was all done in leopard print, like Iris' skirt. There was a pair of black circles high on the sides of his head like panda ears. 'Number 22, in honour of you, your bus and your loyal friend.'

Iris let the tears flow openly this time. 'That's so sweet... I... I don't know what to say. Thank you, lovey.' She gave him a big bear hug.

'Promise me I'll see you again. When I am Señor 106 or 107? I might need your help. Find me again. Or maybe I'll find you.'

Iris choked up. 'You might at that, chuck! I promise.' She leapt into the bus, slamming the doors and revving the engine. And in a spray of gravel, she was gone.

Señor 105 turned and returned inside his house. It was getting late, so he dismissed his staff. He turned off all the lights and spent the entire evening listening to records, quietly chewing gum, and basking in the soft glow of his now fully functional Zodiac jukebox.

Why? Because We Like You

Jonathan Dennis

Panda teetered through a forest of human legs, clothed or bare, hairy or stubbly or greasy with sunscreen, all in constant motion to carry their owners to the next great attraction. He struggled to hold a plastic cup so large its contents had their own tidal system. A plastic bag hung from his neck by its handles. Every surface inch of the bag and the cup were smeared with brightly coloured cartoon characters and their accompanying tiny yet intimidating trademark notices. In the half an hour it had taken him to find the drinks cart, wait in the line, and return to Iris in the queue for the submarine, she had moved maybe twenty feet.

It seems to me,' he said, while handing her the cup, 'that the job of fetching things should go to the person with thumbs.'

'I couldn't do that, Panda.' Iris fished a flask from her shoulder bag and poured a shot into the cup.

'What if you'd got to the front of the queue while I wasn't here? You know they wouldn't let you on the ride by yourself. They all have signs that say 'You Must Be This Tall to Ride' and you're barely ten inches. The wait would have been for nothing.'

'As opposed to the staggering progress you've made,' said Panda.

'Stop being such a spoil sport, Panda. It can't be exciting adventures every day. Sometimes, you have to take some time off. Relax. Have a holiday. Look at these people, enjoying themselves. Look at that beautiful castle, straight out of a storybook. This is the happiest place on earth and the only one not enjoying it is you.'

Panda pried the handles of the bag from around his neck and let it drop to the ground. It fell over and out tumbled the hat he had refused to wear, a cap with a pair of brittle plastic animal ears glued to the top and his name stitched in mechanically perfect cursive across the front. Its partner sat atop Iris' head at what she had assured Panda was a sufficiently jaunty angle. It wasn't easy finding the proper headwear for a silver and black faux leopard coat trimmed with Crayola blue fur but, come to think of it, the ears were appropriate. They made her look like a Muppet. Panda punted his hat into the nearby bushes.

'The castle is plaster. The people are horrific. And you told me the happiest place on Earth was Tijuana.'

'There's all different kinds of happy, chuck,' she said, and pulled a long sip through her straw.

It was true that Iris seemed to be enjoying herself, though Panda imagined it was just a matter of time before a combination of booze and things that spun combined to end her enjoyment. The upsetting part was her disregard for his feelings. Sure, she could spend the day enjoying the black lights and sharp turns of things like Mister Frog's Bad Trip. He was only allowed on if she clutched him as if he were just some common toy. It was undignified, as were the endless parade of sticky-fingered children chasing him. He could take no more. It was time for the silent treatment.

Panda folded his paws across his chest and stood with his back to her.

'Come on, Panda,' Iris said. 'As soon as we've gone on the submarine, you can pick the next ride.'

She had said the same thing in line for the Mountain Coaster and he was not going to fall for it again. Panda refused to budge.

'Come on, Panda,' she repeated and nudged him with the toe of her shoe. He merely stepped out of reach.

'Suit yourself, you daft toy.'

While Iris stood on her toes and tipped from side to side trying to catch a glimpse of the front of the queue, Panda saw the approaching commotion. A small group of people turned the nearest corner, between the faux-storybook gift shop and the flying hippos. They stopped by the people queued up and pointed excitedly behind them, toward the exit. Those in line turned away, gesturing to be left alone. When the newcomers insisted on being heard, one man took it upon himself to shove them away. They gave up and ran to the next queue, stopping directly by Iris and Panda.

There were about a dozen people in the group, including two couples with their children. The man leading them was a non-descript middle-aged man in a tropical green shirt and khaki shorts. An ugly welt swelled red just under his right eye and what was left of his camera dangled from his neck by its strap. There was a ring around his neck where it looked like he had been choked with it. He gasped for breath from the effort of running. Iris had failed to notice him.

'Iris,' Panda called. Iris made a point of ignoring him and continuing to look ahead. He repeated her name and nudged her leg.

'Changing your mind, already?' She still refused to turn around. 'It's too late now, love. You might as well go off on your own. I'll meet you at the bus when I've had my fill.'

'Iris, there's trouble.'

Trouble was the one thing guaranteed to get Iris' attention and she turned just in time to hear the man begin to speak between gasping breaths.

'They've closed up the entrances. Walled up. Guards. I asked them what was going on and they hit me.' He pointed to the welt under his eye. 'They told me to get in the nearest queue and wait to be processed. I ran. They grabbed at me but I got away. We got away. We need to hide. You need to hide.'

The man didn't wait for a response. He took off towards the next queue to spread his message. Iris and Panda had been the only ones in their queue to pay him the slightest bit of attention. They'd seen genuine panic enough times to recognise it.

'How are we going to get back to the bus, Iris?' Panda asked. The bus was in the parking lots and the only way to them was either by boat or monorail, and both of those were on the other side of the entrances. Swimming was out of the question. They'd seen the electric crocodiles on the way over. They seemed quaint and amusing at the time.

'Never mind that, Panda. How are we going to get all these people out of here? They're in danger.'

'So are we if stay here.'

'And if we break out of the queue on our own, we'll attract attention like that chap. We'll have an easier time of it lost in a crowd.' Iris pulled the boa from around her neck and waved it over her head while she shouted for attention. A couple of people glanced in annoyance at her, but the rest ignored her, hoping she'd stop. Then the trumpets started.

It was actually an old tape of trumpets, recognisable under decades of decayed crackle and hiss, emanating from the fairy tale castle that dominated the park's skyline. That was only enough to momentarily distract those in the queue. Panda urged her to leave while she still could but the decrepit fanfare had given her an idea. She turned around and faced in the other direction. The woman, who had been, until a moment ago, behind Iris, took a step back, bumping into the man behind her in the queue.

'What are you doing?' she asked.

'I'm waiting in the queue,' Iris said.

'The front of the line is that way,' the woman said. The man behind her nodded in agreement and pointed.

'No, it's not.'

'Yes, it is. The submarine's that way.'

'This isn't the line for the submarine,' Iris said. 'It's the line for the special event at the castle.'

Iris pointed to the fairy tale castle just as the sickly trumpets piped up again. The woman looked uncertain now. She looked to the castle than back to Iris, who nodded with a sincere 'I forgive you for being so dim' look. The woman wavered a moment before spinning on her heels to face the other direction. The man behind her frowned but did not argue. He turned as well. People on either side of Iris took notice of the growing shift in direction and moved to join in. The effect spread in a wave outward from Iris until everyone in the queue had turned about and, with nothing to stop them, filed out into the park and towards the castle. Panda re-joined Iris as soon as he could get through the dispersing crowd.

'Good heavens, Iris,' he said. 'You reversed the polarity of the moron flow.'

Iris tapped her temple. 'I've been around the block a few times, Panda. I know people.'

They joined the masses of people heading for the castle. The fanfare tape was now on a constant loop, and it had improved, stronger and steadier and louder with each iteration. Iris politely elbowed her way though the growing crowd as Panda held fast to the hem of her coat. By the time they made it all the way to the front, the trumpets were deafening. The press of the crowd jammed them against the wrought iron fence that surrounded the castle. Iris commented on how it reminded her of a Who concert she attended in the seventies, but Panda couldn't hear over the noise.

The trumpets cut off in mid-fanfare. Beyond the wrought-iron fence, a steep staircase led to the massive entrance of the castle. Genuine artificially-antiqued iron bound the lovingly distressed wooden doors that stood twenty feet high. Those doors now opened. Thirty or so smiling guards emerged, awkwardly clutching their rifles with padded, white, four-fingered gloves. Like the rest of the park's staff, they each had a name-tag pinned to the right side of their brightly-coloured uniforms. They lined up on either side of the staircase and stood at attention. A man dressed as a duck scurried out behind them and unrolled a royal blue carpet down the staircase before returning to the castle.

Then he appeared. The founder of the multimedia empire that had built the park, long dead, long rumoured frozen beneath the castle, emerged from the castle in a perfect, fifties-cut suit. His hair was slicked back and a pencil-thin moustache lined his top lip. He looked just like the old pictures, except for the dark blotches of frostbite on parts of his skin, and the clouds of mist that emerged from his nostrils with every breath, and the massive stainless steel mechanical device hooked into his back and pushed on a dolly by a pair of men in seven-foot hot-rod red crocodile costumes.

'He looks like Errol Flynn,' Iris said. 'He fancied me something rotten.'

'I don't believe you,' said Panda.

'Well, that's what Gable said.'

The scuttling duck returned from the castle bearing a microphone on its stand, which he placed in front of the frosty leader. He cleared his throat, producing a cloud so big it obscured his head for a moment.

'Ladies and gentlemen, children of all ages,' he began. 'When I was young, I had a dream of a better world, a happy world full of joy and wonder and the innocence of youth. I know you share that dream. It meant so much to you that you were willing to pay to share it and live it, if only for a day. Now that science has advanced to the point that I can re-join you, I have returned to lead you in making that world a reality for all, every day, every hour, free of charge.

'I believe his brain has turned to mush in the thawing process,' remarked Panda.

Iris shook her head. 'Maybe he's been taking over by some strange and terrible intelligence from before the dawn of time,' she said.

'Maybe he's just an arse.'

'It doesn't matter,' she said. 'I think it's high time we got away from the front of this crowd and found somewhere to plan our next move. Here, get in my bag so you don't get lost.'

Iris held her handbag out for Panda to climb in, but he refused.

'I will not. I've had enough affronts to my dignity lately and will not add that to the pile. I am an adult and I will be treated as such. I'll hold onto your hem the same as before.'

Iris didn't want to waste time arguing, so she allowed Panda to do as he pleased. Getting out of the crowd proved a great deal more difficult that getting to the front had been. That had just involved manoeuvring with the flow. Now they were working against it as everyone struggled to get a better view of the spectacle on the castle steps. The founder continued his speech but Iris paid him no mind. She was getting frustrated. She'd get to what she thought would be the halfway point only to find that the constant flow of people from all corners of the park was continually doubling the crowd's size. Then, under the sound of the crowd and the founder's amplified voice, she heard something mechanical. Once in sight of the edge of the crowd, she could see the cause.

The flow of people was not entirely voluntary. They were being herded by the robotic displays from the rides and exhibits. There were spacemen and pirates and beloved cartoon characters. There were ghosts and zombies and the Swiss Family Robinson. And, most terrifying of all, there were the Presidents of the United States of America. Iris saw a tourist attempt to break Roosevelt's grip on his arm. The robot president responded by twisting the arm behind the tourist's back until it snapped. The founder said something that spiked the anxiety level of the crowd. Iris turned just in time to hear him shout, 'You can't leave. You will stay here and help me build my new world.'

Uneasiness and fear ignited into mass panic. The crowd exploded as people suddenly made for the nearest escape route. Even the robots were momentarily overwhelmed. They snatched at the closest people and immobilised them, which tended to involve the breaking of limbs. This only incited further panicked flight and soon Iris found herself borne on a wave of running, screaming humanity towards the World to Come. It was all she could manage to stay on her feet and go with the flow.

She saw the Home of the Future exhibit. Though its exterior was as well-maintained as the rest of the park, the lack of lighting within marked it as a closed exhibit. Iris steered herself through the crowd towards the nearest door in the building's side, picked the lock with her skeleton hat pin, and let herself inside. The sole illumination inside was a set of dim red emergency lights directly over the exit. It was enough light to see the tear at her hem. Panda was gone.

It happened so suddenly that Panda did not notice until Iris was already out of sight. He looked down to his paws at the tiny shred of leopard skin. He counted himself lucky that he was small and non-human enough to escape the notice of robots, guards, and rioters alike. That said, the stampeding legs were still a danger. He decided his safest bet was to hide under a nearby bench until the worst was over. He would never forget the horrors he saw that day. The pirates were mostly bluster and the ghosts just tended to hold their arms in front of them and make 'wooooo wooooo' noises, but the presidents were brutal. Nixon and Hoover in particular seemed less concerned with subduing people than leaving them broken. Bush just looked confused.

Once the robots had succeeded in subduing and herding the masses to their holding areas, Panda broke cover and ran for the nearest building. The entrance was locked shut. He was able to squeeze through an open window into the basement. The basement was filled with machinery to run the ride in the building above. He had been in such a rush, he didn't even know which attraction it was and the machinery gave no clue. It was just a mass of turbines and pistons hooked up to an old, but well-maintained computer. Panda decided that it would be better to get away from an open window where, however unlikely it was, he could be seen. He wandered through rooms of machinery until he found a staircase to the upper floor.

It was a struggle to climb stairs meant for human-sized legs. Usually, he relied on Iris to carry him, but now there was no choice. It seemed to take forever to scale a single flight and before he could see the top he could hear the small lapping of tiny waves. He hauled himself over the last step and realised exactly where he had taken refuge. It was one of the few rides he had gone on with Iris, a series of small boats touring representations of the different cultures of the world while robot children sang the most annoying song in human history over and over again. By the end, Panda wasn't sure if it was supposed to be fun or an endurance test.

The room Panda found himself in was a gaudy, clichéd reproduction of a German village. Panda found himself offended on behalf of the German people. Where was the Bauhaus? This was just flimsy tin models of beer halls populated by children in lederhosen. There were hundreds of the ghastly little things and every head in the room turned to face Panda.

'Hallo Valorgenpanda.'

Iris let in as many people as she could before they needed to secure the door against the guards and robots. She led a couple of dozen frightened tourists deeper into the building in case someone decided to break down the door. They found an abandoned theatre and were thankful for a place to rest until they saw the robots on the stage. The set depicted a house of the distant future, the year

2000. Everything was labelled as atomic powered and both parents smoked because, as the sign said, it promoted healthy lungs. None of the robots were moving, not the dad in his silver business jumpsuit, nor mom with her plastic apron and gloves, not even little Jimmy with his jet pack or the space dog raised on Mars. Still, they refused to enter until Iris, tired and wanting a comfy place to sit and plan her next move, went in on her own to reconnoitre the situation. She came out, unharmed, a couple of minutes later.

'They're not like the other robots,' she said. 'There's no power to them and they're bolted to the floor. They're not going anywhere.'

'How can we be sure?' asked a voice from the back of the crowd.

'Look, I poked one. It was dead. Come on, you lot.'

She went into the auditorium, took a seat near the back and waited for the rest to work up the courage to join her. Once they had, she began to explain that she had been in much tougher situations than the current one and, even now, she was formulating a plan to stop the bloodshed. The others were not very receptive. A man in his late thirties walked to the front of the room. He wore khaki cargo shorts, a pair of Crocs, and a t-shirt that said 'I see dumb people.'

'Iris,' he said. His accent was depressingly American. 'My name's Jeff. I'm a sales manager and I can appreciate your go get 'em attitude. It's something I'd love to see on a member of my team and who knows, once we're out of here maybe you could swing by and I could get you a position in the office pool or something, something low stress for someone your age. But this isn't really the time or the place for it. We're safe here. We just wait for the proper authorities to come in and we'll be fine.'

Iris eyed him suspiciously.

'How do you know my name?' she asked.

'It's written on your hat.'

The debate didn't go well for Iris after that. These were born spectators, trained since birth in indolence. They had no interest in Iris' vivid descriptions of the joy of toppling despots who are in serious need of toppling. She sulked in a corner away from the rest, who, despite their belief in imminent rescue, were terrified. After an hour, she pulled a cheap paperback from her handbag and tried to read it in the dim light from the stage. After a couple more hours and a couple of hundred tawdry pages, she set the book aside and returned to the main group of refugees.

'So,' she said. 'Who thinks our rescuers are coming any minute now?'

Most of the group just looked to the floor like scolded children. Jeff, however, still had a bit of fight.

'Maybe they don't know yet, or they're getting ready,' he said.

'Don't know?' Iris repeated incredulously. 'This isn't bloody Brigadoon, chuck. It's the most popular fun park on the planet. Hundreds of people work here. Thousands of people come here every day, most of them with mobiles. This place should be swarming with Special Forces. At the very least, we should try to find out what's keeping them out. It might be something simple that we can disable and then your rescuers can waltz right in.'

A woman held up her phone. 'You can't call out,' she said. 'There's no signal. Maybe that's why they haven't noticed.'

'You think no one's noticed you can't call anyone in the park? What about the people who tried to get in after the gates were locked?'

Not even Jeff had a response to those questions.

'So what do we do?' the woman asked.

'We need to see what's going on outside the gates,' said Iris.

'They're guarded,' said Jeff.

'We don't have to walk up to them. I have a spyglass in my bag. I just need to get up where I can use it. What's the highest place in the park?'

'The castle,' half the group responded simultaneously.

Iris frowned.

'What's the second highest?'

The StratoSled was a thrilling ride that Panda had refused to board. He claimed it would make him nauseous, but Iris called him a chicken and rode it three times while he waited outside with her bag. It reproduced the concept of traveling in space while in no way resembling the real thing and it delighted her. The entire thing was encased in a massive geodesic dome of stainless steel. Iris had climbed more than her fair share of domes in her time and the thing about geodesic domes, she thought, was that they were relatively easy to climb compared to plain domes. Lots of handholds.

Rather than look a coward, Jeff came along. The park was practically deserted above ground. The tourists had been herded into the buildings for 'processing' or 'conversion' or whatever the hell was going on. There were small patrols of guards and robots but they were more concerned with intimidation than stealth and were easily avoided. Other than the group guarding the entrance to the StraoSled, that is. So, they found themselves climbing up the outside.

Iris took the lead. She made a comment about Jeff keeping his eyes from straying up her skirt to which he only responded with annoyed grunts. The metal supports were covered with ceramic insulation to protect against the Florida heat. It cracked and fell off under their hands and feet. More than once, one of them found himself losing his grip and needing to be helped by the other. It slowed their progress enough that Iris hoped aloud that they would make it to the top before dark.

As it happened, they made it just in time. They had to stop a moment to appreciate the gorgeous view before them. The sunset to the west spread streaks of orange and violet light across the sky. Gorgeous multi-coloured light that, even with the naked eye, could be seen reflected in the metal tanks, personnel carriers, and landed helicopters surrounding the park.

'We've established that they know there's something going on here,' Iris said.

'That's great,' said Jeff. 'But why are they just waiting there? Why aren't they doing something?'

'Something's keeping them out,' she responded. 'Hand me my spyglass.'

Jeff had been stuck slinging Iris' bag over his shoulder for the climb. Now that they were comfortably seated at the top, he handed her the whole bag. Iris pulled out her spyglass. It was made of dark, varnished wood with brass fittings, very traditional looking. She'd nicked it from a gift shop in Tampa. Opened, it extended close to three feet. She held it up to her eye and pointed it to the parking lot.

'Oh, there's my bus,' she said. 'I should have parked her closer, but she doesn't get a chance to blend in very often.'

'What about the soldiers?' Jeff asked.

Iris lowered the spyglass to the perimeter of the park. She shuddered and slowly lowered the spyglass. It was the first time since all of this had started that he had seen her truly frightened.

'What is it?' Jeff asked. 'What's keeping them out? Is it the guards? Is it the robots?'

'It's worse than that, young man,' she said. 'It's lawyers. An entire phalanx of corporate lawyers probably raised and trained in the harshest law schools of New England. I bet they have statements and injunctions and cease and desist orders. I bet they smell of money and blood.'

'And that's not all,' Jeff said. He pointed to the foot of the dome. There were five robots: a pirate, an astronaut, a ghost, a man-sized dog, and Richard Nixon. They reminded Iris of a previous adventure where she had fought an evil alternate universe Village People. The robots stood in the exact spot where Iris and Jeff had started their ascent. The robots heads tilted up to stare straight where Iris sat. She watched as more robots gathered at the foot of the dome, surrounding it.

'Time to get captured,' she said, and led Jeff down the way they had come.

The ground underneath the park was filled with tunnels and hidden rooms. They were nothing so romantic as rough-hewn rock walls glistening with lichen and vaulted caves, just concrete corridors and windowless offices. To Iris' disappointment, the robots separated her from Jeff and locked her in an office with a young woman whose name tag read Tammy. Tammy explained segregating the sexes was the first thing the robots had done when they had brought the people underground.

'Apparently they don't believe in co-ed prisons,' she said.

'It's not much of prison,' Iris said. She rattled the doorknob. The Clinton robot outside turned and looked in the window at her. Iris batted her eyelashes at him and blew him a kiss. The robot turned back around. She blew a raspberry at him.

'And he's certainly not an accurate reproduction.'

'Just be happy we got the presidents,' Tammy said. 'I hear the redneck bears are brutal.'

Iris ignored the comment and plopped her bag down on the desk. The overhead fluorescents weren't working but there was a lamp on the desk. She pulled it close so she could see while she went through her belongings. She asked Tammy how long she had been working at the park.

'Three years,' Tammy said. 'I worked in systems maintenance.'

'How long do we have before we're sent for processing or conversion or whatever he's calling it?'

'I don't know.' Tammy shrugged. 'Nothing's happened yet. No one knows what this 'conversion' involves. I don't think he planned it out or if he did plan it out, he didn't predict the technology accurately. He thought he'd come back and everything would be atomic. He was surprised that none of us smoke. So until he figures out what he's really doing, we're just locked away waiting. What are you looking for, anyway?'

'I'm not precisely sure, dear,' Iris said. 'There's something tickling the back of my mind. I have something that can help us. I'm sure I have. And when I see it I'll remember it.'

Iris stopped rifling through her possessions and held up her hand for silence.

'Do you hear that?' she asked.

Tammy cocked her head and listened. Her eyes narrowed when she first caught the sound of something far away. She and Iris sidled up to the wall to either side of the door, neither wanting to get in sight of the robot guard outside. They put their ears to the wall. The noise came from multiple sources, like a chorus of voices, but it was annoyingly high-pitched. Then came the sounds of violence, the crash of metal thrown against concrete, the sputtering of shorting circuits, screams both human and robotic. And all the while, the chorus came closer. It was a sing-song chant, almost taunting. Iris and Tammy pulled away from wall and took refuge behind the desk. As the voices reached their crescendo, Iris reached up from under the desk and pulled down her bag.

'I know that song,' Tammy said, and then, as if the possibility of being named frightened it, the chorus ended, the silence broken only by far off moans.

Iris and Tammy peered over the edge just in time to see something small launch through the air at the head of the Clinton-bot. It went down with a crash and struggled noisily for a few seconds before the silence returned. The door swung open revealing nothing but an empty hallway, until they looked down. Iris grinned and ran to the door where she picked up and hugged her friend, who was glad he couldn't blush.

'Oh, Panda,' Iris said. 'I found you.'

'I would say that I found you, Iris, rescued you in fact, with the help of my people.'

Iris set Panda down and looked at the crowd gathering in the hallway. They were robots. Child robots, slightly taller than Panda, dressed in the clothes of all the countries of Earth. They all smiled and about half of them had smears of blood on their face and hands. Iris eyed them suspiciously.

'Maybe you should step away from your people, Panda.'

'Nonsense, Iris. Robots or not, these are merely children. Yes, they can be a little enthusiastic, but like all children, they just need direction. They were abandoned under the new order, discarded as useless. When I found them, they only wanted one thing. Do you know what that was?'

'What?'

'They wanted me to teach them a new song. They've been singing the same one for over fifty years and they yearned for change. I taught them a new song and they made me their leader. I led them here and I rescued you, Iris.'

'But why *Suffragette City*?' asked Tammy.

Panda cleared his throat, embarrassed. 'I had to think fast and it was what was playing on the bus radio when we got here.'

Iris dumped the contents of her handbag on the desk and sifted through the resulting pile, sending empty lipstick tubes and swizzle sticks to the floor. She pulled out a small slip of paper covered in silver foil. She held it out and waved it like she was ordering a drink.

'I knew it,' she shouted. 'I knew I had it.'

'What is it?' asked Panda.

'It's my invite for the grand opening. It's what I was shooting for when we came here but I missed it by a hair.'

'A hair?'

'Never you mind, Panda. This is an all access pass and entitles me to a one on one meeting with our would-be dictator-cicle.'

'And what makes you think a fifty year-old ticket will work?'

'It'll work on the robots. Rules are rules.' She motioned to the hallway full of mechanical children. 'Your people there can take care of the guards, but try and reign in their enthusiasm a bit. All I've eaten in the past few hours are choccies and popcorn and I don't know how much more violence my stomach can take. Now, let's see if we can't cause a little pandemonium.' Iris chuckled.

'You know I hate that,' Panda said, which just made Iris laugh harder.

Iris and Panda released the people in the underground offices. Iris told Tammy to keep everyone safe inside while she went to confront the founder. Once that was taken care of, Iris led Panda and his miniature army to the surface. They immediately caught the attention of a robot pirate. Iris told Panda to keep his people from attacking and she held up the ticket so the pirate could see it.

'I want my meeting,' she said.

The robot paused and stared at the ticket. Iris was just about ready to have the children attack when the robot took a deep bow and motioned to the castle in the centre of the park.

'Right this way, ma'am,' it said.

After that, they made their way through the park with ease. The robots respected the tickets and the human guards were incapacitated by the children. There were a couple of times that Panda had to call them off before they caused permanent damage, but that was early on and they were still learning. They really were like children: cheerful, loud, and horrifically violent.

The founder was still on the steps of the castle. He sat on a massive throne, flanked by rows of robots. The throne had no back so as not to obstruct the tubes and wires connected to his back. A small table sat next to his throne with a pack of cigarettes, a book of matches, and an ashtray. Iris advanced up the stairs brandishing the ticket before her like a cross at the assembled pirates, spacemen, and cartoon characters. Panda remained at the bottom with the children, unwilling to attempt the stairs and avoiding the indignity of being carried like a common toy in front of his people.

At about the halfway point, the founder turned to the nearest robot, a knight in armour, and said something. The knight walked backed to the castle. Iris stopped. The founder smiled and motioned for her to come join him, but she waited until she saw the knight return, bearing a chair that it put on the other side of the table. She climbed the rest of the stairs and handed the ticket to the founder. Without a word, he inspected it and motioned for her to take a seat. The knight held her chair while she did so. The founder picked up the packet of cigarettes and offered her one.

'Cigarette, Iris?' he asked. 'I've been told it's not as popular as it once was, but I see that you, like me, come from a simpler time.'

Iris looked at him with suspicion.

'How do you know my name?' she asked.

'It's written on your hat,' he said, pointing to her head.

Iris snatched the cap from her head and threw it to the ground. It tumbled down the stairs. She took the offered cigarette and put it in her mouth. He lit it for her like a proper gentlemen, but she was only able to take a single drag before she extinguished it in the ashtray with disgust. The tobacco was ancient and stale. He shrugged and took another long draw on his own.

'I can't really taste it anymore,' he said. 'I just like the warmth.'

'Well I certainly can taste it,' she said. 'You should have given me a warning.'

'So, Iris,' he continued. 'You've had that ticket a long time I wager, since you were a young girl.'

'You're no spring chicken yourself,' she said. 'Just because you spent a few decades in the deep freeze. What's the point of all this anyway? Why do you want to take over the world? You already own about a third of it.'

'I don't do this for me,' he said. He swept his arm out at the park. 'This is my dream, a dream of a clean, wonderful world where everyone is happy. Didn't you hear my speech when I arrived?'

'It was drowned out by the screaming,' Iris said. 'Herbert Hoover snapping a man's neck can be a bit of a distraction.'

He frowned. 'Some will resist. But it won't last. Everyone loves it here.'

'It's a great place to visit,' Iris said. 'But they don't want to live here.'

Iris pulled her flask from her bag and took a quick swig. She held it up so the founder could see his reflection in its side. She held it as steady as she could so he could get a good look at the black blotches of frostbite on his face and the arc of the tubes emerging from his back.

'Look at yourself,' she said. 'Go inside and look at the people you have cowering in fear underground. Is this really what you wanted? It's not too late to stop. You could end this right now.'

He stared at the reflection. His face gave away no indication of what he was thinking. His cold breath misted in the warm air with every steady exhalation. He shook his head, slowly at first, then furiously.

'No,' he shouted. He stood up quickly, knocking the table and its contents over. 'I will not stop. Why should I stop?'

Iris stood up as well and closed in on the founder. She stood on her toes and brought her face within inches of the founder's. He just smirked.

'I'm giving you a chance, chuck, and one's all you get. Maybe this will make you more reasonable.'

Iris reached around the founder. At first it looked like she was going to try to hug him into submission. Instead, she grabbed one of the tubes snaking from his back, pulled it free from the machine and poured the contents of her flask down the tube. He shoved her aside and staggered as an astronaut robot reconnected the tube. He shivered as if he could literally shake off the effects.

'You horrible old woman,' he screamed. 'You've poisoned me.'

'Who are you calling old,' Iris yelled back. 'I'm well-seasoned. And stop over-reacting. It's gin, and good gin too. You owe me.'

'Gin! Good god, woman, these tubes run right into my blood stream.' By the end of the sentence, his speech was already slurring.

'Lucky you,' replied Iris. 'I have to do it the old-fashioned way.'

The founder was a lightweight. He staggered, unable to keep his balance. A pair of the robots tried to help him back to his chair but he struggled from their grip. He pointed his finger, wavering between the two of them, and proclaimed that he never trusted either of them. He balled up his fist and took a swing that failed to hit either of them. Instead, it spun him around until he lost his balance and fell down the stairs. As he fell, the tubes and wires between him and the machine went taut and the machine went wheeling to the edge of the stairs after him. Iris grabbed it to keep it from falling on him. The tubes and wires pulled free and fell slack to the ground as he continued to fall. His neck made a particularly nasty cracking noise as he hit the fourteenth step.

Iris froze with her arms around the machine. She darted her eyes between the robots surrounding her, ready to leg it if they reacted poorly to the death of their leader. When they didn't move, she let go and dusted off the front of her coat. She reached up to adjust her hat until she remembered it was gone. She would have to get a new one, a nice red one. It would be the next order of business once they left. She descended the staircase, skilfully stepping over the pools of leaked life support fluid from the pipes and avoiding eye contact with the founder's no longer animated corpse.

'I don't fancy the bill for this mess,' she said.

'They would charge you,' said Panda, horrified.

'You haven't seen the lawyers outside.' She paused. 'Say, you don't suppose your little friends can help us past them?'

A tiny robot tottered forward and grinned up at Iris.

'Teach us a song,' it squealed.

'I will,' Iris said, and smiled. 'Something nice, maybe some Patsy Cline.'

'I shall try to curb their enthusiasm, Iris,' Panda replied.

'For that lot?' she said. 'I think not.'

The children gathered around and started to sing, urging Henry to get off the phone. Iris took Panda by the paw and they walked to the exit, to other, more magical kingdoms.

The Scarlet Shadow

Stewart Sheargold

Iris stared into the bonfire, the flames flickering high, giving off sparks into the deep blue night sky. She had become quite hypnotised by their seductive warmth and playful dance. There were things in the fire, shapes cavorting and enticing her in to their dangerous embrace; but she knew it was the drink making her imagine things. Of course on some planets she would have cause to be worried, planets where fire was a breeding ground for evil spirits and elementals. But not here, here she was safe; here, she could relax. Here among the gypsies, nomadic people after her own heart.

The violins still scythed their plangent melody through the night. The gypsies danced with abandon, the women hitching up their skirts and throwing them about and tossing their long dark hair.

She was thinking about Baba Yaga with her long witch-like nose pushing herself about the Russian forests in her pestle. She was thinking about Baba Yaga's servant, Koschei the deathless, and whether he was more than just a myth these people had created to tell their children. They were a very mystical people, after all.

This had rather worked in her favour when she had appeared in her trusty old bus, as Panda had exasperatedly said, 'Crash bang in the middle of it all again, Iris'. Though secretly she thought he was just as pleased as her to drop straight from one adventure into the next without having to go looking for one. The gypsies had been alarmed to find a great red London double-decker bus in the midst of their camp in the middle of the forest, and had probably taken her to be Baba Yaga herself, such was the fear on their faces when she exited the bus. But she had calmed them down with a few choice words, like an experienced explorer placating a hitherto-undiscovered tribe, and they had welcomed her and Panda (with some joy from the children) into their caravan.

The men danced in staccato bursts, their footwork a stunning, overlapping tap-dance that no one could hope to learn.

Iris was rather enjoying herself just doing nothing much at all. She had rugged up against the cold Russian autumn in a great big fox skin fur coat, one of her favourites in fact, and she had drunk shots of vodka to keep herself warm against the night chill, and she had danced around the bonfire to the strains of frenetic violins until her legs had given way and she'd had to sit down.

Panda seemed to like being the centre of attention (they called him *mishka*), and somewhat revered when Bogdan, the gypsy's elected leader, had discovered his great knowledge of tarot and the magic arts (something which made Iris tremendously suspicious as Panda had never before taken an interest in mysticism, claiming it, 'Archaic, woolly thinking.')

She found herself strangely melancholy, the music evocative of a previous time when she had visited these lands, in a younger older body, and had met an old flame. She looked up at the stars and wondered where he was now, and if she would ever see him again. Who knows, she thought, he could even be here right now. Her time senses had been tingling ever since she had set foot outside her lovely bus. She had a premonition that something untoward was going on here.

A wind whispered through the camp. The fire crackled and threw up sparks. Leaves swirled about her. Iris shivered. Definitely something untoward.

'What is it?' demanded Panda, who had come to sit by her side. He had somehow managed to extricate the vodka bottle from Bogdan and was clutching it rather protectively.

His brusque question brought her out of reminiscence. 'What do you mean, chuck?' she replied a little too defensively.

'I know that look,' he sniffed. 'You have no intention of relaxing. That look means business.'

Iris grinned at him. Bless his black and white furry self; he knew her so well. 'I smell adventure! Something amiss with the timelines. We can't sit on our bums while the planet's in trouble. I'm needed.'

Panda raised an eyebrow.

'Don't you get hoity-toity with me, Mister. I know perfectly well how little you know of tarot and magic, and once that's dried up you'll have lost your charm. Just you wait and see.'

Panda took a sip from the bottle and offered it up to Iris. She took it. The liquid warmed her instantly to her toes, and a delightful fire set itself in her body.

Panda sighed. 'I rather think I've reached that point already.' He frowned and motioned for the bottle to be returned. It was times like these he enjoyed most travelling with Iris, just sitting by a fire drinking with a good friend, someone who knew him through and through and would stick by him come thick or thin. He sighed again, rather expressively.

'What is it, Panda?' she demanded. 'You're putting the grump on, you are.'

He snapped back. 'I was merely bemoaning the fact that you're about to cut my R&R short. You see, I believe I've found your trouble already.'

'Ooh, really?' Iris' eyes gleamed at the thought of peril and daring scrapes.

Panda lifted a paw and pointed across the clearing to a colourfully painted wooden caravan. Sitting just outside the door on the top step was a woman. She was dressed in a baggy red patch-worked cloak with a hood, and though it was evident she was a part of the gypsy caravan, it was also evident to Iris that her cloak was a disguise. Her body language was far too superior to that of these poor but humble gypsies. She was speaking to one of the men, holding his hand, palm up, tracing his lifeline, giving sage advice on his future, no doubt. She carefully folded his hand and with a gentle push sent him on his way. She turned to go back inside her trailer, but lingered to glance over the clearing, at the bonfire, now untended, collapsing in upon itself, at the last dancers who were swaying to the movement of the flames and the mutual alcoholic fire in their bodies.

Her eyes flickered across Iris', and stopped. She paused a second, then with a quick movement she stood up straight, losing the false stoop, and pushed her hood back. Revealed was a very beautiful but somewhat dishevelled woman with an ascetic face, heavily lidded eyes with a supercilious character, a mannish jaw-line, and a great pout. It was a face Iris knew very well.

'Marlene Dietrich!' she shrieked. 'You meddler! What the hell are you doing here?!'

They were having smoky tea in Marlene's caravan. After Iris' outburst Marlene had hurried them inside, determined to keep her disguise intact amongst the gypsies. Iris was not pleased to see her, though absurdly Marlene *was* pleased to see Iris, which made a change.

'I knew there was something amiss here,' said Iris. 'I should have guessed it was you tinkering with the timelines. Is Noel here, too?' She peered suspiciously around the small caravan, at the cramped yellow-painted kitchenette Marlene was currently making tea in, at the tiny bedroom beyond that, at the room where they sat around a small table, laden with tarot cards, gaudily decorated with baubles and trinkets, like a magpie's nest.

Marlene had allowed Iris to pour out her insinuations with barely an eyebrow raised. She brought a steaming hot samovar across to the table and three tiny black stone cups which she sat in front of Iris and Panda. She sat herself, her features brooding and heavy in the dim indoor light. 'I am here alone,' she finally said, her deep Germanic accent sending a thrill through Panda. 'An unfortunate...accident.'

Iris pursed her lips. 'It was those blasted pinking shears, wasn't it? Did he finally get sick of your moody femme fatale routine and kick you down a hole in time?'

'Iris!' snapped Panda. 'You're having a fit of pique. Let Marlene tell her story.' He knew why Iris was annoyed; she was intensely fond of Noel, and intensely jealous that he had decided to tootle around the timelines with Marlene instead of her. 'She puts on airs, she does,' Iris had once said. 'And she steals my ideas! I'm the one who told her about the vicious Scarlet Empress of Hyspero, and Icarus the blue boy angel and she ran straight to old Von Sternberg, didn't she!' It didn't help that those magic pinking shears of Noel's had caused untold havoc again and again, letting all manner of creatures through rips in time, and all because he was almost as careless and cavalier as Iris herself, dashing about on adventures in time. She had placed herself in the position of defender of the timelines, trans-temporal adventuress extraordinaire. Panda had suspected all along that she had piloted the bus here for a very good reason, and had not kept him in her confidence. To find Marlene here only made him all the more suspicious.

'I'm right piqued off,' cried Iris. 'Do you remember what happened last time we encountered *her*?'

Panda certainly did. That was back in the 1970s when they had discovered a plot by vegetables to take over the world by removing government figures from power. Panda remembered clearly the terrible explosive final battle in the streets of London, helped by the forces of MIAOW, and the mess he was getting out of his fur for weeks, and the ultimate horror of seeing a vegetabalised Iris. She hadn't complained then when Noel and Marlene had come to the rescue with his pinking shears; they had been very handy against those thrashing vegetable tendrils that grew from the fingers of the ersatz politicians.

'I remember that I saved you,' replied Marlene, giving Iris a withering look, arching an immaculate eyebrow. 'I think you could repay the favour now.' Her voice was deep and velvety.

Iris paused a moment. 'Well, out with it then. What accident was it that brought you to 18th century Russia?'

Marlene poured the tea into the tiny black cups, the sound soothing, drawing out the telling of her story. It smelled bitter and smoky. 'You will think it nonsense, but in short, I fell into a painting.'

Iris and Panda listened, bewildered and stunned by her sultry tone as Marlene told them how Noel had come visiting one night, right after the wrap party for *The Scarlet Empress*, to pick her up and take her out to dinner to a lovely little restaurant he'd been reading about 15 years in the future. He had wined and dined her and tried to seduce her into another adventure that night, had even said he'd been researching the location of Atlantis, and would she like to pop back a few hundred years and see what happened. Usually when he turned up she found him witty and suave and she could easily be led by his charm. But she had been exhausted after the filming and had only wanted to rest.

She had taken Noel back to the set to show him around. He had been sardonically amused at the expressionist art design, at the leering gargoyles, the ominous dark spaces and the enormous doors. When she had pressed him about his superior twinkle he had claimed, 'Your poor Mr Von Sternberg was misinformed, I'm afraid. Grand Duke Peter preferred neoclassical art and architecture.' Marlene had huffed disapprovingly at him, claiming dramatic licence.

They had stopped in one room where a single painting had taken Noel's eye. He had peered at it and tutted, proclaiming once again that it was entirely out of period, and wondering about the skill of the set dresser.

It was a painting of a tall woman dressed in a scarlet robe, standing in a forest with bare limbed trees. She was half turned away from the viewer, and her profile seemed to be perfectly classical, a straight aquiline nose, thin, long lips, and her eyes were dark but there was a gleam of soulfulness in them, a sense of resignation. Marlene had looked at the scarlet woman and had felt something like fear ripple through her, a strange coolness enveloping her.

She had blinked and then gasped aloud. Noel had raised an eyebrow.

The woman had moved, ever so slightly, so that now her face was turned straight on. Her eyes pleaded. And beyond her, where she had been looking, Marlene could make out a dark figure, hunched over, emerging from behind a tree, a stalking shadow.

'I know, my dear,' Noel had said. 'Improper attention to detail affects me much the same way.'

Marlene had felt a need to reach out to test her credulity, to ensure the painting was only oils and canvas. But as she reached out, she heard Noel shout, and saw her hand pass over the frame and *inside* the painting. Perspective went askew.

She abruptly found herself in a dark, cold forest, exactly the same as that in the painting, improperly dressed in evening wear. Before she could think properly she was set upon by an animal, with glaring yellow eyes and white, biting teeth. She fended it off as best she could, but promptly fainted when it got a grip on her wrist and bit down hard.

'I woke here in the gypsy camp, after Vasily, a youth, had found me whilst out collecting wood. I was fortunate to know a little Russian. I had, after all, just finished playing Catherine the Great. (Iris harrumphed) In exchange for my diamond necklace, I was allowed to stay. I have invented a persona here for myself, that of fortune-teller, which they seem to hold in esteem.' She sighed and sipped her tea. 'I could only wait, and hope Noel would find a way to take me back to the 1930s.' She concentrated her forceful gaze at Iris. 'Instead, I find you here. It cannot be coincidence.'

Iris gazed back levelly. 'As stories it's not the most ridiculous I've heard, but it's pretty close, love.'

'You do not believe me?' Marlene asked, sneering slightly.

'We believe you,' replied Iris. 'And believe me, we've been through a lot of stranger things.' She glanced at Panda who agreed with a slight smile. 'I'm just a bit confounded as to where to start! It's all so,' she looked briefly at Marlene, then let fly, '*Quatsch!* Utter nonsense!'

'I agree with you,' the actress replied smoothly. 'So will you take me back to my own time?'

Panda looked to Iris. She was sitting there measuring Marlene with a cool gaze. Finally she said, 'Eventually. I can't have you staying here meddling with history.' She picked up her tea, which she had not yet touched, and drained it in a single gulp. 'But there's definitely a mystery here that needs solving. We can't have people from the future falling into paintings and ending up in old Russia!'

'I was rather more worried about savage animals in the forest,' remarked Panda, 'considering we have a walk back to the bus.'

Marlene sighed and lit a cigarillo. She blew smoke idly from the side of her mouth. 'I can see you will not leave until you fix these things.' She looked at Iris. 'I will take you to see the Grand Duke tomorrow morning. He has a winter palace beyond the forest.'

Iris preened. 'A Grand Duke! I shall have to choose something particularly swish from the wardrobe.'

Panda, being slightly more practical, said, 'Why would a Grand Duke see you?'

Marlene sniffed, annoyed at being questioned by a stuffed toy, and blew a cloud of smoke disdainfully in his direction. 'He has his fortune told every Tuesday, though he does not wish this to be known, so has to find someone discreet, like me.'

Iris harrumphed again at the notion of Marlene being at all discreet with her lavish, conspicuous airs. 'And why are we going to see him?' demanded Iris.

Marlene smiled. 'Because, as I learned today, a thief broke into his palace a week ago. They took a single painting.'

Wind howled round the bus, swirling leaves in little fitful tornados.

Panda couldn't sleep; indeed he rarely slept at all, having no need to, his curious nature being completely unlike a real toy bear at all, and much more mysterious. Myriad thoughts crowded his mind about Iris and Marlene and Noel and their casual, good-natured rivalry. He kept going back to the last week on the bus, when Iris had been poring over her journals, searching for something, and whenever they would land it would only be for a few moments whilst she got her bearings and then insisted that there was nothing interesting going on and promptly re-set the period and clunked the bus into gear again.

Just what was going on?

He was reclining, as much as he could, on the chintz chaise longue in the centre of the bus, having made himself a brandy in the hope of it helping him snooze. Iris was lying prone on the other couch opposite, snoring loudly. He swirled the amber liquid around in the balloon and gazed at her recumbent form.

What could she want from 18th century Russia? He had to agree that there was something going on here. But it was all as mysterious as her reason for staying. The last five places they had landed had seemed abundantly full of more intrigue than here. And he'd figured that out within ten seconds of materialising.

It worried him that she had not confided in him, her best mate, her oldest friend. It could only mean that she was embarrassed by what she needed, which saddened him. The Iris he knew wasn't embarrassed by anyone or anything! It must be truly terrible if she was keeping it a secret from him. Well, she would tell him in good time; she'd ruddy well have to if she was going to drag him into Marlene's kerfuffle.

Oh Marlene was a shrewd one. She did put on airs, she was artful at dressing up, but she could never get past herself. She was still Marlene Dietrich playing fortune teller, and this time she didn't have Von Sternberg to coach her or light her; she had no illusion to cloak and comfort her off the stage. She knew, now Iris was here, that the Wildthyme act would be larger than her own, and she had gracefully faded into the background, a supporting character, whilst Iris and Panda took centre stage.

The brandy was finally taking affect, and he felt a gorgeous somnolence descend on him.

Wind howled a banshee wail outside. Leaves whispered around the bus. Panda glanced out into the dark and recoiled when he saw two gleaming yellow, intelligent eyes staring straight back at him.

He fell off the lounge with a soft clump. Iris murmured in her sleep – 'Hmm, but I don't like gooseberry jam.'

Panda clambered up a tower of books to the longue and carefully peered out. But the vicious, frightening eyes had gone. The forest was deep with night.

Panda recalled Marlene's story, of being attacked by an animal. He found himself quite wide awake again.

In the morning, Marlene took Iris to the Grand Duke's palace. As she had said, it was a good walk through the forest, the denuded trees clacking their branches together in the cold wind. Iris shivered; she was wary after Panda had told her what he had seen last night, though she hoped the animal would have the good sense to keep out of sight during the day.

Marlene had put on her red cloak, and dressed herself down in a simple skirt and white blouse. To aid her characterisation she had, somewhat stereotypically, thought Iris, clipped on large golden earrings that dangled from her lobes, and tied a colourful kerchief around her forehead. The actress had also insisted that Iris play a part, and she now found herself dressed as one of the gypsy women, and carrying a basket of Matryoshka dolls to peddle, which the gypsies carved from hand. She wondered if they realised that they were actually making models of the universe.

She peeked into the basket to make sure Panda was OK, bobbing along among the Russian dolls, and found him glaring back at her, arms crossed, quite aware of how ridiculous his position was. She hastily covered the basket, leaving him alone with all those wooden grinning faces.

'I feel ridiculous,' said Iris. 'This fabric isn't me at all.'

Marlene sniffed. 'The Duke would not let you in as you were previously. In this case you will have to follow me.'

'So what kind of fortune does this Duke ask for then, eh?'

'He asks only one thing. He asks about his wife. She has been missing for a year. He thinks he sees her sometimes, wandering the palace grounds.' She glanced askance at Iris.

'How mysterious,' she said. 'And exactly what do you tell him?'

'I tell him what he wants to hear. That she is trying to lead him to where she is.'

Iris frowned. 'I think that's a bit in poor taste.'

'You would destroy his hope then?' Marlene snapped. 'You would tell him she is dead, perhaps? Or she had run from him like a caged bird?'

'Flown,' corrected Iris out of habit.

Marlene's eyebrows went upwards. 'I shall send you back now if you utter another word!'

Iris begrudgingly fell silent.

They abruptly emerged from the dim forest onto a vast green lawn. In the distance was a large building with two wings either side of a central colonnaded entrance, and an onion dome situated atop. Iris was struck by the oddity of such a grandiose building appearing in the midst of the forest.

Marlene made straight for the very end of the left wing, bypassing the entrance adroitly with the knowledge of someone who'd had prior engagements. Iris raised an eyebrow suggestively as Marlene knocked at a concealed door. Marlene flashed her eyes angrily.

A small moment elapsed, and then the outline of the door was revealed as someone opened it from the inside. Iris and Marlene quickly went through.

Iris found herself in a luxuriously decorated bedroom, with gilded ironwork on the walls and the ceiling, black velvet wallpaper with fat red rosebuds, a chandelier with a dozen candles, and an enormous four-poster bed covered in heavy, intricately-embroidered damask quilting.

'Where are we?' whispered Panda from the basket.

'Looks like the tart's parlour,' replied Iris.

She was startled when the secret door clicked shut behind her and a man dressed in royal blue kingly vestments stepped from the shadows. He possessed a face that was lined with the worries of age, yet it still maintained a soulful youthfulness. He looked at Iris, intrigued, a slight frown etched on his brow.

'Let me see,' said Panda. Iris shook the basket gently to discourage him. Panda cursed, the noise covered by the sound of the wooden dolls rolling and clacking about.

Marlene bowed. The man said, 'Madame Galina, who is this woman?' He pointed at Iris, his tone devastatingly commanding.

'She is a friend,' replied Marlene, putting on a shocking accent. 'We gypsies must live by some means. Your servants, they like the Matryoshka, the dolls we make, for their children. Please let her do business with them.'

Iris plucked a doll from her basket. 'Oh please your royal highness, I only want to please. I make 'em with me own hands. Beautiful little dolls, every girl needs one.' She was determined to ham it up as much as Marlene was. The actress looked about to hit her for speaking.

The Grand Duke took three swift steps toward Iris and gazed intently into her eyes. 'You will not tell anyone of what you see here. No one, do you understand?'

Iris nodded meekly.

'Now go about your business, and seek my servants. Do not linger elsewhere in the palace.'

As Iris left, Marlene was taking out her tarot cards wrapped in a silk scarf. Iris tapped her on the arm. 'Let me know if The Devil pops up would you, lovey?' she said enigmatically.

'Why?' asked Marlene.

But Iris only gave her a wink and was out the door.

Iris managed to find the room the painting had been stolen from with relative ease. When she had entered the building her time senses had gone haywire, hair standing on end, her lips tingling. Something dastardly pan-dimensional had occurred here.

She traipsed down gilded, luxurious corridors, paintings of Grand Dukes and Princesses in ruffled shirts and puffed up dresses watching her coolly. Her heels echoed on the marble flooring – clip clop clip clop. She seemed to be the only person in the palace, there was no sign of a single soul.

'What was all that about?' asked Panda, peeking out from under the covered basket.

'What was what about?' replied Iris evasively.

'You know perfectly well what I mean,' he snapped.

'I'm not sure I do,' she said.

''Let me know if the Devil pops up, would you, lovey?'' he mimicked in a high pitched tone.

'Well it's a very loaded card.'

'Yes, it is.' Panda was looking at her intently, pulling the reason from her. 'As is this.' And he pulled out The High Priestess and flashed it in Iris' face.

'Panda!' she squealed, rather delightedly. 'You'll have ruined Marlene's tarot spread!'

'Don't change the subject,' he said. 'You must know The High Priestess is mistress of secrets and deceptions. Now just you tell me this instant what it going on here, Ms Iris Wildthyme, or I am going back to the bus and not having another thing to do with this adventure.'

Iris sighed. 'Do you recall our adventure on that lovely planet where everybody was obsessed with gardening and were so nice to each other? And the evil stone statue that tried to tear it all apart, and the wicked man who lived in a clock who tried to steal my body?'

Panda's eyes went wide. 'You don't think he's back again, do you?!'

'Well, it's just a premonition, chuck, nothing I can put my finger on yet. But The Devil is his calling card, and he did go by the name of Koschei at one point.'

'Does that make you Baba Yaga?' said Panda sardonically.

'Oi, watch it, you, or I might just eat you up.' Iris stopped at a large gilded door. 'Here we are.' She reached out for the large brass knockers, and then recoiled as a wave of time washed through her. 'There's definitely time tinkering gone on here, I can feel it in me waters.'

She had to use all her weight to open the mighty gilded doors.

They found themselves in a small square room, decorated robin's egg blue, with white and gold arches forming a number of alcoves on either side of the room. Statues reclined or postulated on stone plinths around the room. The ceiling was a rampant and highly detailed fresco of nude beauties and beasts. At the front, there were three arched windows that looked out onto a lush green garden. There was a single high-backed armchair upholstered in royal blue sitting in the centre of the room.

'A private art gallery,' said Iris. 'Despite his dour temperament, our Duke seems to have a bit of culture about him.'

'I feel distinctly ill,' said Panda. 'And I'm sure one of these dolls just winked at me.'

'That'll be the time distortion, chuck, making you feel delusional.'

'Utter bollocks!' snapped Panda. 'I'm a perfectly seasoned time traveller.'

Iris put a hand to her head. 'So am I, and I'm feeling a bit on the wobbly side.'

They soon found the alcove where the stolen painting had hung. There was a blank space on the wall that was lighter than the surrounding wallpaper. 'I wonder,' Iris mused. 'I wonder if we'd been here a week ago, whether we'd have seen a painting with a scarlet woman and a frightening shadow stalking her in a forest?'

Panda huffed. 'But why this painting in particular? At a single glance I can see a number that would obviously fetch good prices.'

'That, my dear Panda, is what we're here to find out!' With that, Iris began to rummage in a capacious pocket of one of the cardies she had insisted on wearing along with the gypsy outfit. She eventually pulled out a long slim silver device with a rude-shaped nozzle on the end. 'My trusty time anomaly detector,' she said proudly, waving it about.

'Oh Iris, no,' said Panda, frowning. 'That thing gets us into more trouble than it's worth.'

Iris glared at him and pressed a switch. The end glowed blue and a piercing noise was emitted from the device. Iris hummed and ahhed for a moment, her eyes wide at the promise that her spanking new technology would winkle out the problem. It gave a sharp squeal and so did Iris in return. She quickly switched it off.

'Oh dear, oh dear, oh dear,' she said, turning to Panda with a sheepish look.

'What is it?' he asked, worried.

'The thief. They must have used a Micklethwaite extractor.' Her eyes went wide with alarm.

Panda measured her coolly. 'Alas I am unfamiliar with that particular technological gubbins.'

'It means, my old, dear friend,' Iris stressed, 'that the thief created a whacking great time anomaly around this room. And picking an unstable moment they could waltz in and pluck the painting out, and time would simply ignore them.'

Panda raised a doubtful eyebrow. 'That sounds rather unlikely to me.'

'Panda, Panda, Panda! You don't understand. The thieves who stole the Oracle's ear from the Demeter Collection used a Micklethwaite extractor. It was a disaster. They were herding figures and beasts back into paintings for weeks!' She looked around quickly at the dim alcoves.

'You're telling me we may have to deal with inanimate art pieces coming to life?'

Iris glanced at him. 'Anything in this room.' She took another careful look about. The cold sunshine went behind a cloud moving the room into dimness.

Panda coughed. 'This is all rather silly, Iris. I've been through some things with you, but what you're suggesting is just impossible.'

There was a small squeak, like that of an un-oiled door, as all fifteen Matryoshka heads swivelled on their tiny bodies to look at him.

'Oh, my great Aunts,' said Iris, patting her chest. 'That certainly got my hearts fluttering, and no mistake.'

Panda didn't want to admit it but he had felt much the same. He'd leapt from the basket into Iris' arms in a very inelegant fashion.

Iris had lit one of her sobranies to calm herself. She was puffing away, agitated, blowing great plumes of smoke.

They were in the Grand Duke's parterre garden, landscaped with immaculate lawns and topiary-styled trees that had been clipped into imitations of bears. White statues were placed around the lawns in attitudes of alarm, hands thrown into the air.

They had raced here after Iris had dropped the basket of dolls with a messy clatter, neither of them wanting to be anywhere near the small art gallery. Panda had visions of the basilisk crawling out of its frame, or the charging black stallion leaping out at him and Iris, mouth foaming, the soldier bestride him slashing at them with his sharp sword. The whole experience had been quite unnerving.

'I was quite expecting those Matryoshka to start popping open and loosing their smaller kin upon us,' said Panda, seated on Iris' shoulder. 'It is extremely lucky they are made without hands to grab with.'

Iris had sufficiently calmed herself now to bring a sleuthing eye to the proceedings. 'A very close call, as that pompous old know-it-all Holmes would say,' she replied. 'Still, least we know that painting was stolen by an alien visitor to these shores, eh? My waters are very attuned to time spillage.'

Panda grimaced at her phrasing. 'What we need to do now is find that painting.'

Iris glanced at him for a second and blew out a grey plume. 'I have an idea about that, chuck. I think we should use the powers of the peri – ' She stopped abruptly.

'What is it?' sniffed Panda. Then: 'Did the sky just get dark?' he asked, for light had suddenly been extinguished as though by unnatural phenomenon, and grey clouds roiled in the sky.

'Of course we could just ask her, I suppose.' Iris pointed. Before them, down among the statues and the shaped trees stood a woman in scarlet, her dress blowing in the light wind. For a moment time was stilled. Iris gazed calmly into the face of the woman, a wise face, with deep soulful eyes; they measured each other and each came away with the sense of great age and great experience of pain. Iris felt a deep contact, an immense pull from the woman. Then the woman turned and slowly began to walk away, towards the forest.

Panda and Iris looked at one another.

'You don't think—' they both said in unison.

'You do think,' they both agreed.

Iris grabbed Panda and stuffed him in an inside cardy pocket so he could peer out without being endangered. Then she hitched up her skirts and raced after the scarlet woman.

They had barely made the first turn in the garden when they almost piled straight into Marlene, who had come to look for them. 'What are you doing?' she cried, exasperated. 'We saw you in the garden.'

'Oh shut up,' retorted Iris, 'and hitch up that ridiculous skirt of yours, love. We've seen your scarlet woman!' By now she was quite breathless from trying to talk and run at the same time.

They soon entered the shaded forest, the grey clouds stealing all light and making it seem all the more grim. The wind had picked up and was blowing a chill that made them cover themselves. Iris thought of Koschei the deathless again and the rumour of the thunderous skies and the bleak, cold winds that presaged his presence. The limbs of the trees clacked together like witch's fingers.

Iris and Panda raced ahead, catching a glimpse of red between the trees. 'Oi!' she shouted, her voice quickly swallowed by the dim, 'We just wanted a quick word...about a painting.'

A flash of red to the left.

'That way, Iris!' cried Panda, caught up in the action. Iris veered towards it rather slowly; her frame wasn't made for running, which, at times, was a distinct lack in her line of adventuring.

There was a sudden flurry of leaves that came swirling madly toward her, blinding her. She stopped and fought them off. By the time she was free of them the scarlet woman had vanished.

'Damn and blast!' cursed Panda. 'Why couldn't you have been faster?'

Before Iris could begin an angry retort, Marlene, some way behind them, screamed (a trifle melodramatically, thought Iris). She quickly turned and dashed off toward the actress.

They found her slumped against a tree, hands fluttering nervously at her heart. Her usually soporific, dreamy eyes were wide and affright, the whites horribly showing. Iris realised she had to be careful of the poor dear, she wasn't as experienced as her at these real dramatics.

'What is it, my dear?' she asked solicitously.

Marlene stammered out an answer. 'A f-face. A t-terrible face. A horror.' And she reached out an arm and pointed a perfect nail into the forest.

Iris searched the dark tree lanes for a moment, and then she saw what Marlene had seen. A shadow was moving from tree to tree, smoothly and relentlessly like oil. Leaves scattered a path before it. For a moment it seemed to turn toward Iris, aware it was being watched. She caught a brief glimpse of its face and could not repress a shudder. It was a hideously scarred face, dripping with flesh cauterised by flame. It turned away and followed the scarlet woman into the gloom.

Marlene whispered, not wishing to disturb the face of the dark, 'The shadow...from the painting.'

'Are you sure this is going to work?' asked Panda, suspiciously, bobbing along in Iris' inner pocket.

'Of course it will!' replied Iris, exasperated at his lack of faith in her. 'When in old Russia, do as the Russians do.'

Panda huffed.

They were making their way through the night markets in the nearby town. Lanterns on poles sent an amber glow over the proceedings, where night traders hawked their wares: vegetables and fruits, brightly coloured scarves and clothing, wooden children's toys, Matryoshka (Iris and Panda eyeing them warily). Delicious foreign tangs drifted in the night air, making Iris' mouth water. A man was roasting chestnuts in a small oven, competing with the woman beside him who was selling fried bread dumplings. The sizzle and crack of the markets made Iris want to stop and pick through all the stalls. But they had an appointment to keep.

Panda piped up again. 'What makes you believe this Madame Widgerydoodah—'

'Madame Sokorovska!'

Panda paused briefly. 'What makes you believe she could possibly find the whereabouts of the painting? She's likely to tell you any old guff. Besides, you don't have a spiritual bone in your body!'

They had come to the end of the markets and now made their way down a cobbled lane that led to the square and the bookshop where Madame Sokorovska held her readings. It was dark in the streets with barely anyone about, everyone at the brightly lit markets. Iris picked up her pace and walked that little bit faster.

She tsked at Panda. 'She probably will tell me a load of old guff. But time spillage occasionally does boost the psychic power of those few humans who claim to see into the future. Really Panda, you could have a little faith in your Aunty Iris.'

They had arrived at the bookstore in the corner of the square. It had a quaint frontage with the window sectioned into wooden squares. Through each the display had been carefully created to highlight a book with a paper cut-out next to each, presumably to preview a scene. Apart from the lit front window, the shop seemed dark.

Iris knocked on the front door.

As she did so a cold wind billowed in the square. The hackles went up on the back of Iris' neck. Panda shivered and glanced back into the still, grey, cobbled square. For a moment he thought he saw yellow eyes staring back at him from the shadows under a baker's awning. He stared deeply into the space but could not discern anything.

'Come on, Iris,' he said. 'Get inside.'

'Hold your horses, chuck,' she replied. Then the door clicked and opened, and they went in.

Madame Sokorovska was a small woman, wrinkled and prune-like, with eyes so tiny they seemed like raisins pushed into dough, a mouth that was thin and pursed with apparent disdain and white hair that peeked from under a head scarf. Her fingers seemed like claws when she beckoned Iris and Panda inside.

She led them through the dim store, lit only by the candle she held, to a black velvet curtain behind the counter, and waved them through. Iris and Panda hesitated, and looked at one another, wondering what they were getting into. It was all rather mysterious.

There was suddenly an old, brittle voice in the darkness. 'I do apologise. The practice of telling fortunes is seen as ungodly to some, and best kept hidden.' She gave a laugh that turned into a cough. 'Though it is amusing. I have many more customers for the fortune-telling.'

Despite her crooked, fierce appearance Iris found herself instantly liking this little old wise woman, and was certain that if anyone here could help them locate the painting, it would be her.

They went through the black curtain, and found themselves in a tiny backroom, every wall piled high with mountains of books. There was a small table in the middle of the room, draped with a purple tablecloth, and a single candle sputtered in a holder. On the table was a set of tarot cards. There were two chairs facing each other.

'Come, sit,' said the fortune-teller.

Iris sat, checking that Panda was all right in her inner pocket.

'Wouldn't *mishka* be more comfortable on the table?' said Madame Sokorovska with a sly grin. 'Do not worry. I have seen many things. And would he not be able to make sure I am not cheating if he could see me properly?'

Iris raised her eyebrows, and Panda frowned guiltily. Iris plucked him out and sat him on the table. He nodded to the fortune-teller who smiled, her thin mouth breaking into a warm expression.

Madame Sokorovska began to shuffle the cards. She then had Iris pick out seven and laid out a traditional horseshoe spread. She turned over the first card: *Temperance*. A crooked hand hovered over the card, very still. Then she expelled a great breath of air. 'Interesting. There is great restlessness in your past, great imbalance. You...travel, wide and far, so very, very far. How very interesting. You have many relationships. I see specifically one man who continues to become entangled in your life. Wait.' Iris waited with baited breath. 'No, 'life' is wrong. 'Lives'. You have lived many lives, different lives. How intriguing. But it is your life as you are now that you have concerns about. You are not ill, and yet...you are worried.'

Iris coughed gently. 'I'm sure this is all very intriguing for you, love, but I had hoped to find out less about me and more about—'

'A painting. Yes, I know.' The fortune-teller sighed. 'Very well, if that is all you seek, I will tell you. She skipped the second card and went on to turn over the third card: *The Hanged Man*. The old woman gave a cackle. 'There you are: card of the trickster, of thieves, of Odin, the shape-shifter god.'

Panda frowned at her. 'Might you elaborate? That hardly tells us where to find the thief.'

She snapped off her mirth and glared at him. 'You already know, Panda.' She leaned forward. 'You have seen the yellow eyes in the night.' The candle fluttered on the table, and all their eyes went to it.

The bell at the front door went.

'Here she comes now,' said the old woman, smiling, her tiny eyes glittering like jewels in the candlelight.

'She?' replied Iris, confused. 'Panda, what does she mean, you know?'

Panda panicked. 'Quickly, pick me up! Pick me up! We must get out of here!'

Iris eyed him suspiciously. 'Not until you tell me!' She folded her arms.

But Panda was so spooked he leapt off the table and darted under the black curtain. Iris jumped from her chair, and was about to follow when she felt a strong hand grip her arm. Madame Sokorovska was holding her with immense strength. She held out her free hand for payment. Iris rummaged in her pocket and pulled out a few coins that she had nicked from Marlene.

'This is half payment,' said the fortune-teller with cracked disapproval.

'For half a reading!' snapped Iris, and she twisted free from the old woman's tenacious grip, worried about Panda.

As she dashed into the store proper, she heard a terrified squawk, and a muffled growl. The store was dark but a little moonlight illumined the front of the store, and the bizarre scene that presented itself to her. Panda was clutched in the claws of a giant Siamese cat, dressed in a strange lime green spacesuit. The cat's eyes glowed a wicked yellow, and her sharp teeth were bared.

Iris snatched a book off a shelf ('That's four roubles,' said the old woman behind her; she ignored her). 'You get off him, you great big pussy!' she cried and swung her arm up to throw the book.

Then Panda spoke, shocking her. 'Iris, I am perfectly all right,' he said. 'I was just startled.'

She looked at the sharp claws, the white teeth, the glaring yellow eyes. 'But, those claws, those teeth, those glaring yellow eyes,' she said, bamboozled.

Panda managed to look sheepish. 'Iris Wildthyme meet Gemima Smythe, cat burglar extraordinaire, number 3 on the Adjudicator's most infamous criminal list, and,' he paused and went on in a suitably cowed whisper, 'my ex-lover.'

The cat gently placed Panda on the floor, stood upright on strong hind legs and held out a paw, 'Pleased to meet you,' she said in a snooty, aristocratic tone.

Iris' jaw dropped to the floor.

Iris had dragged them all back to the bus – Gemima, Panda, and Marlene (stopping to collect her from her caravan on the way) – where she had promptly pulled out the drinks and had a good, long, stiff, fortifying G&T.

Panda's revelation had been a big shock to her. She knew she had kept secrets from her friend, indeed the real reason why she was here, but she was surprised at such a large secret from him, and what an indiscretion! Panda having it off with a great big Siamese! She shook her head ruefully in the knowledge that no-one really knew anyone, not properly, not completely honestly down to the bone. And this was just the sort of thing friends told each other, juicy gossip about former lovers (she had never shied away from telling anyone of her affections for one man in particular); then again, she didn't know the details of the break-up, it could have been acrimonious. Though judging by their coy smiles and Panda's evident preening that didn't seem likely.

Iris poured herself another gin and tonic, her fourth in fifteen minutes. She now felt capable of getting to the bottom of this mess. That Gemima Smythe had a lot to answer for, causing time spillage that rippled out into the future to pull actresses in, a bona fide thief!, and here she was casually drinking Iris' gin and flirting disgracefully with her ex-love at the back of the bus. Ex-love! She unfurrowed her frown with some difficulty, took another sip, and stomped up to Gemima to interrogate her.

'Now look here, you...minx,' she cried, avoiding Panda's eye. 'This might be a happy reunion for you but you've got some explaining to do! Just what do you think you're doing creating dangerous time anomalies to steal paintings? And while we're at it, exactly where is this darn painting that has caused so much trouble?' She glared at Gemima, waiting for a response.

Marlene came to stand by Iris for support. 'Yes,' she drawled. 'I want to know why you have dragged me into this savage time. I presume it was you who attacked me.'

Gemima gracefully put her drink down, and stretching luxuriously, sat up. For a moment Iris thought she was going to become belligerent, but she flopped back against the red vinyl seat again. 'For that, I do apologise,' she sniffed haughtily, 'but you gave me quite a frrright, tumbling from the painting like that. I had just stolen the painting, my spirrrit was up, and I did not expect to have a middle-aged woman fall on me.'

Marlene's eyes went wide at 'middle-aged', but before she could interject Iris snapped, 'Obviously you stuffed everything up by using a Micklethwaite Extractor! You've made everything in that gallery unstable not only now, but years into the future when the painting will hang on the set of *The Scarlet Empress*!'

Panda looked about to say something, perhaps coming to his ex's defence, but Iris glared at him unkindly.

Gemima was unfazed by Iris' blame. She gazed coolly back. 'I have used the extractor many times and this has never happened. I have never told anyone this but it is my modus operandi.' She picked up her drink again and sipped. 'I did give some thought to this when she appearrred out of nowhere. It is obvious that the issue is with the painting itself.' She sneered at Iris, purring lightly.

Iris paused a moment. 'Perhaps,' she finally said. 'But your meddling didn't help! You realise we now have two figures from that painting wandering loose in 18th century Russia!' She suddenly thought of something. 'And why that painting? There are a number of far more expensive paintings in that gallery – oh, yes, we've seen it. What makes that painting so important?'

For the first time since the questioning, Gemima looked cagey. 'That is my own perrrsonal business.'

Iris snorted. 'Since when was thievery ever a business? You're a wanted criminal, and if you don't tell me what I want to know, I have every right to arrest you and take you to the proper authorities!'

Gemima pushed herself up with her strong back legs. 'I would like to see you trrry,' she purred. 'I don't wear this spacesuit for its fashionable currrves. I am armed.'

Panda coughed. 'Gemima, dear, I don't think that will be necessary. We just want to sort this out and then all go home.'

The great cat turned to him and smiled wistfully. 'That, I'm afraid, is a point of contention. My time capsule – the Catrrrovalva – is damaged.'

'But we can take you back to your own time!' replied Panda, delighted at the possibility of having more time with his ex.

Iris frowned. 'What am I? A travel service for waifs and strays?'

Everyone glared at her. She sighed. 'I suppose I could think about giving you a lift,' she eyed the cat doubtfully, 'if you produce the painting and tell me why you stole it. Fair's fair after all.'

Gemima's eyes narrowed into yellow slits. Iris smiled grandly. 'Very well, if you guarantee me safe passage on this contrrraption, I will tell you.'

Iris nodded solemnly, ignoring the slight on her bus.

The cat held out her glass to Panda who, with a quick guilty glance at Iris, refilled it with a splash of white liquor, and a squirt of tonic. Gemima accepted it with a smile and reclined, her lime green spacesuit squeaking against the vinyl.

'It all began—' she started before Iris interrupted.

'If we're going that far back I need a refill too.' She clunked about in the tiny kitchenette.

Gemima did not wait for her. 'It all began,' she purred deeply, 'when I was sunning myself on the shores of Florrrana, one of the most peaceful planets in the universe, with sands as soft as swan's down and seas like warm milk. I had just pulled off a rather trrricky job on the Museum of Absolutes and thought I deserved some time off.

'The painting I stole had other ideas.'

'The painting?' cried Iris.

Gemima gave her a supercilious look. 'Evidently you haven't been to the Museum of Absolutes. Everrry piece of art it holds does not exist in any timeline anymore. So you can see with such rrrare and expensive paintings available all in one place, it was rrripe for a perfect piece of thievery.'

'Stop preening and get on with it,' snapped Iris.

'To cut a long story short, the painting I stole from the museum is the exact same painting that I stole here. You see, the painting began to speak to me – a crrroaking, ruined voice, but a voice nevertheless. And it told me of untold rrriches in a land far in the past. It intrigued me, so I packed up my bucket and spade and set my capsule for this time period.' Gemima sighed expansively. 'Unfortunately the landing was a little rrrougher than I had hoped for and my capsule was irrrrredeemably damaged. I was marrrooned in this savage, backward time.

'The painting still spoke to me and told me of the Duke's art gallery. Where I was astonished to find the painting I had already stolen. Knowing that the painting existed far in the futurrre I thought I should steal it, in case it could somehow get me back to my own time.'

Iris frowned and broke in. 'Why use a Micklethwaite Extractor then? There is no security here that you couldn't get around with cat-like grace and agility, surely?'

'That was the painting's idea,' said the Siamese.

'Ahhhhh,' replied Iris. 'Now *that* explains quite a lot.'

'Not to me,' said Marlene.

Iris turned to Gemima, grinning broadly. 'You've been had, you daft pussy! Voices in paintings from the far future telling you to steal the same painting in the past. Oh, you've been led a merry dance across the timelines!' She was laughing now, utterly amused at the cat's predicament.

'Iris!' snapped Panda. 'I hardly think the current situation makes for a laughing matter.'

Iris calmed herself with difficulty. Gemima's eyes were fierce slits of yellow. 'Sorry, chuck. But you will agree duping the *infamous* cat burglar Gemima Smythe is quite amusing.' No one agreed. Iris huffed, 'Oh, fine.' They were all looking to her for an explanation. She went to take a sip of gin and found she'd finished; she was very tiddly. 'It's obvious. Through your muddling you've created the perfect escape. Someone wanted out of that painting and went to quite a lot of effort to bring you here to help them.'

Marlene gazed wide-eyed at Iris. 'You don't mean the scarlet woman?'

Iris nodded. 'Though I think it's more likely to be the disfigured man, don't you? He does seem like the type.' She looked pointedly at Gemima.

'What?' asked the cat. 'That is all.'

Iris raised an eyebrow. 'Not quite, lovey. Give us a look at the pics, eh, there's a good girl.'

Gemima stood, and Iris was quite surprised to see that on her hind legs she was a good foot taller. She pressed down on a thigh of her slinky spacesuit and a small drawer opened up with a mechanical wheeze. Her claws extended and she rooted about it the small space, bringing out a tiny old-fashioned tartan purse in red and blue.

'I neverrr go anywhere without this,' she said. She snapped open the clasp and absurdly plunged her whole arm into the purse. A moment later she pulled out a small wooden square. As soon as it was free of the purse it unfolded quickly into its correct size.

Iris had to admit she was impressed. 'A dimensionally transcendental purse. How clever.'

'Just what every lady needs,' simpered Gemima smoothly. 'I never need to take anything else anywhere. This holds all mannerrr of things.'

'If you can find them in there,' said Panda dubiously.

Iris snatched the painting. 'This one is the one you stole from the Duke?' Gemima nodded. Iris gazed into the painting. 'As I thought, no sign of the scarlet woman or her shadow.' However as she looked she began to feel distinctly strange. Her peripheral vision began to blur with tunnel vision. She reached out to steady herself, and perspective went completely awry.

'Iris!' cried Panda. She saw him jump up, his eyes wide with shock. But it was too late by then.

She tumbled over the frame and fell headfirst into the painting.

Panda was frantic. He had been quite happy to sit back and let the drama unfold, his head lovely with a drunken muzziness, occasionally interjecting to defend Gemima, about whom he felt a strange but pleasant fondness now, though that hadn't been the case at the time of their affair. That had been such an intense experience, nights spent in cafes over coffee and brandy chatting about history and art and all sorts of exciting, vivid topics. They had both toyed with one another and had been surprised when they found one another in bed together. Of course he had been slightly taller then, and this was years before Iris. Then he had discovered what she did for a living. It worried him that what he had found so remarkable in her had turned out to be a dangerous disregard for the law, a selfish immediate gratification. He had let himself become her pawn, enjoying the thrill of her danger. Indeed, he found her wicked persona still made him light-headed with pleasure.

Pleasure was now the last thing on his mind. He had been horrified to see Iris reach out, her fingers becoming flat and two-dimensional, and slip into the painting. He'd dashed over, and there she was unconscious on the floor of the forest. He'd shouted, he'd shaken the painting, but she had evidently not been able to hear him. He'd completely discounted the danger of himself falling in. It seemed a solid painting, wood and oils.

'Gemima, help me!' he cried.

She raised an eyebrow. 'Help you what?'

'You must know how to get her out,' he said.

'My dearrr,' she purred, 'I haven't a clue.'

Marlene, seated on the longue, had caught Panda's eye. 'Little one, I think that the woman outside could help.'

He motioned to be picked up. Marlene sat him on the windowsill.

Outside, lit partially by the glow of the interior bus lights was the scarlet woman. She stood there, her dress billowing around her in the windblown night, her face pale and solemn.

'Of course!' said Panda. 'She must have been drawn by the painting.' He turned to check the painting and saw Gemima folding it away in her purse again. 'What are you doing?' he demanded.

'It is still mine,' said the Siamese.

'Give it to me,' Panda said levelly.

Gemima smiled, showing teeth. 'My dear Panda, you aren't going to choose her over me, are you? That would be rrridiculous. She's old, and large, and...well, totally wrong for you.'

'She is my friend, Gemima. I will not have her stuck in a painting for eternity. Now, give it to me or else.'

Gemima meowed with laughter. 'Or else what? I could shrrred you to pieces with a swipe of my claw. I could always put you under my spell. You're just a little toy bear. Now what you are going to do is pilot this pile of junk to Florrrana, and preferably before I ever stole this wretched painting.'

But Panda was utterly still; he saw red. 'A little TOY BEAR!' he shouted. And before the cat knew what had hit her he had thrown Marlene's half-full glass of gin at her. The liquid hit her full in the face. She threw up her paws and yowled. 'Take that! Ha, I know how much you hate being a wet pussy!'

'Quickly, Marlene!' he yelled. She looked to him with a blank face. 'The cupboard!' he shouted. He had raced to the drinks cabinet and with sweeps of his small arms he pushed everything – brandy balloons, champagne flutes, gin, vodka, crème de menthe – out onto the floor, where quite a few shattered to pieces. Oh Iris was not going to be happy with him.

Gemima had recovered from her drenching, and she turned on Panda, claws unsheathed, hissing and spitting. He was shocked to find her bearing down on him with speed. Fortunately this was also just what he wanted. At the last second he leapt out of the way, allowing Marlene to shove Gemima forward. The cat tried to swivel, lashing out, but overbalanced and fell straight into the large drinks cabinet. Panda quickly pushed the door closed. Gemima kicked out and it flew open, but Marlene was suddenly there beside him, straining to hold it closed. Finally, with much effort, the lock clicked, and Panda quickly turned the key. Typical, he thought, that the only door with a lock in the bus was the drinks cabinet.

There was an anguished yowl from Gemima. She kicked against the wood. Panda didn't know how long it would hold. Long enough to find Iris, he hoped.

'Thank you,' he said solemnly to Marlene. She was breathing heavily, shaken by the turn in proceedings.

'It is in my interest to keep you safe, little one,' she replied. 'I hope you can fly this machine.'

Panda glared at her. 'I am going to find Iris.' He pulled the lever that Iris had made especially for him that operated the door lever in the cab. It concertinaed open with a squeal. He jumped down the stairs and into the dark forest.

There was no sign of the scarlet woman. A cold wind whispered through the leaves. The trees cracked together overhead.

Marlene had followed him. 'I am sorry if I seemed selfish in there. I will help you to find Iris.' She smiled. 'I do owe her my life, even if that was in the future.' Her voice was deep and tired and wistful.

Panda was sitting in the leaves, despondent, staring into the night. 'How are we going to find her?'

Marlene shuffled through the leaves and picked him up. She turned him to look at her very serious expression, her seductive eyes sure and capable. 'I have not been here for long but I have found that if there is a mystery to be solved you go to one people. We will ask the gypsies.'

Marlene had only been in 18th century Russia for a short time but she had developed a rapport with Vasily, the youth who had rescued her in the forest, and using her suddenly acquired but limited knowledge of Russian, she had managed to coax from him a story from the gypsies past. At the mention of the disfigured man, he had flinched, and told her of the time many years ago when a seemingly wise, clever man, a foreigner, had come to their caravan asking for shelter from the winter blizzard. The gypsies had offered him food and a warm bed and he told them stories of the places he had been in return. But in the morning, it was found that the man had vanished and the most beautiful girl in the encampment – Vasilisa – had also disappeared. There was a scene of disarray in her caravan. The fortune-teller was called and she divined that Vasilisa had been kidnapped by the clever foreigner. The gypsies decided to go after him.

They caught up with the man in a nearby village where he was being entertained by the Mayor. There was no sign of Vasilisa. When he was asleep, they broke into the house and they took him away stealthily under cover of night. They took him back to their caravans where they interrogated him. Under exquisite torture he revealed that he had killed Vasilisa, had stolen her life energy for he was dying and needed to take other's lives to maintain his, like an ageless potion. When the gypsies heard this they were dismayed and distraught that beautiful Vasilisa, daughter to the toymaker, was dead. They decided to punish him.

The toymaker constructed a frame, in looks quite basic but the perfect frame he had ever made. Into it he poured all his grief and his impotent anger. Then he painted a forest, the very forest into which his little girl had been stolen, a dim depiction of all that was evil in the world. Into the forest he put all his longing. He placed the canvas in the frame. That night the gypsies built the fire high, and the fortune-teller and all the elders sang a strange song into the fire, a song that seemed to warp the very fabric of reality. Then, with great solemnity, they pushed the clever foreigner into the fire, where he burned briefly, and his body died. But when the toymaker held aloft the painting, they could all see, hidden behind a tree, a shadow that was not a shadow but human-shaped.

And so life went on, and though Vasilisa was never forgotten, the toymaker and the gypsies found other worries and pleasures to occupy them. The painting was hung in the toymaker's caravan, but he could not look at it, it was so full of grief and anger and longing.

One day he was working in his caravan, carving out the features of a wooden doll. Some small part of him knew that every face he now carved was the face of his lost daughter. There was suddenly a great wind that surged about the caravan. It rattled alarmingly, and then there was a thump as something fell. When he went to investigate he found the painting had fallen off the wall. He picked it up and placed it back on its hook. And for the first time in many months he looked into the painting. And he got a terrible and wonderful shock.

Staring out at him was his beautiful daughter, dressed in a scarlet robe. Her eyes pleaded with him. He reached out for her.

Though the gypsies searched, they could not find the toymaker. The fortune-teller felt the eerie coldness of the caravan and found the changed painting. She declared the caravan haunted by an evil spirit that had taken the toymaker, and it must be buried under earth in darkness. Nearby there was a mountain range and the gypsies left the caravan in a deep cave cut into the rock. The painting was taken by the fortune-teller, who wanted it banished from their camp. Its whereabouts fell into history.

'The cave, it must still exist,' said Panda to Vasily.

'It does,' he replied, kicking up leaves as they walked. He had been leading them through the forest, telling his story, for seeming hours. 'It is here.' He pointed to the dark hole in the mountain.

Vasily would not enter the cave, so Marlene and Panda went on alone. A river trickled thinly alongside. They went deeper and deeper and Panda flicked on his lighter for a little illumination. Eventually they came to a cavern and the walls opened up around them, and shafts of daylight filtered gently down through holes in the rock above. Dust motes danced as their feet dislodged dirt undisturbed for years.

Panda grinned and turned to Marlene.

In the centre of the cavern was a gaudily painted gypsy caravan, though the yellow and red paint had peeled through weathering.

'Let's get to the bottom of this,' said Panda.

'But the painting is not in there,' Marlene drawled, brushing back her hair messed up by the journey in the dark.

'Ah but if I'm right, my dear, Iris will be.' With that he raced up the stairs and stood there impatiently, tapping his foot, until Marlene opened the door.

Inside, the floor was littered with unfinished wooden toys, some half-painted, some rotting with mildew. Spider webs hung from window to window and in every cornice. A small round table was placed in the centre of the cabin with a single book on it. Panda gazed at it suspiciously. Someone had obviously been here recently. There were webs hanging split in the air.

'Urgh,' said Marlene. 'I do not like insects.' Her eyebrows were going up wildly in affront.

In the centre of the caravan was a deep red velvet curtain. 'Prepare yourself for this,' said Panda. He opened the curtain.

They were in the forest in the painting. He could tell at once, everything was so absurdly still. Marlene almost tripped over him in her disoriented state.

'We are back in the forest,' she said, perplexed.

'We are in *a* forest,' corrected Panda. 'I thought that caravan was probably another portal. They wouldn't bury it unless there was something very strange about it.'

'A portal?' asked Marlene. 'You mean we are in the painting.' She gazed carefully about for the shadowy figure that had so frightened her before.

'See how everything is so still, and almost two-dimensional?' He pointed to a tree. The leaves did not move, the trunk did seem slightly flat.

'What now?' asked Marlene and Panda laughed, suddenly knowing what it was like to have a companion.

He had been walking about in a circle, getting the lay of the land. Now he stopped. 'Well I think we should probably go and ask at that house, don't you?' He pointed to the pleasant looking wooden cottage sitting in a clearing a short walk away.

'I do not remember that in the painting,' replied Marlene haughtily, trying to retain some of her gravitas.

'Exactly!' snapped Panda. 'Now pick me up.'

Marlene made her way to the front door of the cottage, noticing the rather pretty garden of herbs, and rapped sharply. There was a brief burst of discussion from inside. Then a very distinctive cackle.

'Iris!' shouted Panda from Marlene's arms.

Then the door opened. It was the scarlet woman, Vasilisa. She gazed at them both with confused interest. And beyond her, seated at a long table, set with dainty porcelain cups and a piping hot samovar, was the disfigured man in black, and opposite him, one Iris Wildthyme.

She had looked up when the door was opened. 'Panda, dear!' she cried raucously, 'You're just in time for tea.'

Iris played mother and poured. Panda felt a great relief to be by her side again and snuggled up to her warm bulk. He was also slightly cross that she wasn't in a great predicament and didn't need rescuing. After all the anguish he had been through it was only right that she ought to have been in terrible danger, and he would have come swinging in and plucked her from the jaws of death. But here she was having tea with two mysterious figures *in* a painting, blithely greeting him cheerily when he turned up, dirtied and muddied from his spelunking adventure.

'Oh I knew you'd turn up, chuck,' she said. 'I wasn't worried.'

'Perhaps you might have considered that we *were*,' he found himself snapping. 'You had fallen through a painting!'

She turned to him. 'Panda, dear, I had absolute faith in your abilities to find me. You're getting rather good at this now.'

He gritted his teeth against a retort to her patronising statement. From her that was about as much of a compliment as he would get. 'Well you might let Marlene and myself know exactly what you have been doing here while we have searched high and low for you.'

Iris grinned. 'I have the whole story now. It's all very interesting.' She motioned to the scarlet woman. 'This is—'

'Vasilisa,' interrupted Marlene.

'Yes, we know,' said Panda.

Iris huffed. 'And this is—'

'The clever foreigner who stole her life years ago,' finished Marlene again.

The man in black moved, his burnt features twisting strangely into approximation of a smile. Marlene shuddered. Now that she sat close to him she could see the pale marked cauterised flesh. It was as though everything had dripped like wax and dried into new condition.

'This,' said Iris with a hardened tone, 'is a former...acquaintance of mine. A renegade from the Obverse. I had thought him another, a very naughty man I knew as Koschei. But this man is usually known as the Archduke of Autumn. Quite a clever alchemist.' Her tone saddened. 'Or at least he was.'

The man spoke, his voice raspy and unsettling as a box of nails. 'That is too kind a portrait of me, Iris.' He measured Marlene and Panda carefully. 'You have been speaking to the gypsies.'

Marlene nodded. 'What they have told us, is it true?' she asked.

But it was Vasilisa who replied. 'It is true.' She had a soft voice, filled with heartache and sad acceptance. 'He stole my life, centuries ago. But ever since he was placed in the painting, he had no bodily control of me. I was able to claw free from his bitter hold.' She sipped at her tea. 'Though not completely. We are still forever tied by the fortune-teller's curse, and his power over me is strong. When the occasions are right and the moon and the stars are aligned correctly, he can make me pull people into the painting, where he feeds upon them to keep himself alive.' She gazed calmly at the man in black, not hatefully, but with cool disdain and bland futility. 'He killed my father.' A blue tear fell down her pale white cheek. She composed herself. 'But I too have found power over him. Wherever I go, he must follow; he is my ugly shadow, forever chasing the life he once took.' Vasilisa gave a short smile that held a terrible depth of coldness and joy at the man's pain.

The man smiled again, a terrible vision, at their combined power over one another.

Vasilisa sighed. 'But the fortune-teller was kind. Every ten years I am allowed out of the painting. Oh! It is such a joy to be free.'

Iris frowned. 'Excuse my French, love, but you're just a phantasm. How is that possible?'

The scarlet woman looked pointedly at Iris. 'I inhabit a body that has only barely been taken to the realm of the deceased. The last time I was free I found myself in the body of the Grand Duke's wife. She had died quietly, while asleep, from a burst blood clot in the brain. The Duke never even knew a different person had entered her body.' She closed her eyes in happy remembrance. 'Oh that year was such a perfect time. I would dine lavishly and sit and talk with the Duke in the gardens, and play games, and dance. The dancing was divine.'

'The Duke's missing wife,' exclaimed Marlene, and her brow furrowed in concern that now he would truly never see her again.

Vasilisa opened her eyes and they fell upon the Archduke of Autumn. 'It must have been exquisite agony for him to endure this tiny world without my presence. Even at the end of the year I felt him pulling me back inside the painting, back into the prison. But as I saw when I came back, he had not been idle. Somehow, somehow his influence had spread beyond the painting. I do not know how. I could feel how oppressive the air was.'

Iris nodded. 'He was sending out a message to the stars, through the oil and the wood.' She looked at the man in black, almost reverently. 'You always were a master of alchemy, conjuror of the magicks of Autumn especially. No wonder your power increased.'

The man inclined his head to Iris in a small nod of acknowledgment.

'There were voices in the air,' explained Vasilisa.

'Yes,' replied Iris. 'He was putting an escape plan into action, weren't you? You knew the painting was hung in the Museum of Absolutes, in the future. That's where, through the right conjunction of stars and alchemy, you could focus your efforts! Although what you got wasn't quite what you wanted. A daft great pussy!'

Panda piped up. 'That's right. He was the one who instructed Gemima to use a Micklethwaite Extractor.'

'He knew it would fuse the world of the painting with the real world, for a time. Didn't you?' Iris smacked the table, making the tea cups jump.

Throughout this the Archduke of Autumn had been contained, his blue eyes flicking between the conversationalists with keen interest. 'You are right, my old friend,' he replied in a gravelly tone. 'I am sick of prisons. I must have my escape before I go mad with the unenduring Russian autumn.'

Marlene, gaining courage enough to question the man, said, 'But you cannot escape. You are just a spirit.'

He grinned, and they were all shocked at how hideous his face became with the expression. 'I have power over the Autumn. The fortune-teller did not know that when she imprisoned me. Through careful alchemy, of oils and wood and leaves and herbs, I have been able to bestow the same privilege of freedom upon myself that Vasilisa enjoys.'

'No!' gasped the scarlet woman.

'Yes. Although I cannot wait ten years.' He paused a moment. 'Fortunately, through my machinations, the painting has been cared for and is being kept for me ten years from now. I only needed two bodies for my plan to become complete.' His eyes raked over Iris and then Marlene. 'One for my beautiful Vasilisa, whom I am very attached to, and one for myself.'

Marlene gasped with horror, putting a hand to her throat. Rather overdoing it, thought Iris.

'Oh no you don't, lovey,' said Iris, all bolshy and ready for a fight. 'You'll not be suckling on me!'

'But my old friend, you are worried for the end of your life. You have lost count of the regenerations. And this would be a new life: we would share it, as one.' The Archduke of Autumn's voice was oddly soft and compelling even whilst being sieved through glass.

So that was what Madame Sokorovsky had been on about, thought Panda. Poor Iris, wondering if this was her last life, wanting to prolong all the fun and the scrapes and the derring-do and the surreal adventures they found themselves in.

For a moment Iris seemed to waver, considering the offer.

'Oh, Iris,' said Panda with such tenderness. She caught his tone and bucked up instantly, brightening at the trust of a good friend.

'Not on your nelly, you cut-rate phantom!' she cried, and laughed in his face. 'If I'd known you were going to be so disagreeable I wouldn't have had tea with you!'

His face twisted into an ugly grimace. 'You will do as I tell you,' he demanded. He stood and his presence seemed to fill the small room. It was evidently too much for Marlene, who's eyes were wild (Iris didn't think her suited to time-travelling at all, all shock and melodrama; but then she was probably playing a part in her head, knowing how canny she really was). The actress leapt from her chair and raced from the cottage, knocking over the oil lantern on the table. Instantly, flame sprang up hungrily.

The man threw up his arms with a terrified cry.

Vasilisa was alarmed. 'The cottage! It is not real, everything is painted in flammable oils!'

Iris hurriedly picked up Panda, whose wool had already picked up a scent of smoke. Iris went to the curtains and was about to tear them down, when Vasilisa stopped her. 'They are oil also,' she said. Iris looked at them, at the way they didn't move. She pulled and there was a canvas tear.

'Is there nothing we can do?' she asked.

Vasilisa hung her head. 'You can go.'

'Come with us,' she remonstrated. 'The time anomaly will last a little longer. We can find you a proper body, ten years in the future. He has set up his own escape but why can't it be yours?'

Vasilisa's eyes filled with tears. 'I had one good year. It was beautiful and it was the best year of my life. I do not want another now.' She gave a quick smile. 'And he would never let me go. He would come back, somehow.'

'But—'

'No. You must go now. Go!'

The fire had become a quick conflagration, the walls, the floors, and the furniture alight. The Archduke was huddling in a corner, shouting for Vasilisa, terrified of the element that had killed him before.

Iris dashed through the flames, coughing at the dirty smoke, and battered down the door with her shoulder. She fell in a heap in the garden. Panda went 'Oof' underneath her. She quickly picked herself and a very grumpy Panda up, and turned to look into the burning cottage.

She saw: Vasilisa smiling in the flames, holding the struggling figure of the Archduke of Autumn. The flame had just caught her scarlet dress and was lighting her up like a candle. The man screamed and screamed.

The roof caved in, and they disappeared from view.

'A very brave girl,' said Iris gravely.

'Iris, we are still inside the painting,' said Panda. He waited for her reaction. 'The oil painting.'

'Oh heck,' she exclaimed. She raced to the clearing where they had fallen in. Marlene was there, waiting for them, cool as a cucumber. 'Now we have to find the exact place we fell through.'

'It was here,' said Marlene. She raised a snooty eyebrow and vaguely nodded to the tree behind her. As Iris peered closer she saw a great big X printed on the tree with red lipstick.

'Well you are a class act, aren't you, lovey,' smiled Iris.

Everything burned. The cottage and the toymaker's caravan, and the painting (Gemima getting quite a shock as her purse belched out a flame which her spacesuit thankfully put out).

Iris and Panda and Marlene were back on the bus as it chuntered down the multi-coloured timelines, listening to a compilation tape of Cilla and Dusty and Shirley, and sipping a much deserved gin and tonic (which had fortunately not fallen victim to Panda's destruction of the drinks cabinet). Gemima had been released at slimline laser pistol-point (set to stun), and slightly singed from the purse explosion, and much cowed when she realised the damage she had caused (Iris had been as angry as Panda had ever seen her, going on about dangerous time loops and paradoxically destroying paintings before they could be placed in future museums). She sat curled up on the longue where everybody could see her, happy enough that she was going to be taken back to the future.

'You did awfully well out there, Dietrich,' said Iris around a mouthful.

'I am a trained professional,' replied the actress drily, her eyes hooded with suggestion. 'I simply use the set to my advantage.'

'I think the sooner we get you home the better. Old Russia can't take any more of you.' Marlene seethed but decided not to retort, accepting the sly reprimand from the time lady. She would get her own back by telling Noel everything; he would dissect it in his own witty way and end up the hero of the piece with Iris a devilish old nuisance. 'Still, all's well that ends well. The time loop will slowly dissipate without the painting, and we'll take you two muddlers back to your own times, with perhaps a short adventure on the way. You never know where the bus will take you.'

Panda was seated on Iris' shoulder. He was glad to be in her boisterous company again. Though there was one thing he wanted to have a word to her about. He whispered in her ear, 'You aren't really coming to the last of your lives, are you?'

She stiffened but then relaxed. 'My dear Panda,' she replied sotto voce, 'That was me being a very silly, selfish woman.' She smiled. 'Besides, come the end of the twelfth I seriously doubt you could stop me from looking my cadaverous Aunties in the eye and demanding another set, chuck!'

Panda smiled and raised his glass to her. They drank to friendship and adventure and a long life and brave scarlet women and trusty red double-decker buses and that little clothing store in Carnaby St and that mad film director after Iris in the 1970s...

And the bus rolled on through time.

Only Living Girls

Steve Cole

It was blowing up a gale as Ellie and I trudged up the dead road. The ash flew round and round in playful, ragged circles. Little bits stuck to my tights, as always. It's hell to get them off. And I love my tights. They are stripy purple and black. Like bruised bees.

They belonged to Arlene Magus, from the Show. She's one of my favourite supporting actors from series one, so they're extra-amazing. I still can't believe they fit me so perfectly, Arlene always looked much bigger on the telly. Seeing her there, though, alone in her big bed, all grey and stiff... She looked so tiny. And she was staring up at the ceiling all sort of peaceful.

Maybe some day we'll find one who didn't die with their eyes open. I hope so, cos it does creep you out, and makes you feel sort of bad for being in their place. Like they can still see you or something, through the filmy dust on their eyeballs.

Anyway, that first day, I told myself not to be silly and took the tights from Arlene's dresser. I took a silk slip too. I'm wearing that, as well, underneath two of her jumpers and two coats; one hers, one mine from before. And a blue skirt with black cats on that belonged to Mrs Belfast – remember her, the white witch who went missing in episode three? They were going to bring her back in the season two finale, if only—

It's a lovely skirt, but it lets in a draft. Even through tights.

It's cold the whole time, now the world's ended.

The day it all kicked off, Ellie wasn't talking to me. She was probably still furious that I fit in Arlene's clothes and she can't. She tried to put on one of the skirts and it ripped before it was halfway over her arse. It didn't surprise me; Ellie's arse would rip through almost anything. But I had to pretend I hadn't seen or heard a thing, else she'd never have stopped sulking. She settled for taking a ring, Arlene's gold signet ring, which she's squeezed over her little finger. But Arlene never wore it in the Show so it's not really such a trophy. It didn't even fit. As Ellie drove us in the hearse we'd taken from the Co-op, she gripped the wheel really tight as usual cos she didn't really know what she was doing, and the ring bit hard into her flesh, turned it white and then blue as the hours growled past slow as Christmas traffic.

It took a while to get used to the roads being so empty.

We parked, and then Ellie was off and walking as fast as she could, knowing I can't keep up so well. She crumped along through the thick ashen skin of the street, bits blowing up like flies around her wellies.

'Your finger's gone purple,' I said.

'It's fine,' said Ellie, her nose pushed into her big, dog-eared map.

'It could drop off, though.'

'Leave it, Etta.' She flashed me a scornful look. 'Just cos you could wear it as a bangle. Ickle Etta Little.'

I looked away. I wish I'd never told her the kids at school used to call me that. Just cos I was skinny and small. Everyone used to say I had an eating disorder. Even the teachers. But I do eat, it just doesn't go on anywhere. Dad used to say it was cos I have big dreams. Big dreams need feeding. I'm not sure Ellie has so many. She's a big lass, and she never seems to eat so much, not when I'm there anyway. I should never have said anything about the Etta Little stuff. She probably thought I was showing off about being thin. If anyone does anything that Ellie can't do, they're showing off. I bet I could read the map a lot better than her, but if I tried we'd never hear the end of it.

'What if Davydd's not there?' I wondered.

'Shut up. He's bound to be there. All the others were at home when it happened. It was the middle of the night.'

'Davydd might have been out at that observatory,' I said. 'The one they filmed at in the second episode, right on his doorstep. He got into it all, stars and planets and magic and stuff. Davydd gets so lost in his stargazing, he spends whole nights there sometimes.'

Ellie stopped and looked at me, and smiled like I was dumb. 'That was just press release stuff! You don't really believe that, do you?'

'I believe that bit.'

'Davydd probably went to the observatory, like, once and they made a big thing of it. That's what they do, especially when it fits with his character.'

I'd been going to bite my tongue. 'No, though,' I said, 'because Davydd also said it at Shadow Con.'

I could almost hear Ellie stop breathing as we walked. She had missed Shadow Con, of course. The only proper Shadow-Monger convention and she wasn't there. She started her first period that afternoon, in the back of her dad's car. While I was watching Davydd in the front row, she was in a services outside Coventry in tears, wearing a dog blanket while her dad swore and scrubbed at the back seat.

Actually *being* there at Shadow Con goes beyond showing off, of course. For a while, Ellie can't even speak.

'The Work,' she says thickly, 'was all my idea.' The words are coming out sticky, like her tongue's swelling up with her finger. 'And it was me who found Arlene's address book. Just remember that.'

She's right, of course. I only broke into Arlene's house to see what sort of place she had. Someone had said she lived on that street, but Ellie and me, we didn't know for sure. Before the world ended, me and Ellie used to hang around there, hoping for a glimpse.

See, I reckoned she brought back Other Cast Members for parties. Big wild parties where they summoned shadow-demons, just like they did on telly. Only ruder here, away from the cameras, behind the lead glass and heavy drapes. Here you would see the stuff they'd never allow on TV. And so we drank red wine from a Coke bottle, stood under the streetlamp and imagined what Davydd would be doing at the party. He was the hero, Marc Gaslyght, the demon-slayer – but away from the cameras he might find himself seduced by this evil. He would gyrate with the other acolytes. He would go up against Hecate Jones, head to head, face to face. But instead of vanquishing her with a kiss like in season one's finale, he would kiss her and nothing would happen. He would have to do more to her. He would start kissing her harder and harder, and Hecate Jones would be shocked but then start getting into it, and he would start touching her, and she would touch him back, and Davydd would be lost for all time to wickedness…

We would plan it all out, giddy on the wine, never minding the cold. Sometimes we would burst in and save Davydd. Or sometimes we would be taking part in the revels, two virgins to be sacrificed, and Davydd would save us and we'd be so grateful and beg him to make sure we could never again be menaced in that way. Ellie would carefully describe what he did to us, holding nothing back, keeping us warm. And then when we'd stretched it out as long as we could and it was dead late I'd sneak back into my house and creep to the bathroom without waking Dad and brush my teeth, and the toothpaste would come out like blackcurrant foam and I'd look in the mirror and my sticky-out cheekbones would be strips of white in the red flush and my elfin lips would be black and it looked awesome.

Ellie was nicer, back when it wasn't just her and me in all the world. The apocalypse had brought out her mean streak. Then again, most people left us alone when the world was still standing. They didn't get us, thought we were weird for loving Shadow-Mongers so much. They called us the Shadow-mingers. I didn't really care; it made a change from the other names they called me.

But I never expected to see Ellie again when the ash fell.

Dad had died that night. And the neighbours. And the school was empty, the children and teachers dead in their beds or their armchairs at home.

After two days spent crying – and a couple more to be sure no one was coming to help – just for something to do, I went to see if Arlene's house was really Arlene's house. It wasn't. Thirty broken windows later I found she lived in the next street.

The weird thing was that her body wasn't charred to ash like everyone else. She was dead, but with her eyes wide open she looked as though she was just lying there. It was such a relief to see her, to touch her and know she was real. To find that her clothes fitted me and that actually her makeup looked pretty good too.

I lived with her for a day and a half, and then Ellie showed up. I don't know why it's just her and me left. Why us? There's nothing special about us.

Unlike Arlene's address book, which Ellie found while nosing about in the dresser.

It was a Religious Conversion. Suddenly, we had Work to do.

'Etta,' Ellie hissed, dragging me back from god-knows-how-many-weeks ago and stopping dead in her tracks. She grabbed hold of my wrist, almost crushed it. The signet ring on her purple finger pinched my skin.

'What is it?' I asked.

'Davydd's house should be just down this street. But I can hear something...'

She was right. It was the noise of an engine.

We rounded the street corner and saw a gleaming red double-decker bus parked outside. The number 22 to Putney Bridge. Shaking with the rumble of the engine. Like it was laughing.

We hurried silently through the ash, Ellie and me. She's big, but she can move quickly when she has to. Who says you learn nothing at school?

Behind the bus was a black sports car. It looked shiny new, not coated in the grey, smoky fug that had settled over the world. We stared at our reflections in the paintwork. Red and black. Exciting, dangerous colours. Well, except on ladybirds, maybe.

'Omigod!' I whispered. 'You know what this means – someone is alive!'

'It's Davydd!' Ellie hissed back. 'Maybe he *was* at the observatory. Like you said.'

I nodded. 'And he wasn't touched. Just like we weren't.'

We stared at each other.

'Omigod, omigod.' Ellie started trying to smooth her black hair a bit. Her cheeks were pink; the colour sat strangely on her face. 'Imagine if it's just us and him left in all the world?'

'But he doesn't drive, remember? He failed his test twice.'

'Three times,' Ellie corrected me instantly.

'No, though, cos he overslept the morning of the third test, so he missed it rather than—'

'He still failed it. Technically.'

'All right, all right.' Ellie's like a little kid sometimes. 'So, since Davydd can't drive, who came here on the bus and in the sports car?'

I should have felt excited by the idea of finding other survivors. But it felt wrong to me, just then. I'd been trying to get my head round the idea of it just being Ellie and me and that the Work was what we did to fill the time until, I dunno, whatever, and suddenly—

'I can hear voices,' Ellie declared in a stage whisper. I listened hard over the sound of the engine chugging, and realized she was right.

'Let's get closer,' I mouthed at her.

We held hands and crossed the road to the pathway of a nice looking house. Not show-offy big, not nasty. It was a good size but tasteful. Just the sort of place you'd imagined Davydd would have. But I didn't have much time to think about that then because we were crouching down under the window, and my heart was swelling so I could feel it in my throat, and a man's voice and a woman's voice were cutting through the grey daylight from the front door, which stood a little way open.

'...next thing I know, he's disappeared!' The woman sounded like she came from up north. There was an earthy, smoker's rasp to her voice. 'I checked all over the bus, thought he might be trapped inside the drinks cabinet like last time. But no, not a sign!'

'My doctor said something about reality crossing wires,' the man was saying. 'You know, like, if he pushed off in the middle of fighting some alien nasty who wanted to destroy the world and arrived in the same place the next week—'

'Oooh, I know, Fritz, chuck,' the woman declared. 'He'd find the world had been destroyed. Alternative time, they call it. Like dropping through a ciggie burn in the lining of the Very Fabric of Space and Time. And to think we've landed up in it! That's not supposed to happen...' I could almost hear her shiver. 'The place where maniacs' dreams come true... where they're never defeated and have their wicked way with whole planets... Oh, lovie, and here we are – stuck!'

'We'd better not be, Iris,' Fritz said. He sounded North London, like me. And scared, too. 'I need to get back to my own adventure, where the good guys win. This place... it's horrible.'

'I'm taking steps,' said Iris.

Iris. That's a nice name, I thought.

Then her voice rose as she called: 'Would you like to come in out of the wind, my little dears?'

Ellie looked at me in horror, and my face must've mirrored hers. How did this woman know we were out here? We both held still. She couldn't know. She couldn't have seen us.

When the woman spoke again, she was standing behind us on the path.

Hunched over in her floppy, wide-brimmed hat, ankle-length leopard-print coat and crimson trouser-suit, Iris was like some fantastical figure from a costume designer's sketchbook, brought to life and left out in the rain for thirty years or so. Her face was lined but her brown eyes were bright as the conkers I used to find as a kid. I'd hardly seen any this autumn, and we were well into December now. But Iris' eyes, they reminded me of so many things I'd forgotten.

'Come on, then,' she said kindly. 'You'll catch your deaths out here. And there's been enough of that, don't you think?'

I got up. Reluctantly, so did Ellie, glowering and shifty. 'Who are you?' Ellie said. 'What are you doing here?'

'I'm Iris Wildthyme, transtemporal adventuress!' she declared. 'And I'm looking for a friend.' She turned back to the open front door. 'See, Fritzie? I told you – leave your engine running and others'll come running and all.'

Fritz came out. He was tall and gangly, unshaven but sort of nice-looking. He smiled at me. 'All right?' Then he saw Ellie and his smile cooled a bit. 'Er, hi.'

'Where's Davydd?' Ellie demanded. 'Is he in there?'

'I'm sorry,' said Iris, with a bat of her lashes. 'I'm afraid he's dead.'

The news hit me like a fist. It was stupid, I know. Everyone else was dead and I didn't really think that his being at the observatory would have helped him. Did I? Perhaps I did, cos when she said he was dead I just wanted to be sick. I leaned against Ellie.

'Oh, dear,' said Iris, her face falling. 'There I go, opening my big mouth and upsetting you...'

'Fuck off!' Ellie exploded.

Fritz took a step back. 'Oi! No call for that—'

'You fuck off too.' Ellie always swears when she's scared. 'I bet you're not even real. Or you're ghosts or something.' She grabbed my hand and yanked me towards the front door, pushing Fritz out of the way. 'But we're real, and we came here to see Davydd and that's what we're going to do.'

I let myself be pulled along by Ellie's gravity. I was so freaked out by seeing people again I didn't look left or right or take in any detail of Davydd's house. Ellie's bum filled my view, and in a daze I watched it trying to fight its way out of her black leggings as we hurried upstairs...

Ellie stopped. Slowly, I lifted my head and saw over her trembling shoulder.

There was Davydd, lying on his bed, skin as white as his cotton pyjamas. Dead, like Iris said. Staring peacefully up at the ceiling. I was even closer to him now than I was at Shadow Con. I wanted to scream at him to wake up but he was dead and I couldn't breathe. I wanted to throw myself on top of him. Lie beside him on that perfect, creaseless duvet. His room was so clean. Minimalist, you'd call it. The dark carpet was spotless, really spotless.

And soft, as I fell face first into its deep-pile blackness.

When sound and muted colour crept back into the world I was downstairs again, sat beside Ellie on Davydd's couch, in Davydd's lounge. Ellie was holding my hand, so tight she was cutting off my circulation; I realized it was more for her comfort than for mine. *Davydd's dead*, a dull voice in my head insisted. I didn't want to believe it. It's like when the Show was almost cancelled after the first season. It was brought back by Fan Outcry. Now I wanted to bring Davydd back.

Back home to where the others were waiting.

Fritz hovered by the lounge window, looking out while Iris sat in an armchair, watching me sympathetically. 'You had a turn, lovey.'

'Shock, probably.' Fritz ambled over and offered me a hipflask. I took it, and swigged. It was brandy or whisky or something. I'd not tasted that since the second day of the apocalypse, working my way through Dad's drinks cabinet. Ellie looked disgusted with me for taking a drink and shook her head curtly when Fritz offered the flask to her. 'So, what're your names, girls?'

'I'm Etta,' I muttered, like I was owning up to something terrible, which maybe it is. 'She's Ellie.'

'Don't tell them stuff!' Ellie shot at me. 'I mean it, they're ghosts or something.'

'Don't be daft!' said Iris. 'My talents might tend towards the preternatural, but just look at me! The rest is all woman.' She looked meaningfully at Fritz, who passed her the hipflask. 'Ta, lovey.'

'They're alive, like us,' I whispered. 'I knew we couldn't be the only ones.'

'Oh, but you are,' said Iris, watching us closely. 'I scanned from my bus out there. Not a living soul on the planet apart from you two.'

'Where did you come from?' I asked quietly.

'And what are you doing *here*?' Ellie added.

'Good question,' said Fritz.

Iris took a swig from the hipflask herself, and got out a silver cigarette holder already loaded with a silver cigarette. 'I'm looking for a panda, as it happens. One of Davydd's co-stars.'

I sat up. 'Pandastro, the black-and-white demon?'

'The toy that comes to life in 'Enemy Bared'?' Ellie said just as quick.

Iris' eyes widened. 'You've seen him?'

I nodded. 'Yes, we—'

'We've seen him on TV.' Ellie was keeping her lips tight. As well as swearing when she's scared, she can't help smiling when she's lying. 'I love that episode. You would never know that wasn't a real bear.'

'He's a remarkable little feller,' Iris agreed. 'I thought he might be here. I could tell he got on well with Davydd during filming...' Now she scabbed a match off Fritz. 'They recognised each other's star quality. Struck up a fine friendship, they did.'

'What are you on about?' I said. 'Were you working him? Only I couldn't see any secret buttons or where the wires would—'

'You do sound intimate,' Iris said, watching me like a bird eyes a worm.

Ellie nudged me hard in the ribs. 'Don't encourage her. I bet she's nothing to do with Pandastro. She's crazy.'

I wasn't so sure. I was starting to think this weird couple could have come through a crack in the fabric of time. Like the Shade-Blade did in *Demonoid* part one.

'Iris isn't lying,' said Fritz. 'I saw that Panda at Davydd's Winter Solstice party. Right here in this room.'

'You went to a party with the Shadow-Monger cast?' Ellie sneered as she shook her head. 'As if.'

'I was!' Fritz protested. 'I'd been told there might be trouble. *Things* gathering in the atmosphere, crowding about the place, so I was keeping an eye.' He lit up a cigarette, arched a knowing eyebrow. 'It's just what I do.'

I felt breathless. 'Was it a good party?'

'Not bad.' Fritz grinned. 'Your mate Davydd was loving it, too, all dressed up in his little cape, pretending he was Marc Gaslyght's bad brother. The birds lapped it up! Especially when he got this book out and started reading spells...'

'He really did that?' I felt quite faint and clutched hold of Ellie's arm. 'I said so, didn't I! I said they met for parties.'

Ellie shook her head. 'Don't listen to them. They're telling us what we want to hear.'

Or what I already knew. All that time we spent imagining those wild, decadent parties... I felt giddy, as though I'd somehow brought those illicit dos into being with my thinking and wishing and dreaming beneath the streetlamp.

I leaned forwards towards Fritz. 'What happened when Davydd read the spells?'

'Not a lot.' He shrugged, took a deep drag. 'Panda got himself in a bit of a state. Then someone put on a Fleetwood Mac album. It sort of broke the mood. People went home. I crashed out in a hotel room. When I woke up...'

'Alternative time had taken root,' Iris declared. She turned to me. 'You probably think things have been this way for months, don't you?'

'They have,' I said. 'Haven't they?'

'Not really, no.' She lit up her cigarette and shook her head. 'It just seems that way. Like you're caught in a dream.'

'It does feel like a dream sometimes,' I admitted.

'It does not,' Ellie insisted, fidgeting. 'You're so gullible! Don't let them trick you.'

'Speaking of tricks...' Iris took a long drag on her ciggie. 'What happened to this book you saw, Fritzie, love?'

Fritz shrugged. 'I dunno, I've checked all the shelves, it's nowhere.'

I watched a scattering of ashes dance around his Cuban heels. The stuff got everywhere. I felt suddenly sick. I turned and staggered to the front door.

And saw a big cloud of ash blowing up about the bus outside. Heard the noise. Low and booming. Then a little higher.

Two noises, talking to each other.

I tried to call Ellie's name. But it was like being in a nightmare when your voice has dried up and frozen and you can't say anything at all.

The ash was buzzing down the path towards Davydd's house like black bees.

'Bugger me!' Iris declared, there behind me, looking over my shoulder. 'It's a visitation!' She slammed the door shut. 'Come on, we'd better try to get out the back way.'

I came back into the lounge, as Iris bustled through into the kitchen. Fritz was looking pale, pacing about. 'Oh, great. Fab. Why does this stuff always go down when you're around, Iris!'

'Well, we're not leaving without Davydd,' Ellie announced, fists bunched. Her eyeliner had smudged and made her look well fierce.

I nodded quickly. 'We can't leave him.'

'But you saw it out there!' Fritz protested. 'Scary black stuff! Aliens! Incoming!'

There was a crash at the door, which nearly banged off its hinges.

Something was after us.

Ellie barrelled upstairs, and I ran after her. For a moment I just wanted to get away. But then I saw Davydd lying there, and he looked so vulnerable, and I thought, *We can't leave him,* and *Nothing is gonna get him if we can help it.* 'Come on, then!' I told Ellie. I grabbed his ankles. His skin was cold. My fingers felt hot. Ellie leaned over and moaned in fear, in love and disbelief, as she grabbed him under the armpits (Davydd's armpits!!!) and hauled him up off the bed. His head squashed between her boobs and her belly. Why didn't I take that end? I pressed his feet up against my chest. I've got no boobs, I could feel his soles against my ribs. My heart was pounding and my mouth was dry.

'We're saving you, Davydd,' I whispered, though I didn't know what we were saving him from.

Not just then, anyway.

Wood cracked and split; the noise carried like shouts. I think it was the front door. Fritz came running up the stairs rubbing his shoulder, Iris wheezing and gasping behind him.

'Can't get the bloody back door open,' Fritz moaned. 'And it's getting in!'

'Come on! Out through the bedroom window,' Iris panted. 'Onto the garage roof and jump into the shrubbery. We can double round.'

Fritz ran to the window and threw it open. 'You know a lot about it.'

'Davydd's girlfriend had a proper temper on her,' said Iris, swinging an immaculately stockinged leg over the window frame with the sureness of a pro. 'So Panda told me,' she added quickly.

Fritz was about to follow when he glanced at us and stopped guiltily. 'Go on then,' he told me. 'Girls and dead people first.'

I smiled at him. Ellie and I manhandled Davydd through the window as gently as we could. Iris was a glimpse of leopardskin in a big bush below. Behind us something was crashing up the stairs.

'Shift!' Fritz yelled, pushing behind us. 'Just leave him, can't you!'

We never would, of course. Ellie and me jumped off the garage roof, holding Davydd like our parachute. We crashed into the bushes. Davydd's eyes looked glassily into mine for a long, incredible moment as Ellie hooked her hands round his chest and hauled him up. Fritz almost landed on my head, swearing as he hit the shrubbery. Iris was shouting at us to hurry up as something black and bitty buzzed up to the window we'd climbed out of and—

The house blew up.

Huge, roiling flames shouldered through the windows. Glass shattered and brickwork broke apart as the fire took wing. My eyes burned and ears rang with that laughing, ecstatic destruction. *Davydd's beautiful house…*

Next moment the fire was gone and ash was falling like blankets of dead flies.

'That's my hairdo gone to buggery,' Iris complained, brushing herself down. 'Talk about being dragged through a hedge backwards…'

'What happened?' asked Ellie.

'I left my ciggie in the kitchen, next to the gas ring,' Iris explained. 'Now come on, everyone on board my bus. You too, Fritz lovie. And you can leave your snazzy sports car behind.'

'Oh!' Fritz complained.

But once we'd skirted the blackened stumps of Davydd's house and got back out onto the street, we saw that the bus was still chugging away while the shiny black sports car had been tipped on its side. An avalanche of ash was heaped over it.

Fritz got into the bus without another word. We all did, and Iris made a quick getaway.

'I'll drop you home,' Iris told us grandly as we lurched off along the street. 'This business is shaping up to be a nasty one. You're too young, too innocent to take part.'

'Don't take the piss. We just want to be dropped at Etta's house.' Ellie looked at Fritz. 'And don't get any ideas.'

Fritz shrugged. 'You're the one cuddling a corpse, love.'

Ellie ignored him. She was cradling Davydd protectively, like he was hers, but I didn't mind cos she could only look down his ear squashed up like that, while from the seat opposite I was able to look at the whole of him. It was amazing, watching him up close like this.

'Where'd you live, then, Etta?' Iris said cheerily. 'Where can Aunty Iris drop you?'

'Willesden Green, please.'

'Only we'd better be quick,' she went on. 'The *Spiritus Mundi* homed in on the bus's paranormal vibrations and came looking, just as I'd planned. Now they won't be far behind us.'

'The who?' Fritz wondered.

'World spirit,' said Iris cagily. 'Though the spirit of quite a different world to this one. It's trying to sew this patch of alternative time over good old reality!'

'Was it this *Mundi* thing who made the world end?' I asked.

'Of course it was!' Iris swung right. 'I sent it packing to the outer darkness, years back. Jenny helped, mind. Her finest hour, it was! Anyhow, it looks as though it was all in vain. The *Mundi's* found a way back into the physical world.'

'Something to do with Marc Gaslyght here and his dodgy book?' asked Fritz. 'One of those spells and incantations he read out, maybe...'

'Might have given the *Mundi* a way in,' Iris agreed. 'But now we need to kick the bugger out.'

I didn't say anything. I kept glimpsing something on Davydd's lap. Something small and dark and square. But when I looked too hard, it wasn't there. I kept looking, looking away, looking again.

We turned onto the North Circular. With a sudden thrill of dread, I knew our secret would soon be out.

The house was very different from when Dad was alive. There were little candles and oil lamps everywhere you looked. I loved the light they gave off, all warm and Christmassy, and the smell too – that ruffian spice of smoke and paraffin.

Iris had turned off the bus's engine this time. She and Fritz followed Ellie and me and Davydd into the house. As we stepped inside onto the worn hall carpet, my legs prickled in the stolen tights. Ellie's finger looked black and fit to fall off and point up at her from the floor, accusingly. I knew our story would sound odd and awful, but it wasn't like that. It wasn't like that at all.

Iris gave us a reprieve by disappearing upstairs to use the loo. Then, as I opened the door to the lounge with my elbow and helped carry Davydd inside, a funny sense of calm and warmth settled over me. Fulfilment, maybe.

Here they all were at last. Friends and enemies, safely gathered.

On the sofa, Arlene Magus was sat awkwardly beside Bill Butler, her ardent admirer with the sinister secret. Dolly Mink, the scheming witch, watched them both with Jake Walleye, her familiar, at her feet. Hecate Jones, pale, devilish and beautiful, straddled the pouffe. They all crowded together, cheek by jowl on the rug, or by the imitation fire, or propped up against the clotheshorse – posed extravagantly in death's stony sleep. And now Ellie was completing the tableau, carefully arranging Davydd on the plinth we'd made from the ironing board, erected in the middle of the lounge and waiting for this day. I watched her set out his limbs with reverence, lost in a different world.

'Bloody hell!' Fritz stood alone in the doorway, shaking his head, looking pale. 'You two come on like a couple of regular schoolgirls. But all the time you're breaking into houses and nicking bodies.'

'Not *bodies*,' said Ellie indignantly. 'Just the principal cast from seasons one and two of Shadow-Monger.'

'And we didn't nick them,' I mumbled. 'We just... didn't like to think of them lying all alone. We saved them. We wanted them to stay together.'

Ellie nodded proudly. 'It's a shrine.' She looked at me, wetness shining in her eyes. 'And now they're all here, Etta. The Work's done.'

Iris burst in. The lines on her face seemed deeper in the soft, greasy flicker of the lamps as she barged up to me. 'So where is he then, eh? The Great Pandastro was in series two, episode 11, so—?'

'We haven't got him,' Ellie protested, looking down at the floor and smiling despite herself. 'We… we were *going* to move onto the non-human characters but—'

'He's tucked under Arlene's skirt, Iris,' I said. 'We found him in her spare bedroom, just like he was in the show. I'm sorry, we should've told you sooner…'

'God, Etta,' said Ellie, looking disgusted.

'Panda, poppet!' Iris picked her way through the bodies and started rummaging under Arlene's taffeta folds. 'I'm here, I'm here…'

'Get off!' Ellie snapped, grabbing hold of Iris' shoulder. 'Don't muck up her costume! You're spoiling it all!'

'And you're a nutjob!' said Fritz. He tried to pull Ellie away but she elbowed him in the stomach. He fell against Nathaniel Crump in the armchair. I gasped, and Ellie shrieked, and Fritz yelped and tried to scramble away in horror, but old Crump's finger had hooked into the waistband of his jeans somehow and as Fritz rose he started dragging the body with him. Yelling in alarm he tried to smack the old man's hand away. Ellie gasped, sank down beside Crump, fiddling with his fingers. 'Stop moving about!' she barked at Fritz. 'Stop bloody moving!'

'Everyone shut up!' Iris yelled. And we did, and we held still and stared. She had Pandastro in her arms now.

And the little black-and-white figure was stirring!

'You're working him,' I breathed.

'Working me?' The disapproving croak came from somewhere inside the panda. 'How dare you!' His voice was just like off the telly. I couldn't believe it. Neither could Ellie. Her jaw was dropping.

'He's not dead. He's like Fritzie and me, from Outside all this.' Iris smiled as the panda's head turned slowly towards her. 'Only he was at the epicentre of things, and it's given him a turn. My charms have brought him round.'

'You reek like a brewery,' Panda moaned.

'Less of your cheek, we haven't the time,' said Iris. 'Do you remember what happened? You went to that Christmas party – without me, I might add, – and you came back feeling queer.' She squeezed his paw. 'Then you disappeared all together, dragged away into alternative time.'

'*Spiritus Mundi*, summoned here as you feared, Iris,' Panda muttered. 'It should've been the end of the world. I tried to stop it happening… Mystery to Me…'

'Mystery to me, too,' I muttered.

'No, that was the album he put on,' Fritz interrupted. 'Fleetwood Mac.'

'Of course, I'd rather jack, personally, but in the cicumstances...' Panda looked at me again, his eyes suddenly sharp inside their black smudges of fur. 'Wait. It's her.'

I gulped. A member of cast had recognised ME?

'Her from the end of season finale...' Panda blinked. 'Her and Davydd, they *make* it...'

I felt a shiver run through my bony back, and Ellie's eyes on me like death-rays. 'Her?' She folded her meaty arms. '*Her* and Davydd?'

With a jolt, Panda craned his furry neck to look at her. 'It's you! Her big friend.'

'Oi!' Ellie scowled. 'You can't call me—'

'You saved the world, my dears,' Panda said.

Ellie's complaints died on her lips.

I forced out a whisper. 'We did *what*, Pandastro?'

Fritz cleared his throat. 'Er... have you seen the world lately, Panda? Doesn't look very saved to me.'

'No, but think about it, Fritzie...' Iris looked up at him from beneath the floppy brim of her hat. 'We're stuck in the shadows of what might yet happen. And our plucky cast of characters are the only ones who haven't rotted away to ash...'

'Which is a bit weird, seeing as they're the ones who let in these *Mundi*-things in the first place,' Fritz noted.

'Something's keeping them safe... Aha! Iris jumped up – or attempted to, it was more of an arthritic clamber, really. 'Of course! Their biggest fans!' She swung round to Ellie and me. 'You two!'

Ellie stared. 'What?'

'Uncertain belief brought the *Mundi* through,' Panda gasped. 'But the strongest belief is holding them at bay...'

Oh my god! I thought. And I looked at Ellie and there she was, thinking it too. Strongest belief! *We're Shadow-Mongers' biggest fans, ever, in the whole world!* It was official. I mean, you might tell someone you love them but you can't prove it, or how *much* you love someone, can you? Except here and now, me and Ellie could. Our love of the Show had marked us for life. It had preserved us, along with the heroes and villains we loved so completely, those characters we held so close. And we looked at each other, Ellie and me, and I could see she was going to cry and she *never* cries, not about anything, and that made me feel like I was going to cry too. She grabbed me in a rough hug, and I hugged her back, and it was like when the world was here and we stood under the streetlamp, and it was cold except for that sodium glow above us. That hard, orange glare we thought was gonna be the only spotlight we'd ever know.

Then a huge cloud of ash exploded into the room.

'Shit!' Fritz yelled, and Iris threw Panda up in the air in surprise. Candles hissed out and lamps were sent clattering to the floor. Ellie screeched and dropped to the floor. Ash was everywhere. There was a noise like pressure in your ears, when you need to swallow to clear it. But if we swallowed now we'd get a dirty, scratching, foul-tasting mouthful of evil ash. Iris was fanning it furiously with her big hat. Ellie hid her head under Arlene's skirts. Fritz was flailing his arms about as if warding off wasps.

But the sudden violence couldn't stop me thrilling to the knowledge of what we'd done, Ellie and me. Through the storm of black and grey I saw Davydd on the ironing board. Something dark and solid lay on his chest like a slab of strange chocolate. It was a book, I realized, the leather cover dimly reflecting the light of the lamps and candles.

He sat up, as sound and light fell away. The book threatened to fall but he grabbed it without even looking. I could see him and hear him perfectly.

'Etta,' he said, grinning that wolfish, dangerous smile Mrac Gaslyght is famous for. 'Things seem serious.'

'They are,' I said quietly. Shock and terror were catching up with me, but to see him sat on the ironing board like that, I couldn't help smiling back just for a moment. 'They really, really are.'

'Then it's down to us to put things right,' he said, waving the book. 'You and me. Marc and Etta.'

'But you don't like it when people call you Marc Gaslyght,' I protested, 'you're keen to keep your own identity separate from the fiction of—'

He grinned. 'You never really believed that, did you?'

I smiled, breathless. I shook my head as he took my hand. His skin was warm, his breathing was fast and his brown eyes danced as he looked at me. 'Only we can complete the ritual as it must be, Etta.'

I looked for Ellie, but she was somewhere in the dark now, arse stuck up in the air and her head buried between Arlene's ankles. Arlene herself looked none too happy about it. She was alive again, looking flushed and astounded. Butler took her hand protectively. Walleye prodded Crump cheekily in the ribs, trying to get him to stand up, to join the others in the circle that Hecate Jones and Dolly Mink was bidding them form. Hecate had her eyes on me, but as the ash flashed about like flies in summer I knew there was no evil in that look. Just a recognition of strength.

Marc put his face closer to mine, his sharp features more heroic than ever in the moody lighting. 'Well?'

'Ellie can help...' I began.

He shook his head. 'Not quite strong enough. Was she at Shadow Con? I don't think so.'

You noticed! 'I queued all night to be near the front.'

'I was really glad you did. You could tell, I think, when I looked at you towards the end...'

'Then you really *were* looking at me...'

I heard a high, choking shout from somewhere past the Great Pandastro, who was sat now on Arlene's shoulder. 'Etta, love! Oh, Etta...' I saw the suggestion of Iris at the fringe of the circle, face black with ash, holding Pandastro's furry paw and nodding encouragement. She looked so sad as the ash piled up around her, settled like dark, glistening snow, weighed down the brim of her hat. 'The dam is breaking...'

'It has to be now, my dear,' Pandastro said firmly.

I looked down at the book Marc had opened. There were words there, etched in hard lines of indigo. I didn't know what they said, but Marc knew. He was already shouting them out. Each syllable was snatched hungrily from the air by the busy darkness outside the circle of the Shadow-Mongers. The room grew blacker, as though the words were feeding the living ash. I couldn't even see Iris now, couldn't see anything beyond the circle. I laughed, though the darkness was thickening. The Shadow-Mongers had come together here in my lounge. My world was theirs. The darkness was pressing in, black as leeches and cold as snow. The circle was growing tighter.

'It is the winter solstice!' Pandastro boomed fruitily. 'The nights have drawn in ever closer... now let that darkness be repelled!'

And Marc and Davydd leaned in to kiss my mouth. Soft and wet and sexy and perfect. No acting. No pretence. My lips were melting, I was rupturing inside. Nothing could feel as good as this, I thought. Nothing in my biggest dreams could ever be as good again.

It was OK to let go now.

'I'd die for you,' I thought.

'I know,' he said, as I did.

Daylight hit me first like it does when you're little and it's a school day and your mum comes in and yanks open the curtain. The morning gobs brightness into your eye. It's the worst way to wake up.

But I soon saw that this was proper sunlight I was looking at. The sunlight of a real world. I could feel its warmth. It lit queues of cars in the road, still frosted from the long night. It shone for commuters hurrying for their trains. It hung over the poor bastard schoolkids on their tired trudge to see out the end of term.

I watched them all. I flitted past them in saintly specks too good to be seen.

'No battle is won without sacrifice,' Marc Gaslyght said in *Enemy Bared*. He said it with such raw conviction, with such a look in his eye. Of course, I know now he was speaking to me, reaching out to me in the very room where one day we'd see off the darkest of shadows on the longest night, as autumn ended and winter began. *My* sacrifice was won without battle.

Now they've started filming a new season of Shadow-Mongers. I get to watch it as it's put together, of course. Unlimited access. I sit and laugh with the cast in their trailers. I prompt poor old Crump when he forgets his lines. I plague and harangue the writers and tell them a thing or two about saving the world. I hug Davydd's white pyjamas, and I can feel the warm cotton stripes of Arlene's tights around my legs.

And always, as I feel that beautiful burn on my lips, I remember how everyone came together to make me light up the dark.

Fritz got back to his friends, and I still see Iris and Panda about. The things they get up to! I wave to them, and Iris waves back when she remembers to see me. She has a lot on her mind, a lot to contend with. Always off gadding about, she is. But she gives me the biggest smile sometimes.

And sometimes, late at night, she is maudlin. 'Never give all the heart, they say! But if you hadn't, Etta, love, where'd we be now?'

We're here, I call to her. That's what matters.

'I envy you sometimes,' she goes on. 'I've waited a lifetime for a kiss like that. I'm always waiting.' She downs her drink. 'One day he'll capitulate. Till then there's travel. Isn't there, pet?'

I'm nodding. I feel the sunshine.

Ellie doesn't look for me. I smile down on her as she stands beneath the streetlamp, her breath steaming out into the air, swigging from her wine bottle and trying to remember. She makes her plans and thinks how things might be but I used to give shape to those thoughts. She's not the same without me. She wishes she had a friend who would make her sweeter. Someone she would share everything with.

I watch her wonder, 'which is Arlene's house?' In her drunken fug she glances down at that golden ring tight on her finger, wonders who it belonged to, how she ever got it on and if she'll ever get it off again.

She watches a big red bus go by. Misses the panda waving at her from the fogged up window.

Silly cow, I do love her.